Glimpse Of Never Ending Love

Evanell

A Wings ePress, Inc.
Paranormal Romance Novel

Wings ePress, Inc.

Edited by: Diana Greenwood
Copy Edited by: Leslie Hodges
Senior Editor: Elizabeth Struble
Executive Editor: Lorraine Stephens
Cover Artist: mpmann

All rights reserved

Wings ePress Books
www.wingsepress.com

Published In the United States Of America

Wings ePress Inc.
3000 N. Rock Road
Newton, KS 67114

What They Are Saying About
Glimpse Of Never Ending Love

I like the intimate feel of Glimpse of Never Ending Love. The heartfelt attraction between Catharine and Tyler is perfect.

—Eden Robins,
All Our Tomorrows

Evanell penned a wonderful and delightful tale to show us Catharine and Tyler's romance. Fairy Fey and guardian angel Rey add touches of magic. Extra spice for this paranormal story comes from time travel and a villain. From beginning to end, this tale entertains.

—Cherie Lee, Associate Editor
Sun Life Magazine
Author and freelance writer
Otherworlds Sci-Fi 2003 Anthology
Sun Life Magazine

Dedication

To William,
my webmaster,
also my husband
and the love of my life

* * *

I asked God for water
He gave me an ocean
I asked God for a flower
He gave me a garden
I asked God for a tree
He gave me a forest
I asked God for a friend
He gave me you

Anon

One

Catharine clutched the telephone with both hands. Her stomach knotted sickeningly as Dillon McKenzie, a pompous, troublesome co-worker growled, "I'll be there in a few minutes. I won't be put off any longer. Tonight I intend to sleep with you, whether you're willing or not. And if you don't open the door, I'll find a way to break in."

The tiny hairs on the back of Catharine's neck stood on end, piercing her tender skin like sharp pinpricks. She slammed the phone down, grabbed her navy backpack, and dashed out of the small Denver house she had lived in since coming to the twenty-first century. Grateful she still had her coat on, she tore down the snowy sidewalk as though the devil himself pursued her.

She didn't have many friends and could only think of one place to go. To Tyler's apartment. Tyler was Jennifer's cousin, and Jennifer had said Tyler would help if Catharine ever needed help. And tonight she definitely felt needy.

With her heart pounding as loud as the overhead thunder, she raced against the fierce February wind, hoping she wouldn't fall, praying Dillon wouldn't find her and force her into his car.

At the corner of Humboldt and Evans, she stopped to catch her breath. Bitter bile marched up her throat. She jammed her gloved hand against her mouth and willed the awful taste back down. She had left England because her step-papa had threatened to have his way with her. What was wrong with men? Why couldn't they take no for an answer?

Shaken by those memories and terrified of Dillon's threat, Catharine shivered in the cold, doing her level best not to slip and fall on the treacherous unshoveled footpath as she continued to the bus stop.

While she waited for the bus, she sucked in huge gulps of cold, exhaust-fumed air. In spite of the snow-packed roads, traffic whizzed by her. Thankfully she didn't see Dillon's black sporty car among them. His threats made her skin crawl, but being out alone at night frightened her, too.

The bus finally arrived. Relieved, Catharine scurried off the curb. Pain shot up her right leg as she twisted her foot. All that running and she hadn't fallen. Now, like a ninny, she'd crimped her ankle. She nearly buckled, but someone behind grabbed her arm.

"No," she wailed, trying to jerk free, but failing and slamming her shin against the bus step.

"I only want to help you board the bus," said a stocky elderly man, who reminded Catharine of Rey, the guardian angel who had brought her to the United States two years ago. "You might have sprained your ankle."

"Thank you," she mumbled, choking back the sudden urge to cry.

With her leg throbbing painfully, Catharine climbed the steps and displayed her monthly bus pass. After the driver nodded, Catharine limped to a seat and plopped down. Heaving a silent sigh, she set her backpack down and bent over to inspect her ankle. Not only did it hurt like holy heck, her shin burned as though the bones had caught fire.

The bus turned a corner. She braced herself against the wheels sliding on the icy road. When that didn't happen, she unclenched her hands and tried to relax.

To reach Tyler's apartment near Cheeseman Park, she needed a transfer. With a grimace, she collected her backpack, limped back up the aisle and forced herself to talk to the bus driver. It took a lot of courage, though. She hated speaking to strange men.

About three quarters of an hour later Catharine reached Tyler's apartment building and mimicked what she had seen Jennifer do; waited for a lady to insert her security card, then followed her inside to the twin elevators at the far end of the lobby.

On Tyler's floor, Catharine slipped her two-inch high heels off. With her feet flat, some of the pain in her ankle eased. The new maroon hall carpet smelled pleasant, and the plush tufted yarn caressed her feet as she stuffed her shoes in her backpack and hobbled to Tyler's door.

Then her nerve faltered. What if he wasn't home? Or if he were, he might not be alone. Perhaps she should have called. But she didn't have a cell phone. Truth be told, until this very moment, she hadn't ever felt a need for one.

Despite being worried about Tyler and his reaction, Catharine summoned her courage. Her heart pounded madly as she rang the doorbell. Although she felt foolish and embarrassed, her throbbing foot hurt too much to retrace her steps. Besides that, she didn't have anyone else to turn to.

The door opened. She glanced up. Tyler, as tall, dark and handsome as any man she had ever seen, smiled down at her from his six feet height. Tongue-tied, she tried to speak, to explain why she had come. But words failed her. All she could do was stare.

"What's wrong?" he asked, his gray-green eyes filling with concern.

Catharine knew she should say something, but the words she'd silently rehearsed vanished. Had she made a mistake by coming here? Presumed too much? Jennifer had assured her she needn't fear Tyler. He would never harm her. Why then was her heart pounding at a terrible speed?

No matter how many deep breaths Catharine took, her heart continued to thump. Most men made her heart race, but always in fear. Yet with Tyler it raced for an entirely different reason. No other man had ever made her feel this way—wary, excited and frightened all at the same time. Why did he wield such power?

She drew in another deep breath. The expression on Tyler's handsome face was one of welcome. She unclenched her fists. Tyler's looks weren't his only asset. In a peculiar way she felt as though she'd always known him and would miss him if he ceased to be a part of her life. Still, she had kept him at arm's length, so they didn't know each other very well.

Finally, after a silence that lasted an embarrassingly long time, she managed to blurt, "I'm afraid."

Tyler blinked at the girl he'd known all his life. As he had anticipated, she'd turned into a stunner. But why had she rung his doorbell on a cold Friday night to tell him she was scared?

When she didn't elaborate, he swept his gaze over her. Petite, with long blonde hair and brilliant blue eyes, she tugged at his protective male instinct. The tiny scar on her right cheek that turned into a dimple whenever she smiled, quivered. He smiled again, hoping to put her at ease. Kacy always used to have a warm smile for him. But not anymore, and tonight was no exception. She looked as though she'd rather be anywhere but here.

Almost three years ago she had told him in no uncertain terms that there could be no romance between them. He thought he had accepted that, and had gone on with his life, but now his body refused to believe what his brain had been told.

"Come in and tell me what you're afraid of, Kacy."

Her bottom lip trembled. So did her voice when she spoke. "Pl—please call me Catharine."

"Sorry," Tyler mumbled. Last year she had legally changed the spelling of her name, and asked everyone to call her Catharine instead of Kacy, short for her initials Kathryn Cassandra. "Guess I forgot."

"How could you, when you facilitated the change?"

Tyler spread his hands in mock surrender. "I plead guilty. Am I forgiven?"

She furrowed her blonde eyebrows. "Do people usually forgive attorneys when they forget?"

He grinned. "Their friends do."

"I see."

"Are you going to come in?" he asked. "Or do you want to stand in the hall all night?"

"Are you alone?"

"Yes."

"I shouldn't have come, should I? This is not at all proper, is it?"

"When have we ever been proper?"

She shrugged, looked behind her, then up and down the empty hall before she asked, "Do you have plans for this evening?"

"No.

"Do you mind that I have come?"

"Not at all."

"Are you certain?"

"I think you should come inside before we continue this discussion."

She nodded hesitantly.

Tyler backed away to give her a wide berth. "Come in. The hall's cold, and I'm losing all my heat."

"You? Or your apartment?"

Ty grinned again. "Got me Kacy. I mean Catharine. I owe you one."

"You don't owe me anything. However, it would please me no end if I could consider you a friend."

"I thought you already did."

She pursed her lips and didn't comment.

Beginning to feel like he'd accomplish something as major as winning the trial of the decade if he could get her inside, Ty waved his hand, motioning her in. "C'mon. I don't bite. You don't either, do you?"

Catharine shook her head. He raised his hand to hide a grin as she peered inside his apartment before she cautiously entered. Was she trying to decide if the place was safe? Wired with booby traps... or what?

When he shut the door, the fear in her eyes started to worry him. He reached for her arm. But she jerked away, her face flaming a bright red.

"What's wrong?"

"I told you. I'm afraid."

Ty had a sudden urge to pull her close and kiss her fear away. Instead he folded his arms so she'd know he wouldn't try to touch her again. "I'm not a mind reader. You'll have to tell me what you're afraid of."

She clasped her hands together, and stared down at them. "There's a man where I work who makes me uncomfortable." Her bottom lip quivered.

The desire to pull her into his arms battled with Ty's legal training. He wanted to draw her close and promise he would protect her and never let anyone scare her ever again.

"Has he done anything specific to make you feel that way?"

She nodded. "Sometimes he touches me, or tries to, when no one else is around."

Tyler's gut clenched, his protective instinct kicking into high gear. "That's sexual harassment."

"I know. Jennifer told me months ago that I should press charges or file a law suit against him."

He winced at the painful mention of his cousin. "How long has this been going on?"

"About nine months."

Furious on Catharine's behalf, Ty ground out, "There are laws to protect women from that kind of treatment."

Mentally he calculated how long she'd been working... About twenty months. After her accident in London a couple of years ago, she had decided not to return to college, and taken a job as a receptionist at an oil and gas firm in downtown Denver. Although her parents, like Jennifer's, had left a substantial trust fund, he knew Catharine had only used a small portion while in college. Ty admired her for working now, rather than squandering her legacy or sponging off her grandparents.

"Have you told your boss about the man?" he asked.

"No. He, Mr. McKenzie, said I couldn't prove anything, and he would deny everything if I accused him of sexual harassment."

"McKenzie? What's his first name?"

"Dillon. Dillon McKenzie."

The name sounded familiar, but Tyler couldn't put a face to it. "Do you want to file charges against him?"

"I—I don't know. I didn't come here with that in mind."

"Why did you come?"

"Because I didn't know who else to turn to. I wonder, would you mind if I slept with you tonight?"

Tyler's hormones slammed into overdrive. "You want to sleep with me?" He barely got the question out of his dry, stunned throat.

"Yes. Perhaps over there on the settee, I mean couch, that is, if you don't have an extra bedroom. I truly don't wish to stay alone tonight."

"Why?"

She looked away before she answered. He watched her intently, saw her shoulders tremble. "Mr. McKenzie has repeatedly asked me to go out. Always I have refused. He often accuses me of being a 'stuck up broad.'" She shuddered. Again Ty fought the impulse to gather her in his arms.

"Tonight he cornered me in the hall before I could escape to the elevator, and..."

"What did he say? Did he threaten you?" Ty knew he was leading her, but he couldn't seem to stop.

"Yes." She licked her lips. A nervous tic wiggled her smooth cheek, the cheek with the tiny indentation that dimpled whenever she smiled. "He—Mr. McKenzie said he knows where I live and that I live alone now, and he would come tonight, and he intended..."

"What?"

"I cannot repeat the word he used. It sounded so vulgar."

"Did it start with an f and end with a k?"

She nodded, her face bright red again. "I escaped when another co-worker came by. However, Mr. McKenzie called shortly after I arrived home, and made his intentions clear. I was too frightened to stay home because he said if I didn't answer the door, he would find a way to break in. Please, may I stay here with you tonight, Tyler? I don't know who else to ask."

"Of course you can stay. But what about your grandparents? You could've gone there."

"No." She shook her head again.

He clenched his hands to keep from reaching out to touch her.

"My grandparents aren't home. They're in Arizona. I think they want to move there. And, in any event, there isn't a bus route near their home."

"You could've taken a cab."

"Taxicabs frighten me. The drivers do, too. I cannot face riding alone with a stranger. The bus has other passengers, so I am never alone with the driver."

Baffled by her fear, and wondering where it had come from, he motioned toward his couch. "Let's sit down."

She took one step, and stopped. He looked down, noticing her bare-stockinged feet. Concern rocked him. Had she walked here barefoot? Frozen her feet in the process? "What happened to your shoes?"

"They're in my backpack."

"Why?"

"I crimped my ankle before I caught the bus."

He frowned. "Crimped?"

"Twisted."

"Let me help you." Without giving her a chance to disagree, he curled his arm around her waist. And felt her tremble as they walked across his living room.

He helped her out of her black winter coat and waited for her to sit down before he went back and made sure the door was shut tight. He crushed the temptation to ram the dead bolt home just to see her reaction. Would she jump? Scream? Yell? Squeal?

Striding back to the couch after he hung her coat in the closet, he sat down beside her, and spoke quietly. "Tell me what I can do to help you."

She looked up and finally smiled. Her dimpled cheek winked at him. He wanted to lean close and kiss the dimple, taste her lips, inhale her sweet scent, hold her in his arms.

"You have already helped, just by being home and listening." She paused, licked her lips. "I think Jennifer was right. You are a nice man."

"Nice?" He'd rather be handsome. Sexy. Irresistible. Mysterious. So damn attractive she couldn't walk away from him ever again. How odd to be more attracted to her now than ever.

They were sitting side by side, their hips so close they were touching, the sides of their legs, too. Suddenly Ty felt a familiar stirring in his groin. Of all times to feel horny. He shouldn't have sat down so close. He drew in a sharp breath. And inhaled her sweet fragrant scent. Horny hell, he was on fire!

She shifted, moved a little away.

He frowned, missing the contact. "You can't be afraid of me." But the look in her eyes said otherwise. "Are you?" he asked, unable to believe that. He'd never done anything to frighten her.

"I don't wish to be afraid of you. Jennifer said I could trust you... that you would be a good friend. And since she's gone, I find myself very much in need of a friend."

Again Tyler winced at the mention of his cousin. Orphaned at the age of four, Jennifer had lived with him and his parents until she started college three and a half years ago. Then she'd rented a house with Kacy, near Denver University.

Jennifer had been like a beloved daughter to his parents, and a sister to him. Her sudden death two weeks ago had left a gaping void in all their lives. His grief, still raw, was on edge and at times difficult to live with.

Swallowing his sorrow, he concentrated on Catharine. She'd made it clear there could be no romance between them. Why then, did he still find her so fascinating?

He shifted, stared at the muted TV, and smoothed his hands over his blue jeans. A believer in reincarnation, Tyler was positive he had known Catharine in prior lives. In most of those lives other people had kept them apart. Now she was responsible. Even so, he had proposed once. She had let him down gently, with tears sparkling in her pretty blue eyes. But she'd been firm when she said, "I'm not in love with you, Ty, and I can't marry you."

He had given up. A man didn't have to be hit over the head to know the attraction was one-sided.

Now, her shy, uncertain expressions held more appeal than when she had been bold and unafraid of anything she encountered. In spite of telling himself that a relationship with her was hopeless, he was enchanted. Or demented.

She licked her lips. He wondered what they would taste like if he kissed her.

"Perhaps I should explain..."

"What?"

"That I am uncomfortable around men."

"Really?"

"Yes, really."

"Well, bite me."

She looked shocked. "I beg your pardon?"

He had almost said 'bite my ass,' but he'd cleaned it up for her because ever since her accident in London two years ago, she seemed prim, proper, and shy. Not at all like her old self. "That's just a slang expression."

"Slang. Yes. I know what that is."

When had she started to act and talk differently? And with a British accent? Had they avoided each other so long, he couldn't remember? "When did you pick up that accent?"

Her cheeks flamed red again. She raised her hand to her throat. "I—uh—didn't pick it up. It's always been in here." She fingered her throat above the collar of her pink blouse. "Is something wrong with the way I speak?"

Tyler couldn't help himself. He threw his head back and laughed. It was the first good laugh he'd had since Jennifer's funeral, and it felt good.

"You're delightful Kacy—Catharine."

"Thank you very much. You're kind to say so."

Ty stopped laughing. He didn't feel kind. He felt odd. Horny again. And that irritated him. He shoved his fingers through his hair. Over the years he had seen Catharine in all kinds of situations, but he'd never seen her like this, wide-eyed scared as a brand new baby bird.

As he stared, her shoulders shook. Silently he cursed Dillon McKenzie, the man responsible for the stark terror in her blue eyes.

When she shifted beside him and wiggled one foot, Ty looked down and saw the swelling on her right ankle. Concern slashed through him. She'd arrived barefoot and said she crimped her ankle, but he'd been so startled to see her, he hadn't noticed the swelling. "Would you like an ice pack for your ankle?"

"No. My feet already feel like cubes of ice, I mean ice cubes."

"How about soaking them in some hot water in my bathtub?"

She tilted her head, her brow quirked. "Would that be proper?

"Does being proper matter?"

"Not to most people perhaps, but to me, yes."

"I see." He rubbed his six o'clock whiskers, wishing he had shaved after work. But he hadn't expected company. "Since we've known each other about seventeen years, I think it's safe to say it's proper for you to soak your feet in my bathtub."

She looked like she was about to object, or disagree. Instead, she said, "Very well."

He helped her to the only bathroom in his one bedroom apartment. The scent of his spicy aftershave lingered. He had spilled some that morning and wiped it up with a towel. His electric razor and shaving kit made the white-painted room with dark green carpet look very masculine. A few feminine items—hers—scattered around, wouldn't bother him one bit.

She stood in the doorway, looking nervous and uncertain. He shoved the striped shower curtain to one end, bent over, secured the bathtub plug, and turned the water on.

"I assume you'll want to sit on the side of the tub. If not, you're welcome to undress and have a full soak."

Her face flamed again. He wondered why. She seemed so—what? Old-fashioned? Yes, that's exactly what she appeared to be. An old-fashioned lady. He hadn't thought there were any left on the planet.

"I'll just sit on the edge of the bathtub, thank you."

"Can I get you something to drink?"

She offered a timid smile. "If it isn't too much trouble."

"I have hot spiced apple cider or soft drinks."

"Do you have hot chocolate?"

A little hesitant, he said, "Yes."

"A cuppa would be a wonderful treat."

Cuppa? Tyler forced himself to act calm. "Take your pantyhose off and soak your feet. I'll be back in a jiff."

He left the bathroom trying to decide which bothered him most— her red face that indicated she was uncomfortable, or his eagerness to return. But he knew one thing for certain. Kacy Rose never drank coke, coffee or hot chocolate. Caffeine in any form didn't agree with her. And cuppa? When had she concocted that word?

Two

Catharine closed the door behind Tyler. Her pulse was racing. He'd given her a lingering stare. And she'd stared right back. A little embarrassed by her boldness, she slipped her royal blue suit coat off and hung it on a metal hook on the back of the door. Then she raised her full blue skirt and petticoat and wiggled out of the sheer silk pantyhose.

Seated on the edge of the bathtub, she tested the water with her fingers before she swung her feet over the side. The shock of hot water stung her cold feet, but she forced herself to keep them submerged until they thawed. Once they stopped tingling, the water felt wonderful.

She closed her eyes and concentrated on the exquisite sensation of warm water licking her ankles. Never would she take for granted the comforts so easily available in this century. It still amazed her how easy it was to do for oneself, with no need for servants.

The air held a spicy scent, reminiscent of Tyler's cologne. Breathing in the essence floating in the warm steamy air, she decided to let her hair down. The French twist she had arranged that morning had lost most of the hair grips during her mad dash to escape Dillon. Knowing she must look a sorry sight, Catharine removed the few remaining grips. She kept a brush in her backpack, but she'd left that in Tyler's parlor, so she combed her fingers through her hair, untangling the long blonde locks the best she could.

As she stared at her bare ankles, hoping the sprained one wouldn't give her a peck of trouble, she thought about the differences between clothes in the nineteenth century where she'd been born, and here in the twenty-first. Although ladies here wore trousers often, Catharine considered them men's clothing, and couldn't bring herself to put a pair on. The shorter hemlines had taken some getting used to, but she loved not having to wear a corset and so many other cumbersome underclothes.

Another oddity in this time was Tyler living alone and fending for himself. She'd never known a man who could prepare his own meals. True, Tyler had all the modern conveniences, but having offered to make hot chocolate for her was both surprising and endearing.

While she sat there, she recalled the vague dreams of Kacy's tiny fairy godmother urging her to tell Tyler the circumstances that had brought her to this time.

"I wish you were here, Fey," Catharine muttered. "I'd like to talk to you."

While she chided herself for talking to herself, a small female voice, said, "I am here."

Catharine's startled heart fluttered while her gaze searched the room. "Where?"

"Up here."

She looked up and saw Fey. The two inch fairy was poised on the metal curtain rod, her silver-tipped wings spread behind her tiny shoulders.

"Oh, Fey, how wonderful to see you again! When did you arrive?"

"When you did." The smiling fairy flew down to perch on the ceramic soap ledge across from Catharine. "After Miranda's accident, I promised Rey I would watch over you. I heard Dillon McKenzie threaten you tonight. I wouldn't have let him hurt you."

"If I'd known you were nearby," Catharine gasped, "I would've stayed home."

Fey shook her head, her blonde springy curls whirling with the motion. "That's one of the reasons I didn't tell you. Tonight is not the night to confront Dillon."

"But I've inconvenienced Tyler by coming here."

"No you haven't. Bringing your problem to share with him was a stroke of genius."

"I cannot see why."

"Thinking about protecting you will take his mind off losing Jennifer. And now that you're here, you should heed the advice I've been imparting every night whilst you've slept."

Small beads of perspiration broke out on Catharine's forehead. "You think I should tell him about Jennifer and Kacy?"

"Absolutely."

Catharine grabbed a dark green towel to mop her brow. She feared her tongue might lose touch with her brain when she saw Tyler again. The mere thought of him created indescribable joy, another first for her. Most men frightened her speechless. *Why didn't Tyler? Because he was a kindred soul? The man she had admired and respected in other lives?*

That thought robbed her breath. The first time she had seen him in this century she'd sensed they had known each other in past lives. Now she believed it not only possible, but very probable.

She cleared her throat. "I have a strong feeling I've known Tyler before—in other lives."

"You have," Fey said.

"Then may I assume the memories that have flooded my thoughts and dreams are valid?"

"You may."

Catharine regarded the fairy for a moment. "Can you tell me how many times I have known him?"

"A score or more. The memories are within you. Eventually you will remember them, each and every one."

Catharine pursed her lips as another question popped into her mind. "Will Tyler be able to see you?"

"No." Fey spread her wings. "Is there anything you want me to do for you?"

Caught off guard, Catharine shook her head, unable to think of a single thing.

"Very well, then." The fairy raised her tiny wand.

Catharine frowned. "Are you leaving?"

Fey nodded. "I must. I have other mortals to watch over. Not to worry. You'll be safe with Tyler." She waved her wand and vanished.

As soon as she was gone Catharine realized she could have asked Fey to heal her injured ankle. Would that be too presumptuous?

She stared at her bare knees. In the mid 1850's her reputation would be in tatters if she spent time alone with a man without a chaperon. Truth be told, she felt wicked, bare-naked beneath her skirt with Tyler mere steps away in the other room.

Uncomfortable with her knees and legs exposed, she spread the soft green towel over them. When Tyler returned, she didn't want to look improper. Bad enough she felt that way.

~ * ~

In his small kitchen, Ty filled two mugs with water and popped them into the microwave. When the water was hot, he stirred a packet of Swiss Miss into each mug and added coffee creamer, a trick he'd learned from his mom, to make the chocolate taste creamier.

He needed to discuss Dillon McKenzie's threats more fully with Catharine, but first he wanted to make her comfortable. That's why he'd suggested she warm her feet in his bathtub. A sudden thought flashed. If things had gone the way he'd once wanted, they might be in the tub together right now, buck-naked.

Ty shook his head to clear the erotic image that thought had spawned, and drew in a deep breath to relieve the tightening in his groin.

After Kacy—Catharine—had refused to marry him, he'd told himself he wasn't in love with her anymore. He had almost convinced himself too, until Jennifer passed away. He didn't know what he or his parents would have done without Catharine then. Her presence had been a pillar of strength to all of them, perhaps more to him, because she had rarely left his side. It was as though she knew he needed her without him having to say a word. But then, maybe she had needed him, too. She and Jennifer had been best friends all their lives. They had lived together for more than three years. Now Catharine lived alone and she had come to see him because she was afraid.

Thinking a strong drink might help put her at ease, he rooted around until he found the bottle of Peppermint Schnapps Sloan had given him for Christmas. He felt guilty as he poured half a jigger in each mug. Sloan expected to share the Schnapps with him. She didn't expect him to break up with her. But that was what he intended... why he hadn't gone out with her tonight.

He carried both mugs to the bathroom.

Seated on the edge of the tub, Catharine had removed her suit jacket and folded a towel across her lap. Her face had lost the blush of embarrassment, and she smiled as she accepted the hot mug, exposing the single dimple that made her so unique.

He smiled back, and tipped his mug to hers. "To the future."

"The future," she repeated, looking doubtful... and adorable.

Steam from the hot water made the bathroom humid, and small curls framed Catharine's beautiful, oval face. She had unpinned her French twist, and her long, blonde hair now hung loose down her back, in semi-wild disarray. Tyler raised his mug and took a slow sip, fantasizing about the silky strands sliding through his fingers, while he held her close. Would she resist? Or melt against him?

Catharine sipped her chocolate, then licked her lips. He wanted to lick them, too. He sipped his hot chocolate instead.

"The chocolate tastes different somehow," she said. "As though it contains mint of some sort."

"I added Peppermint Schnapps. A friend claims that once you've tasted hot chocolate with Peppermint Schnapps, you'll never want it any other way." Again he felt guilty about Sloan. He needed to tell her they had no future. Soon. He took another sip.

"Your friend could well be right." Catharine sipped again, too. "It's delicious."

So are you, Tyler thought, but left the words unsaid, and sipped more hot chocolate. The soft glow in Catharine's blue eyes enhanced her low, softly spoken words. He told himself not to get his hopes up. She might never return his affection.

"My feet are warm now." She stared up at him, waiting.

He knew she expected him to leave. But he set his half-full mug on the tan Formica vanity, grabbed a green bath towel and spread it on the tiled floor. "Step out and use that to dry your feet."

She did as he suggested, without dallying. That trait pleased him. Another woman might have argued... told him to leave.

Ty helped her limp back to his living room, each carrying their own half-filled mugs. After she sat down, he picked up the remote and shut the muted TV off. Sitting down beside her, he laid the remote back on the coffee table, by the Chinese takeout he'd been eating before the doorbell rang.

For a few seconds Catharine stared at the blank TV screen. Ty finished his drink, wishing he knew how to put her at ease. Maybe the Schnapps hadn't been such a good idea after all. The liquor relaxed his control. Made him want her. Made him horny.

He glanced at her bare feet. She was so petite they didn't reach the floor. Realizing they might get cold again dangling in midair, he plunked his empty mug on the coffee table, and pulled the blanket off the back of his striped couch, then spread it over her lap.

"Thank you." She smiled, tucking the fuzzy fleece blanket around her legs.

"Would you like to discuss Dillon McKenzie more fully now?"

"Would you like to discuss the weather?" she countered.

Ty grinned. In spite of the accident in London that had hospitalized her two years ago, and the coma she had been in for two long, worrisome weeks, she still had a sharp mind, quick wit, and dry humor. Somehow he found those traits more fascinating than ever before.

"All right, we'll discuss your fear first. Where did all this fear and distrust come from? I can't remember you ever being afraid of anything."

Catharine leaned back, pressing her shoulders against the couch. Then she clasped her hands together, looked down at them, then up at him. When she spoke, her voice was scarcely more than a whisper. "You cannot remember anything about me because you don't know me very well."

Ty cleared his throat. "I think I know you well enough. We lived in the same neighborhood for about fifteen years."

She shook her head. "You're under the misapprehension that I'm Kacy. But I'm not."

For half a second shock stunned him speechless. "Look," he said, ignoring the desire to take her hands in his, "you don't have to pretend you're not yourself just because you changed a little after your accident."

She stared into his eyes, deeply, without blinking. "You truly believe I'm her, don't you?"

That shocked him anew, knocked him off balance. "What?"

"Kacy. You think I'm her. It flatters me that you do. I hold her in high regard."

Ty tensed his jaw, eyeing her with deepening concern. "If you're not Kacy, who are you?"

"I am someone," she hesitated and swallowed before blurting, "—someone who is afraid of most men."

He didn't comment. He didn't know what to say. *Had she lost her mind? Gone off the deep end?*

"Kacy and I switched places twenty months ago because she wished to live where I did, and I couldn't bear to live there any longer. I call her grandparents mine, however, they're not."

Ty couldn't believe his ears. *Was she crazy? Or was something else wrong?* Had he fallen asleep while watching the news on CNN... Was this a dream?

He raised his hand to the back of his neck to rub a rigid muscle.

Cold goose bumps greeted his fingers. Neither the gesture nor the goose bumps were something he ever recalled having in dreams.

He slid closer and caught a whiff of Catharine's faint perfume. Different from the flowery fragrance he'd always associated with Kacy. Slightly sweet, like maraschino cherries with a hint of almond.

"So, who are you?" he asked to humor her. "If you're not Kacy Rose?"

"I was born in England, in Kent, a very long time ago, and my parents christened me Catharine Paice."

"How long ago?" Would she claim she'd been born the same year as Kacy? He didn't know why he wondered that. The ripe old age of twenty-one, going on twenty-two wasn't all that long ago.

"Do you truly wish to know?"

"Sure."

"In 1837."

Shock was Tyler's first reaction. Disbelief came next, then anxiety. She'd flipped, toppled over the brink of sanity. She was nuts, possibly certifiable.

"Kacy—Catharine, I'm Tyler, your friend. Remember? Don't make up stories. I want the truth."

"But what I just told you is the truth. Two years ago Kacy traveled back to the year eighteen fifty-four with her guardian angel. That's where I met her. The angel brought me to this century because I didn't wish to live in the nineteenth any longer, and Jennifer agreed to help me learn how to live in this time so Kacy could go back."

Ty jumped to his feet, rammed his hand through his hair, and started to pace. "This nonsense has gone far enough. Tell me…"

"Pardon me, please, for rudely interrupting." She clasped her hands together, and frowned up at him. "Would you please sit down?"

Ty stopped pacing and searched her eyes. "This is ridiculous."

She shook her head. "'Tis not. My real name is Catharine Paice. Not Kacy. Nor Kathryn Cassandra Rose. And I have more to say. About Jennifer."

As an attorney Ty was trained to read people, and he knew she wasn't faking. This was no joke. She was in dead earnest. He sat down, not as close as earlier. "What about Jennifer?"

"Please brace yourself. What I have to say may come as a bit of a shock."

"I'm ready."

"She isn't dead."

Ty wasn't ready. Not to hear that.

"Of course she is. We buried her ten days ago. You attended the funeral. Have you forgotten?"

"No. But I knew she wasn't Jennifer before the funeral. I didn't know whether to tell you or leave it be after the automobile accident. Then Jennifer returned, and I left the matter in her hands."

"What?" Ty jumped back up to his feet. "How can somebody return from the dead?"

Catharine, who was beginning to seem more like a stranger with each passing second, shook her head again. "Jennifer didn't return from the dead. The girl who died, the girl you and your parents buried, was someone else. Her name was Miranda. She assumed Jennifer's identity after Jennifer went back to live in the same time as Kacy."

"This is crazy," Ty ranted. "How dare you trump up such stories? And why tell them to me? What's your reason? And if Jennifer's alive, why did you wait this long to mention it?"

He paused, giving Catharine a chance to answer.

She licked her lips and lowered her head, breaking eye contact. "I can prove what I say is true."

"How?"

She opened the navy backpack she'd plunked on the floor by the couch, and ransacked until she found a VCR tape.

"Jennifer left this. She returned the morning we planned the funeral. I think she considered calling to tell you she's still alive. But if she had, there would have been no easy way to explain her disappearance if she returned to the past. And then that man came, and she decided to go back with him."

Dumbfounded, Tyler could only stare as Catharine extended the VCR tape.

"Jennifer made this for me, and for you, in the event I decided to share it with you. And now I have made that decision."

Tyler seized the tape, but he didn't insert it into the VCR. He had too many questions, but didn't even know where to begin.

Had the only girl he'd ever truly been attracted to gone off her rocker, into some other dimension? Was her mind now incapable of discerning fact from fiction? Is that why she acted so differently? Why she sat there looking innocent, fragile and demure after spinning such unbelievable tales?

He rammed his hand through his hair again and paced the carpet. *Kacy and Jennifer had not traveled back in time and decided to live in the mid 1850's any more than two strangers who looked exactly like them had traveled to the future and taken over their identities as well as their lives.*

The whole thing was unthinkable.

Impossible.

Too far-fetched even to consider.

Catharine had flipped out of her ever-loving mind.

That thought sobered him. He must handle her with care. Humor her and find a way to get her medical attention without causing more harm.

Three

Catharine watched Tyler pace the floor, the VCR tape in hand. Uneasiness thrashed through her when he examined it, then paced again. How could she make him believe she had spoken the truth? That she wasn't a twister? A liar?

Jennifer had talked about him so often, Catharine felt as though she knew him. But he was a virtual stranger. She had deliberately kept it that way, and couldn't quite believe she had worked up the Dutch courage to come here alone tonight.

Her fear of men had lived inside her ever since her papa passed away when she was seven years old. Except for him and Rey, the guardian angel who had brought her to the twenty-first century, Catharine had always been nervous around men, and afraid to be alone with one. Until now. She thought Tyler top-drawer. And oddly enough, with him she felt safe.

Almost two years ago she had run away, knowing she might never return to her home in Kent, England. At the time she hadn't known she would leave the nineteenth century. But she didn't regret her decision to live in the twenty-first. In the 1850's she would have been expected to marry. Here it wasn't at all uncommon for women to remain single. That suited her. Wilbur, her step-papa, had been a repulsive, domineering bully, who imposed enough rules to last several lifetimes. She didn't want any man to control her life ever again.

Catharine thought she had adjusted to this time quite well. For fourteen months Jennifer had been a very patient house mate, teacher and friend. She had answered Catharine's questions, introduced her to hundreds of modern conveniences, taught her how to use many of them, and showed her things that still boggled her mind.

Tyler captured Catharine's full attention again when he set the VCR tape down, and cleared the remains of uneaten Chinese food off the coffee table.

While he carried the plastic fork and white food cartons from the room, her thoughts wandered again. Last August after Jennifer flew to England; Miranda had arrived from the past and announced a wizard had brought her forward in time. For five months Catharine had enjoyed the role of teacher. Although they were friends, Catharine had been appalled by Miranda's flagrant misuse of Jennifer's credit cards, and her total disregard that Jennifer's trust fund wasn't hers to spend as she wished.

In spite of disagreeing about that, they had lived together until Miranda drove Jennifer's car during a perilous snowstorm, and got herself killed. Catharine hadn't had a decent night's sleep since then. She felt somewhat responsible. If she had been more firm with Miranda, insisted that her behavior was out of line, Miranda might still be alive.

Tyler returned from disposing of the food. Without a word he picked the tape up again and inserted it into his VCR.

Catharine started to shake. Even her teeth chattered. How would he react to seeing Jennifer on his TV screen? Would he believe the tape had been made after Miranda died? Whether he did or not, would he keep Catharine's secret that she was an imposter? Or expose her as a fraud?

Anxiety attacked. She nearly jumped up and dashed out of his flat. But where could she go? It wasn't as though she had scads of friends. Besides, her gammy ankle hurt too much to walk, let alone run.

Tyler interrupted her turbulent thoughts when he sat beside her and picked up the remote. After he pushed a few buttons, the fuzzy TV screen cleared, the static buzzing stopped and Jennifer appeared.

"She recorded the tape when she returned to this century the morning after Miranda died," Catharine quickly explained.

Tyler frowned his disbelief, but said nothing, merely returned his gaze to the TV.

"Hi," Jennifer said from the screen. "I'm making this tape for you, Catharine, and also for Tyler, in case you decide to share it with him. If you're watching it now, Ty, I'll assume Catharine has done as I suggested and told you she isn't Kacy. Please don't worry about Kacy. She's alive and well in the nineteenth century, and as you can see, I'm also alive and well. I'm terribly sorry Aunt Rachel and Uncle Mack think I'm dead, but I've been living in the past for five months now and I don't think I could live here in this time again and be happy."

Jennifer paused, presumably to catch her breath. "You see, a wizard switched Miranda and I. She's the girl who died while driving my car. Apparently she looked exactly like me. I'll let Catharine explain more about Miranda, if you have questions."

Tyler pushed the remote to stop the tape, and turned his scowl toward Catharine. "Tell me about Miranda."

Catharine clasped her nervous hands together, trying not to flinch under his intense scrutiny. "Miranda and I met at Miss Treacher's Academy for Young Ladies when I lived in the past."

"How did she switch places with Jennifer?"

"As she said on the recording, a wizard arranged it."

"A wizard?" Tyler scoffed. "You can't expect me to believe that guff."

"Perhaps not, but wizards do happen to exist."

Tyler smirked. *Perhaps deservedly so,* Catharine thought. Still, she frowned. "Should I continue or not?"

"Yeah. Go ahead."

"I understand the wizard wanted Miranda's soul, and told her I was here to whet her appetite. When he bragged that he could bring her to the future, she made him prove it before she promised her soul. Even then, she didn't promise it. I think that made him angry, which might be why she died."

"If that's true, and I'm not saying I believe it, did Jennifer strike a bargain with the wizard?"

"No." Catharine shook her head. "At least not to my knowledge. However, when she came back the morning after Miranda's accident, I was in a hurry to leave for your parent's home to help you plan the funeral. Therefore, I didn't have much time to talk to Jennifer. I hope to see her and hear about her experiences before she leaves this time."

"Leaves this time?" He looked confounded. "Where is she?"

Catharine cleared her throat, summoning more courage. She truly disliked being interrogated. "In England."

"Can you prove that?"

She nodded. "There's more on the tape."

Tyler blinked, but instead of asking more questions, he pressed the remote again. A few tension-filled seconds later, Jennifer reappeared on the screen.

She smiled before she said, "Ty, you know Kacy and I believe in reincarnation, as you do. We believe we have and will live more than once, and we've both decided to live out our current lives in the nineteenth century. We've found love there, with the men we knew and loved before, and we expect to be happy. Wonderfully happy."

Grinning, Jennifer added, "I have another surprise, Ty." She stretched out her hand. A man with platinum blond hair and a neatly trimmed mustache walked to her side and slid his arm around her waist.

"This is Drake, the man I've always loved. I'm sure you'll recognize him because he used to be our neighbor, Dirk. He's my husband now. Again. If you're curious and want to know more, please fly with Catharine to London and we'll tell you all about the events that led to my decision to live in the past."

"Catharine," Jennifer continued, "Kacy wrote a journal and put it in Barings Bank to explain what happened after she switched places with you. I understand people don't have safety deposit boxes in England, but they may take a box of their own and have it locked in the bank's vault. I'm hoping to retrieve Kacy's journal from the vault when I fly to London, and I'll give it to you when—if I see you."

"Ty, Catharine has never flown before, and I'd really appreciate it if you could fly with her to England before we leave. We're hoping you'll want to see us as much as we'd like to see you."

Jennifer smiled up at the man beside her and waited for him to speak.

"Hello, Catharine. Hi, Ty. Jennifer and I hate to leave Denver without seeing you, but we can't stay here. We're too tempted to try to see you, your parents, and my own. I feel needed in the past, and Jennifer agrees that's where we belong." He smiled down at Jennifer. "I think she has more to say."

Jennifer's speckled green eyes sparkled as she spoke. "If you can manage to get away from the office, Ty, and fly to London with Catharine, she'll know where to find us. I hope you can come. We'd love to see you. I'd like to give you a hug and tell you goodbye in person."

"If we don't see you, perhaps we'll meet again in another life. If we do, I hope we retain our memories, so we recognize each other and remember what we've shared. Don't mourn for me, Ty. I'll try not to mourn too much for you, also. Please accept that I'm alive and happy somewhere."

Jennifer placed her fingers on her lips and blew a kiss. "Always remember that I love you, both of you. Farewell now. Until we meet again."

Jennifer blew another kiss, and her husband smiled down at her before the screen went fuzzy once more.

"Will you fly with me to England?" Catharine asked, anxious to hear Tyler's reply and unable to gauge his mood.

"Why did you wait so long to show me this tape?" he demanded instead of answering.

"I had a score of doubts. I still don't know if I have done the right thing. Jennifer made the recording for both of us, but I wasn't sure you would believe she traveled back in time, or that I traveled forward."

"Right," Tyler said. "The whole idea is too improbable to be anything other than fabrication."

"I'm sorry you feel that way."

He studied her so long she felt like squirming, but she had no reason to act like an intimidated twit.

After a prolonged silence, he said, "Why don't we sleep on it, and discuss my decision in the morning?"

Relieved he hadn't refused outright, Catharine said, "As you wish."

"I'll go get some blankets and a pillow."

"Thank you."

"They're not for you. They're for me. You can sleep in my bed. I'll sleep out here."

"No. I couldn't. It wouldn't be at all proper for me to sleep in your bed."

When he didn't reply, she asked in a trembly voice, "Would it?"

"Nobody gives a rip about being proper any more. Haven't you learned that?" Without waiting for an answer, he added, "You look bushed, but I'm not tired."

"I couldn't sleep yet either. The hour is still quite early. Perhaps we could watch TV together until we're both tired."

Tyler frowned before he walked away. A few minutes later he returned with an armload of blankets and a pillow.

"I put clean sheets out. My cleaning lady changed them yesterday, but if you want clean ones, I hope you won't mind changing the bed." He stood by the couch gazing down at her, an unreadable expression on his handsome face.

Catharine relaxed her stiff posture. Tyler hadn't tried to touch her. Nor did he give her that creepy-crawly feeling other men did.

He piled the blankets and pillow on the couch between them, sat back down and picked up the remote. But instead of turning the TV on, he said, "Tell me more about Dillon McKenzie. What's his position at the company?"

"He's a petroleum geologist."

"Does he spend most of his time in the office? Or in the field?"

"In the office."

"How many times a day does he try to touch you?"

When she didn't answer right away, Tyler probed, his darkened gaze intent. "Once? Twice? More or less than that?"

"At least two or three times each morning. That many or more in the afternoon, especially if he drinks during the noon hour."

"The bastard," Tyler growled, staring at the blank TV screen.

Catharine flinched at his harsh tone.

"We'll nail his butt to the wall."

Unable to imagine how, she asked, "How does one go about doing that?"

Tyler turned an exasperated glare at her. "I didn't mean it literally. I was speaking figuratively."

"I see."

He shifted sideways on the couch. "Do you want to stop him from harassing you?"

"Yes, of course. But I hoped there might be an easier way."

"Do you have something in mind?"

"I suppose I could try to find employment elsewhere."

"Don't you care that he might treat other women the way he treats you?"

"Croikey, I didn't think about that." She ducked her head. "I just want to avoid unpleasantness, if at all possible."

"Why?"

She looked up, met his gaze. "Because I dislike up and downers."

Ty's brows shot up. "Drugs? You use drugs?"

Catharine shook her head. "A row. A disagreement."

He relaxed the crease in his forehead. "Do you consider this discussion difficult? Contentious?"

"No."

He smiled then. She liked his smile. It was very handsome, just like him. He reached out to squeeze her hand before she knew what he intended. She tensed, but didn't pull away.

"Does my touch make you nervous?"

"Yes."

"Why?"

"I don't know. I guess—I don't like to be touched."

"By anyone?"

"By men."

"Why?"

"You ask that a lot."

"I'm an attorney. My job is to ask questions."

Catharine tried to smile. He still held her hand. It startled her that she didn't mind. She actually liked the feel of his warm skin against hers. And that surprised her mightily.

"Why don't you like men to touch you?"

"Mother said I had a harrowing experience when my father passed on. I must have blocked it from my mind because I don't remember what happened."

Ty let go of her hand, leaned back and crossed an ankle over his Levi-covered knee. "Let's assume I believe everything you've told me. That you came from the distant past. Let's further assume you're Catharine, a prim and proper young lady who grew up in Victorian England, and we're not well acquainted."

Catharine liked it that he sounded cooperative, and she relaxed again.

"Let's further assume that the girl my parents buried ten days ago wasn't my cousin, Jennifer, but an imposter you knew very well, having lived with her for—how long did you say?"

"I didn't. I attended the academy where I met Miranda for only half a year before my stepfather insisted that I return home. Miranda and I carried on a lively correspondence until I left the past. She was here five months before she died."

Ty hiked his brows in disbelief. "Miranda impersonated Jennifer, used her identity for five months?"

"Yes."

"And not once during all that time did you think it important to tell me or my parents?"

"I didn't know what to do. Miranda said the wizard wouldn't bring Jennifer back as long as she was here, and she wanted to stay. Besides, you and your parents thought she was Jennifer. I don't know if I could have convinced you otherwise. I wasn't even sure Jennifer could when she returned."

"Yet now you want me to believe Jennifer's still alive, somewhere in the past?"

"Not yet in the past," Catharine corrected. "At the moment she's in England."

Ty stared at Catharine, sitting stiff and tense again, her back ramrod straight beyond the mound of bedding he'd stacked between them. Nothing he'd seen, heard, or said since he opened his apartment door seemed real. But she looked upset, so he tried to soothe her by gently asking, "Is it true that you've never flown in an airplane?"

"Yes, and the thought terrifies me. Although, I doubt it can be much more harrowing than traveling through that spiraling time tunnel to get here."

Spiraling time tunnel? Ty forced his expression to remain bland. "I assume that's how you supposedly came to this time."

Catharine nodded. "Rey held my hand all the way. If we fly together in an airplane, would you hold my hand?"

Confused, Ty frowned. "Rey? Who is Rey?"

"An angel."

"Are you afraid of him?"

"Goodness no. He's Kacy's guardian angel. I wish he were mine as well."

Goose bumps dribbled down Tyler's spine. Years ago Jennifer had told him about Kacy's imaginary guardian angel. She'd even given him a name. Rey. She'd claimed she had a fairy godmother named Fey, too. Ty had always admired Kacy's lively imagination, although he'd never told her. Admiration wasn't all he'd felt. He had loved her. Still did.

During their teenage years, he and Kacy, and Jennifer and Dirk, were together as often as possible. They had dated so long he assumed Kacy was as crazy about him as Jennifer was about Dirk.

Shortly after the girls graduated from high school the four had all flown to Vegas so Jennifer and Dirk could elope. Tyler had considered suggesting he and Kacy tie the knot, too. When she hadn't given him any encouragement, he decided marriage should wait until he graduated from Harvard Law School.

Even after Dirk died, Ty still believed Kacy loved him. A full year passed before he discovered she didn't feel the way he did.

So, who was the girl sitting on his couch? This dead ringer for Kacy who didn't act anything at all like her? Was Kacy merely acting out her vivid imagination? Had she lost her memories when she'd been hit by that London taxi two years ago? Or was this really Catharine? A woman who had come from the past?

There seemed to be one way to find out. Fly to England with her and see for himself whether Jennifer was alive or dead. He'd believe Catharine's cockamamie claim only if he saw Jennifer in person, and she told him Catharine wasn't Kacy.

In spite of his doubts, he no longer believed she was crazy. She sounded rational and had an answer for every question. But she could still be acting, although he couldn't imagine why she'd do such a thing.

"If we fly to London, what would you do about work?" he asked.

Catharine blinked rapidly, signaling a crack in her composure. "I thought I might call and leave a message that I've been called out of town."

Ty decided he could, and would, take care of that for her. He'd always been a sucker where Kacy was concerned. And now, even though he called himself ten times a fool, he found himself more infatuated than ever. *With her? Or this stranger? Was she truly a stranger?*

He cautioned himself not to get too emotionally involved. He'd been disappointed previously. It could happen again.

Four

Although nervous about spending the night in Tyler's bed, Catharine climbed between the bed sheets around eleven p.m. The covers smelled faintly of Tyler, and his spicy cologne. She closed her eyes, fell asleep, and slept like a baby cocooned in her mother's warm embrace.

Refreshed when she awakened in the morning, the first thing she did was check her gammy ankle. Still swollen. Croikey, it hurt, too. She winced, wishing she could somehow come up with a quick miracle cure. "Fey?" she whispered. "Are you here?"

"Yes, sweetling." The fairy flew across the room and hovered in midair a few feet from Catharine's face. "What can I do for you?"

Catharine hesitated, not sure she should ask, but finally did. "Do you have the power to heal sprained ankles?"

Fey nodded, waving her glittering silver wand. To Catharine's surprise the swelling in her ankle disappeared. She poked again. No more pain. "Thank you."

"You're welcome." Fey smiled. "Anything else?"

Catharine smiled, too. "Clean clothes would be appreciated. But Tyler would probably wonder where they came from and I've already given him enough to swallow without explaining you."

"At least I can provide new underclothes." Fey giggled, waving her wand again. A pink lacy bra with matching panties and new pantyhose appeared out of thin air.

"You're wonderful, Fey." Catharine laughed. "Thanks ever so much. I guess I should bathe and get ready to face Tyler."

Fey wrinkled her pixie forehead. "He's not an ogre."

Catharine smiled. "You're right." A huge thrill splashed through her. Soon she would see him again. "He's actually rather nice."

"Of course he is. Otherwise you wouldn't love him."

"I don't love him," Catharine protested, frowning, but unable to control the erratic pounding in her chest. "I do like him though."

"Whatever," Fey said. "You mortals place such importance on trivial words."

With a silvery flash of her tiny wand, Fey disappeared, leaving Catharine to wonder what trivial words meant. She thought love was rather profound. Not one bit trivial. And she ought to know. She'd lived without it in several lifetimes. Without Tyler's love. Without Tyler.

Sometime during the night she had recalled a number of past lives. In each one she had known Tyler. More often than not he had been involved with other women. They had admired and respected each other as friends, and mostly from afar. She had loved him in secret but never told another soul. Except in one life. Then, when she had told him, he had admitted he loved her, too. But The Plague had struck. And claimed both their lives.

A wave of longing struck. Catharine sighed. Would the memories influence her current life? Dare she let them? What about her decision never to allow any man to control her life? She felt her resolve weakening, her heart melting. And that frightened her. She didn't believe she could be a good wife, no matter how much love might enter into the equation.

Ty waited for Catharine in the living room. She came out of the bathroom dressed in the blue suit and pink blouse she'd worn the previous night. She looked very appealing, although she still had that shy, timid expression.

Her makeup, the little she wore, lipstick and mascara, had been carefully applied after the bath he'd heard her taking about thirty minutes ago. Except for pantyhose she was barefoot. But she no longer limped.

He stared at her ankle. The swelling appeared to be gone. With her hair coiled in a French twist and her blouse collar neatly tucked beneath her suit jacket, she looked prim and proper. Tyler wanted to reach out and muss her up. But he didn't dare touch her. She might bolt.

If she was as scared as she looked, everything she'd said could be true. He still had doubts though. Believing in reincarnation followed logic. Time travel, guardian angels and wizards did not.

Another thought intruded. If Catharine wasn't Kacy, what had happened in her youth to make her so afraid? He hated the images that question conjured—a man molesting a young girl, using her to satisfy his sick lust, while the terrified child cried and fought and failed to get free, and was left feeling defiled and unclean and unable to trust a man ever again.

Shaking his head to clear those images, Tyler wished he knew how to make Catharine unafraid. He hated having her watch him as though she expected him to pounce any second.

"Good morning," he said, breaking the silence she seemed to favor.

"Good morning."

"How's your ankle?"

"Much better, thank you."

"Are you sure? If not, we could go see a doctor. You might have sprained it. If so, you should probably stay off it for a few days."

"My ankle couldn't be better." She smiled shyly, yet a puckish gleam brightened her blue eyes. "Perhaps Kacy's guardian angel or fairy godmother healed it for me."

Ignoring that implausible statement, Tyler asked, "Are you hungry?"

"I don't wish to be coddled. However, the truth is I'm famished. I didn't eat last night."

"Why didn't you say something? I would have been happy—"

She raised her hand to cut him off. "Last night I was too upset to eat, or even think about it. Please don't feel you must feed me. I can take care of myself, after a fashion, that is."

"Did you sleep all right?"

She nodded, her cheeks turning pink. "I slept quite well, thank you very much."

Ty suppressed a grin, forcing his mouth into a straight line. The becoming blush made her look adorable. Shy too, but a little less frightened. He squelched the urge to ask if she had enjoyed sleeping in his bed... in his apartment. If she admitted she had, he'd feel what? That he'd made some progress because she wanted to sleep under the same roof?

Telling himself he was beginning to think like a nut, he moved the stack of blankets he'd folded over an hour ago to the end of the couch. Now she'd have to sit by him, if she sat down.

"Would you like something to drink?" he asked.

"Yes, please. Do you have tea?"

He nodded.

"Would it be too much trouble to brew a pot?"

That was definitely not like Kacy. She never drank anything that contained caffeine. Is that why he suspected the young woman standing so rigidly ten feet away had told the truth? Or was it because he had known Kacy so well and loved her so long, he knew she would never lie or try to put something over on him?

"I don't have a teapot, but I can fix a cup or two of tea in the microwave." He headed for the kitchen, pleased when she followed.

Last night before he slept, he had reluctantly concluded that Catharine, not Kacy, might be the girl he had known and secretly loved in prior lives. Although still not certain, he couldn't ignore the heroic thrill of knowing she had come to him when she was frightened and needed help. Perhaps, just as she had in prior lives? The girl he'd known then had always held a special place in his heart, but not in his life.

After he filled a mug with water and popped it into the microwave, he rummaged in a cupboard until he found the flowered tea caddy somebody had given him as a housewarming gift when he moved in. While they waited for the water to heat, Tyler refilled his mug with coffee, then slid the tea caddy across the counter toward Catharine.

Her eyes lit up, sparkling as she read, "Mrs. Bridges English Breakfast. It's from England."

Ty nodded.

"I thought everyone in Denver and Colorado drank those herbal teas that are made in Boulder."

He grinned. "I imagine a lot of Coloradoans do." The microwave bell sounded. He pulled her mug out, and set it in front of her along with a clean spoon. "Do you want cream?"

"Yes, please." She smiled. "You're very well stocked for a bachelor. I wouldn't have expected that."

"I like my coffee strong and with cream." He shoved the carton across the shiny counter, grateful Ginny, his cleaning lady, had cleaned on Thursday this week instead of Tuesday. Otherwise, there likely would be dishes in the sink and crumbs on the counter.

"How about sugar?" he asked.

"Yes, please."

As he reached in a cupboard behind him, the phone rang. He snatched the covered sugar bowl and plunked it in front of Catherine before he picked up the receiver. "Hello."

"Hi, Tyler. It's me... Sloan. I'm going to be in your neighborhood in about an hour, and I wondered if you'd like to meet me for coffee and one of those decadent cinnamon rolls, like we ate last Saturday."

"Sorry. I already have plans." With Catharine now less than four feet away—only the counter separated them—he knew his free time would be tied up for quite awhile. And that bothered him not at all. The mysteries that lay behind her quiet demeanor fascinated him, and he intended to do all he could to unravel them.

"I'm sorry, too," Sloan said. "If you change your mind, you know where I'll be."

Ty said goodbye and hung up. He'd been dating Sloan for six months, but they hadn't slept together. She was willing, eager even, but he wasn't. He considered her a friend and colleague but knew she wanted more than friendship. That might have been possible a month ago. It wasn't now, and hadn't been since the accident that claimed Jennifer's life... or Miranda's, the person who might have impersonated Jennifer. Shortly after they heard the awful news, Catharine had rushed into his life and acted like an anchor. Not only for him, but for his devastated parents as well. Ever since, she had claimed a good portion of his thoughts.

Ty knew he had to break off with Sloan, but she hadn't given him a chance. The fact that he'd turned down her invitation to a party last night didn't seem to faze her.

Dismissing Sloan from his thoughts, Tyler smiled at Catharine. "How about some toast, and bacon and eggs?"

"They sound delicious." Catharine offered another smile, a feeble one, but a smile nonetheless, before she spooned the tea bag from her mug and set it on a paper towel she had folded with precise neatness while he talked on the phone. After she added cream and sugar and stirred, she took a dainty sip. Then she asked, "What can I do to help?"

"Nothing. Just keep me company and enjoy your tea."

She watched him turn a gas burner on, select two frying pans, and collect eggs and bacon from the fridge. "I've never seen a man cook before."

"Then you're in for a treat, aren't you?"

"I would like to think so." Her eyes twinkled with the first merriment he'd seen in them since when? Christmas day, when she and Jennifer, or rather Miranda, had stopped by his parent's home, delivered gifts and stayed for dinner.

Delighted that Catharine's mood had lifted, Tyler winked.

"Prepare to see a man of action."

He separated the bacon and placed it in one frying pan. When it sizzled, he turned it over, then cracked two eggs against each other and dropped each one, separately in the other frying pan.

"Tyler?"

"Yes?"

"I really would like to help."

"Good. You're in charge of the toast. The bread and butter are in the fridge. So's the marmalade."

"I can lay the table, too."

"Lay?" His pulse throbbed with sudden physical awareness. "You must mean set the table."

"Where I came from we sit on chairs and lay the table."

"Makes sense to me," he said with good-natured humor.

She smiled again, this time with less timidity. Tyler felt as though he had gained entry to a locked door. What would he discover inside? He couldn't wait to find out, but then he'd always been anxious to uncover her. His Miss Right.

Jolted by that thought, he frowned. He was thinking like a smitten swain in one of those romance novels Jennifer had enjoyed so much.

His gut feeling told him Catharine wasn't Kacy. Even though they looked exactly alike, right down to the tiny scar on her dimpled cheek, Catharine acted very differently.

After she helped him set... or lay the table, they sat down to eat. "Do you think it will be possible for you to travel to England with me?"

Ty nodded. "I checked flight schedules to London on the Internet this morning, and..."

"And?" she prompted, her blue eyes bright with interest.

"I made reservations."

A full-fledged smile covered her beautiful face. "Wonderful. When will we leave?"

Amused by her eagerness, he winked. "Early in the morning. We'll have to get up at the crack of dawn."

"You don't waste time, do you?"

He grinned. "Not if I can help it, Cath."

"I like it that you have shortened my name. No one ever has before."
She lowered her head, as though she shouldn't have admitted that.

He reached across the table and cupped her cheek. Instead of
trying to raise her chin or force her gaze to his, he waited for her
to do it on her own. When she did, he said, "And I like it that you
came to me last night when you were frightened. That you trusted
me enough to share your secret and show me the VCR tape. Also,
that you stayed here and slept in my bed."

She blushed. Swallowed. Licked her lips, as though she didn't
know how to respond. Then she said, "If we're going to London, I
should probably show you Jennifer's postcard."

Ty hiked his brows in surprise. "Postcard?"

Catharine nodded. "I was so nervous last night it slipped my
mind. It's in my backpack. I'll go get it."

He watched her slip away. For a few seconds he had the oddest
sensation she might disappear without warning. He shook the
thought away, and was relieved when she returned.

She extended a postcard. The brilliant Las Vegas night scene bore
a week-old postmark on the back, and Jennifer's familiar scrawl.

> *Loved talking to you last night, Catharine. Sorry
> Dillon's still bothering you. Tell Tyler. He'll help. Hope
> to see you in England. Call and let us know your plans.
> Leave a message if we're not in, and we'll call you back
> ASAP.*

The card had been signed simply with the initial, J.

Goose bumps prickled Ty's neck and arms. It had been written
by his cousin, Jennifer. All the capital letters had familiar curlicues.
One more piece of evidence to indicate Catharine had told nothing
but the truth.

He raised his gaze to hers, feeling a bit short of breath as that
thought sunk in. "When did you talk to Jennifer?"

"On Friday, a week past. She called from Las Vegas."

Rubbing his goose bumps and still wondering why he was willing to accept circumstantial evidence, he asked, "Do you know where they are now?"

"I expect they're in London. At the Grosvenor Hotel."

Ty's legal training and experience had made him cynical, yet part of him believed Catharine hadn't lied. He couldn't doubt the sincerity in her eyes anymore than he could doubt the postcard in his hand. She had no reason to fake any of this. At least none that he could fathom.

"When we finish eating," he said, deciding to trust his gut, "I'll drive you to your house to pack. I think you should stay here again tonight. It'll be more convenient to go to the airport together from here."

She nodded in agreement.

That she made no comment didn't surprise him. Sometimes she didn't speak unless she had a very good reason. He'd discovered that at the funeral. At the time he'd thought grief and sorrow kept her quiet. Now he realized it might just be her way.

"I'll do the washing up," Catharine said, when they finished eating.

"The what?" Tyler asked, confused.

"The washing up. The dishes. You did the cooking. I'll clean up."

Sipping his coffee, he enjoyed watching her clear the table and bustle around his kitchen. It would be easy to get used to having her around all the time. Once again he cautioned himself not to get his hopes up. If she had truly come from a different century, she might go back.

"We had servants to do this sort of thing in the past." She smiled as she rinsed the plates before stacking them in the dishwasher. "I never learned to cook or clean until I came to this time. It's quite a novelty. I've discovered I enjoy domestic chores."

"It's a good thing," Tyler said, since I doubt you can afford to hire help."

"I may not even be capable of paying my rent if I quit working before I find new employment," she said, then quickly changed the subject. "Maybe we should call Jennifer?" Catharine consulted her wristwatch. "It's about four in the afternoon in London, so now might be a good time. If we wait much longer, they may be out."

"Do you have the phone number of the Grosvenor Hotel?"

"Yes. In my backpack." Having brought it to the kitchen when she went for the postcard, she rummaged around and pulled out a scrap of paper. "Here 'tis."

Ty stared at the digits. The handwriting didn't resemble Kacy's bold scrawl. Someone else had written those small, neat numbers. Must have been Catharine, this timid young lady who twisted his insides into knots and suddenly made him want to take care of her for the rest of his life.

Wrestling with that startling thought, he asked, "Whom should I ask for when I call?"

"Mr. or Mrs. Castlebury."

A frown puckered Tyler's forehead. Seeing Jennifer alive on the VCR tape after thinking they had buried her had shocked him. Seeing Dirk, his best friend, who'd been killed in a car crash almost four years ago, had shocked him even more. It also confounded him. Although the man on the tape looked older and sported a mustache, he had Dirk's eyes and voice. He even had the same small mole under his left eye.

Ty stared at the postcard, knowing he could no more refuse to fly to London, even if the trip was nothing more than a wild goose chase, than he could quit breathing. He'd already called his dad and told him he needed some time off. His father had assured him the family law firm could get along without him while he was gone.

This morning Ty had also called Catharine's office and left a message on the recorder, stating he was her attorney and she had been called out of town unexpectedly and wouldn't be back to work. They should hire a replacement. He wasn't about to let her work any longer in an office with Dillon McKenzie. She might not like what he'd done, but he'd acted in her best interest.

Picking up the phone he dialed the international code for England and the number for the Grosvenor Hotel in London. He could hardly believe his ears when Jennifer answered.

"Hello."

"Jennifer?"

"Yes. Tyler! It's wonderful to hear your voice."

"Yours, too. I can't tell you what I'm feeling right now."

"Shell shock, I imagine."

"Right."

"Are you coming to England?"

"Yes."

"Good grief, I'm so happy I think I'm going to cry. I'll let you talk to my husband, and I'll talk to you again in a few minutes."

Ty heard her sniffle, then a familiar masculine voice. "Hello, Ty. This is Dirk. How are you?"

"Astonished. How are you?"

"Better than I've been in years." He didn't waste time on any more formalities. He simply asked, "Can you fly to England? Jennifer and I would both like to see you."

"I've made reservations. We should arrive at Heathrow late tomorrow night."

"Have you booked rooms in London?"

"Not yet."

"We'll be happy to book them for you here at the Grosvenor."

"Please do."

"Consider it done. And don't worry about the expense. This trip, including your airfare is on us."

A few seconds later he said, "Hold on a minute. Jennifer wants to talk to you again."

"I knew you'd take good care of Catharine," Jennifer said. "Thanks. Now I won't have to worry about her, and I can't wait to see both of you."

"We'll see you soon."

"Please be careful. I couldn't bear it if anything happened to you, Ty. And be gentle with Catharine. She's kind of fragile."

"So I've discovered."

He hung up, staring at Catharine as though seeing her for the first time. She really was a stranger. He hadn't known her all his life. Yet he had a strong hunch she was the girl he had dreamt about, on and off, for years. Was he still hung up on Kacy, who had always made him laugh and feel like a hero? Truth be told, he didn't know. This pretty stranger had claimed his full attention, and he had a strong premonition she would continue to do so for quite some time.

Ty reached in his pocket and pulled out his car keys. "Let's hit the road."

Catharine scrunched her forehead in a frown. "Whatever for?"

"We need to drive to your place so you can pack."

She nodded, although she looked a bit confused. He had to hand it to her. If she was Kacy, she was doing a damn good job of acting like someone else.

Five

The peacock blue sky contrasted with the frosty winter chill when Catharine and Tyler climbed in the taxicab early Sunday morning. She sat on the edge of the seat, drew in a deep breath, and let it out slowly. They were on their way to Denver International Airport, and she couldn't get rid of the butterflies in her middle. She was actually going to fly in an airplane. One of those huge metallic jet-birds that soared through the sky and left what Jennifer called contrails, that looked like long, thin clouds.

"Are you nervous?" Tyler asked.

Catharine nodded. "I've been out by the airport to watch planes land and take off, and I saw a program on the PBS Channel that explained flying and jet engines. However, I still don't understand why planes don't drop out of the sky. They're so heavy. And their wings are immobile. Nothing at all like a flapping bird's."

Tyler grinned. "It isn't necessary to understand the aerodynamics as long as the manufacturer does. Our plane won't fall out of the sky. Trust me."

"I do, Tyler. You must know that by now."

"I'm beginning to believe you do."

Catharine loosened her grip on her reticule—backpack, and stared out the window. She had adjusted to most modern words but backpack sounded like something that should be strapped on an animal, not a human.

Outside, last night's new snow glistened on rooftops, tree branches and lawns. Fat snowmen with black top hats, carrot noses, lime green tennis balls for eyes and colorful red, yellow, and blue scarves draped around their thick necks, decorated several front yards. The snowmen conjured images of her youth, cavorting in the snow, playing in the garden with Papa before he died. A wave of nostalgia wobbled through her.

When the taxicab skidded on the snow-packed road, she pressed her feet against the floorboard. Modern modes of transportation might be more convenient, but they all frightened her. Buses were the only form of transport she had conquered. She hadn't learned to drive. Doubted she ever would. Too shy to join a car pool, she was also afraid to hire a taxicab by herself. In her own time, being alone with a strange man would be considered highly improper. That wasn't her only reason for disliking taxis. Most men scared the bejinks out of her. Now she had another reason to dislike taxis. They moved too swiftly and didn't feel nearly as safe as horse-drawn carriages.

When she leaned back, her feet lifted up off the floor. Tyler reached for her hand, and winked. Her heart reacted joyously. He truly was an amazing man, so very fine; masculine and handsome, too—everything a man ought to be.

As they approached the airport, Catharine's racing pulse accelerated. Silently she congratulated herself. She had survived another night in a strange bed, and the drive in a taxicab at breakneck speed on slick, snow-packed roads.

If she weren't such a milquetoast, she might enjoy this holiday. But at the moment, she could barely control the tempest rumbling inside her.

She drew in a slow breath. "Without you I couldn't have done any of this, Tyler. Well, I could have made the airline reservations because

I do that for the bosses at work. However, I wouldn't have had the courage to ride in a taxicab by myself."

Tyler winked again. "Stick with me, Cath, and you'll go places."

She would like to stick with him, she thought, admiring the ease with which he paid and tipped the driver, then summoned a uniformed porter to take charge of their luggage.

Her head swam as they checked in, then cleared security, and proceeded through the airport to their gate. Everything seemed second nature to Tyler, as though he did this sort of thing every day. She didn't have a clue what to do next, or even what to expect. Each new experience reminded her how very much she still had to learn about living in this century.

"Are you still frightened?" Tyler asked, taking her backpack after she tucked her black leather gloves inside.

"Yes."

Switching his briefcase and her pack to the same hand, he clasped her elbow with his other. "Let's talk to take your mind off your nervousness."

She smiled, happy to be with him, and happy to be on her way to England to see Jennifer. "What shall—will we talk about?"

He grinned, hiking his brow in question. "The difference between will and shall. Is there one?"

She winked as he had winked at her. "There is if you're a Scot or a Brit."

"Would you care to explain?"

She nodded. "Broadly speaking, the Scots use 'will' where the English use 'shall', and vice versa. I can illustrate by telling a story. A Scot fell into a lake. Afraid he might drown and wouldn't be rescued, he cried, 'I will drown, and no one shall save me!' A passing Englishman, believing the man was determined to commit suicide, left him to his fate."

Tyler chuckled. "You delight me, Catharine."

"You delight me as well, Tyler." And he did, she realized, smiling.

Then she recalled her dream of the night before, and frowned. It had been about Tyler in a prior life. He had been betrothed to another and his friendship with Catharine forbidden. She hoped history wouldn't repeat itself and that they would always be friends, good mates in this life.

Before they boarded the jet, Tyler guided Catharine to a small kiosk. "We need to exchange some American dollars for British pounds."

She watched him make the transaction, and wondered how he knew so much about traveling. Obtaining British currency hadn't crossed her mind. She hadn't even known the small kiosks at the airport were banks until he explained.

About an hour later they entered the plane and found their assigned seats.

"Will it be safe, flying over the ocean?" she asked.

"Yes." Tyler reached for her hand. Comforted by the gesture, she smiled up at him. Her heart fluttered while pleasure settled deep inside her.

Tyler held her hand as the huge DC 10 jet taxied down the runway. When it lifted into the sky, the air left her lungs. She felt muzzy. Would she faint?

When Tyler squeezed her hand gently, Catharine turned, clasped his hands with both of hers and clung. The combination of fear and excitement sizzled inside her. She closed her eyes, hoping she wouldn't be ill and embarrass herself by losing her breakfast.

Then they were airborne.

The improbability of flying kept her on the edge of her seat, at least as much as the confining seat belt allowed. She told herself they weren't going to crash into a building, or fall from the sky. According to Jennifer, thousands or millions of people flew every day. So surely they were safe.

"What are you thinking about?" Tyler asked, gently rubbing her fingers.

Physical awareness made her heart throb. She tucked her bottom lip between her teeth, trying to think of a reply while turmoil churned inside her. Finally she said, "The strange dream I had last night. And also about the different modes of transport."

"Please elaborate."

"I don't wish to bore you."

"I doubt you could if you tried. We have a long flight ahead of us, and I'm a good listener."

I doubt you could if you tried? Was that a compliment? Or merely an attempt to soothe her?

Very aware of what his touch was doing to her insides, she drew in a long, slow breath before she began. "In England I traveled from Kent to London and back, always on the train with my mother. Sometimes my step-papa accompanied us. In 1851 we went to London to the Crystal Palace for the Exhibition. I still marvel at what I saw." She closed her eyes, recalling the memories. "A palace built entirely of crystal, used as a museum to display marvelous exhibits and inventions from all over the world. Truly a wonder then, I believe the crystal palace would have been an amazing feat even now in the twenty-first century."

She looked around, wondering if anyone else was listening. When she realized the other passengers were absorbed in their own conversations, she continued, her voice quiet and low. "When I left Kent to attend Miss Treacher's Finishing Academy in Surrey, I traveled by horse-drawn coach, and when I returned home in mid-term, I traveled the same way."

"Why did you leave in the middle of the term?"

"Because Wilbur, my step-papa, ordered me to. And at the end of the day, after profuse arguments, he refused to pay the remaining tuition. As Mother's husband, he controlled her fortune."

"Do you know why he wanted you to leave?"

Catharine nodded, a frown puckering her brow. "He wanted to be intimate with me, and he was furious that Mother said I could go to the finishing academy. They had a terrible row the night before I left. However, Mother and I thought it the best way to keep me safe."

"Did your stepfather ever have his way with you?"

She shook her head. "Mother and I always contrived ways to thwart his attempts to be alone with me."

Chills crawled down her spine and she shivered as the memories returned. Unwilling to explain any more details, Catharine closed her eyes, pretending she was tired. She must have been because she dozed off... and dreamed.

~ * ~

Back in the past, her arrogant, thick-stomached step-papa glared at her in triumph, his ruddy face redder than usual. "I have betrothed you to Mr. Albert Smytheton.

Catharine's heart fell. "I cannot wed him," she whimpered. "Mr. Smytheton is old enough to be my grandpapa."

"You will do as I say," Wilbur bellowed. "You shall wed him, and you will do so soon."

Tearfully shaking her head, Catharine dashed from the parlor to find her mother. When she found her in the solarium, among plants and beautiful flowers, she sobbed, "Wilbur says he has betrothed me to Mr. Smytheton."

Her mother's expression saddened as she closed the glass door behind Catharine. "I fear the betrothal is hideously true."

"But I cannot wed him!" Catharine gasped. "He's ancient. Nearly at death's door. And I'm afraid Wilbur will force himself on me whenever he chooses to visit me in Mr. Smytheton's home."

"I share your fear, dear one." Her mother gathered her close and stroked her long hair. "Calm yourself and we shall discuss your alternatives."

"There seems to be only one," Catharine cried after they discussed several possibilities, none of which seemed feasible. "Leaving... Running away. But I cannot bear the thought of going without you, Mother."

"I cannot bear that either, my dear. However, it may be our only course of action."

Catharine dabbed at her tears with a lace-trimmed handkerchief. "Oh, Mummy, I wish you hadn't married Wilbur."

"I wish that as well. I have asked for a divorce, however, Wilbur won't hear of it."

"What shall we do?" Catharine asked, fresh tears trailing down her cheeks.

"If we think of nothing else by morning, you must leave with my blessing."

Catharine felt her head slide in the airplane seat and knew she was dozing. She twisted, found a more comfortable position and let her mind return to the past.

Without a plan she had taken the train to Victoria Station then, afraid of being pursued by Wilbur, she boarded the next train she saw. During that southbound ride, she chewed her fingernails, half-expecting Wilbur to appear at any moment.

When the train stopped at Warlingham in Surrey, she got off, left the station, and wandered through the woods. In the back of her mind she hoped to find Miss Treacher's Academy.

But she didn't.

Night fell.

She bedded down in the woods, using her reticule for a pillow, her cloak to cover her, and wishing she could make herself invisible so no one would harm her and Wilbur couldn't find her. She dreamt she had succeeded in becoming invisible, because the night turned so dark she couldn't see her own hand in front of her face.

Stiff and sore the next morning, she wandered again, wondering how to find her way out of the woods, and where to go when she did.

After three days and nights with neither food nor shelter, she caught a chill and the sniffles. Early in the morning of the fourth day she found herself standing in front of a huge pink and white striped tent in the middle of the Surrey woods. While she debated whether to approach the owner and ask for nourishment, she found herself miraculously transported inside.

A girl who looked exactly like her stood beside a jolly looking white-haired, white-bearded man who made the introductions. "Catharine, this is my charge, Kacy Rose, and I am Rey, her guardian angel."

Shocked at being miraculously transported inside the tent, then meeting a real live guardian angel, Catharine fainted.

Ensconced in a comfortable feather-ticked bed when she came to, she was startled to see Kacy Rose sitting by her side on a chair in the humongous tent.

"Where is yo-your guardian an-angel?" Catharine had stammered.

Kacy smiled. "Rey went to fetch someone to help you."

Marveling at her good fortune, and meeting the girl she had dreamed about for years, Catharine smiled, too.

She and Kacy had talked and talked, confided, shared, and become fast friends.

After a while Catharine said, "Running away is the bravest thing I have ever done."

"I know." Kacy smiled and touched her arm. "I wish I could heal your cold." And to both their amazement she somehow magically did.

A few moments later, Kacy said, "I have a feeling you're on the threshold of a brand new life."

Catharine found it almost impossible to believe Kacy and her guardian angel were more than figments of her imagination.

Then Rey returned, his white hair spiked and his white waistcoat and trousers rumpled as though he had traveled a great distance in a short time. "Unfortunately no one is available to help you just now," he announced.

Tears filled Catharine's eyes.

"Fear not," the plump, wingless angel said. "I shall."

And he did.

He befriended her, provided food and shelter, and insisted she catch up on lost sleep.

When she felt good enough to travel, the angel Rey took her to Europe to collect information to prove Wilbur was a bigamist.

Not long after that she traveled forward in time, and agreed to switch places with Kacy.

~ * ~

In the airplane, Catharine's head fell against Tyler's shoulder. Jolted back to the present, she opened her eyes. Every time she recalled the past and her decision to leave, she wondered about her mother. Did she know that she and Kacy had switched identities?

While Catharine sucked in gulps of dry airplane air, Tyler asked, "Are you all right?"

She swallowed over the huge lump in her throat. "I was thinking about Mother. I don't expect to see her again, but I miss her terribly."

"I'm sure you do," Tyler sympathized, patting her hand that was once again nestled in his. Then he said, "Before you fell asleep, you mentioned your dream. Tell me about it."

"Twas sad." Catharine stared at the seat back in front of her, knowing she should reclaim her hand, but reluctant to do so. Tyler's touch felt so comforting... so wonderful. "I dreamt about a prior life where I knew you. I was fond of you. However, you were betrothed to someone else, and our friendship was forbidden."

"Why?"

"Because your betrothed was jealous and suspicious. If you hadn't married her, your family would have suffered and been forced to live in shame. Therefore, you renounced our friendship. But when your betrothed became your wife, she accused us of having an illicit relationship. One day she threw a tantrum then jumped into the moat. You jumped in to save her, but she fought you and sadly you both drowned."

"I've had similar dreams," Tyler surprised her. "For years I thought the girl in my dreams was Kacy. Now I wonder if she might have been you. And our friendship isn't forbidden now, nor will it ever be."

Thrilled by his words, Catharine wished they would always be friends. She also wished she would never have cause to be afraid of him.

When he tightened his hold on her hand, she let him keep it. His touch eased her fear and some of her nervousness, although it created a tumult within her heart.

Six

During the frightful landing, Catharine worried that she might lose her late dinner. Thankfully she didn't. The plane bumped, jolted, shuddered, and finally jerked to a hissing stop.

She pasted a smile on her face. "I couldn't have had a finer first flight," she said with false brightness. "Not even if I had rubbed a magic lantern and had a genie pop out to grant three wishes. I wouldn't have known what wishes to ask for, but you have made more than three come true, Tyler."

He smiled. "I have a feeling you're trying to camouflage your nervousness after the bumpy landing. They're not all that rocky."

"But they must all be abrupt."

"They are." He nodded. "By necessity."

She shuddered, like the plane did when it landed on the ground. "They're a bit like having a horse come to an abrupt stop after a mad gallop."

"Yes," Tyler chuckled. "They are."

Sudden tears misted her eyes. "I am so happy to be here."

He offered his handkerchief.

She dabbed at her eyes before they stood to disembark. Then she gathered her backpack and belongings. As they left the airplane, she glanced at her wristwatch. "It's nearly midnight. Are we in London?"

Tyler shook his head. "Heathrow's west of London."

"Do you know how long it will take to get there?"

"About an hour. Depends on how we travel."

Just then they heard their names being paged over the P.A. system. "Mr. Tyler Quinlane and Miss Catharine Rose, please check with a British Airlines agent." The words echoed in the large room that was devoid of passengers except for those who had traveled on their plane.

The British lady, dressed in the same blue uniform worn by the flight attendants, said, "A Mr. Castlebury hired a limousine to drive you to London. The chauffeur will meet you after you clear Customs. He'll be holding a sign with your names so you don't miss him."

"Thanks," Tyler said.

A bit overwhelmed by Jennifer's husband's thoughtful generosity, Catharine was impressed with Tyler's ability to take it in stride.

~ * ~

"Does anything look familiar?" he asked as the black limo sped along the motorway sometime later.

"I've never been west of London, and it's too dark to see much. However, I do notice changes."

"What are they?"

"The motorway for one thing," she whispered so the driver couldn't overhear. "Paved roads for another."

"Many of England's streets are crooked and twisty," Tyler said, "far different from Denver's north-south, east-west orientation, except for that quarter wagon-wheel in Denver's downtown area."

"Yes," Catharine agreed. "Those roads are similar to the lanes in Kent where I grew up." She spoke in jerky spasms. The speed on the motorway robbed her breath and made her wonder if traveling by train wouldn't have been more safe.

"Try to relax." Tyler closed his hand around her clenched fist.

"I am trying. Please believe me."

He smiled, stroking her fingers. Catharine's pulse raced with more than fear of the limousine's speed. Tyler made her yearn for things she knew she could never have. A good husband, children, a happy family, and love. Her fear of intimacy would rob her of all those things.

In spite of her misgivings, the taxi reached London without mishap.

As they checked in at the Grosvenor Hotel, the concierge said, "I believe there's a message for you. Yes, here it is."

Tyler unfolded the message and held it where Catharine could also read.

Tyler and Catharine,

>*Call us as soon as you get here. We won't be asleep. We're anxious to see you.*

>*Jennifer and Drake.*

After Ty tipped the bellboy for delivering their luggage to their rooms, he called Drake and Jennifer.

"Are you sure you want to see us now? It's almost the middle of the night."

"Yes," Drake said. "We have a suite and plenty of room to visit. Come as soon as you can."

Ty and Catharine headed there without delay.

Drake opened the door almost as soon as Tyler knocked. When Ty saw Jennifer he grabbed and hugged her, then he gave Drake a big bear hug before he embraced Jennifer again.

"You're a sight for sore eyes," he said.

Jennifer laughed. "So are you." She opened her arms to Catharine, and they embraced.

As far as Catharine was concerned, the reunion was anything but awkward—happy, joyous, and full of delight.

"How much longer can you stay in this time?" Tyler asked.

"Our guardian angel said we could stay here for a month. We spent three days in Vegas and a week in New York so we have more than a fortnight left and we intend to spend it here."

"How long is a fortnight?"

"Two weeks," Catharine said, surprised she knew something Tyler didn't.

"I'm still finding it difficult to believe you're alive," he said, staring at Jennifer. "That you traveled back in time, met the man you've loved for eons of mortal time, and intend to return to live with him in the past."

Jennifer grinned. "Well, seeing's believing, isn't it?"

"I'm not sure. I might be dreaming."

"I know the feeling." Jennifer laughed again, and swatted him playfully on the chest. "This is all quite out of the ordinary."

"You can say that again."

Jennifer's expression turned somber. "What reason did you give Aunt Rachel and Uncle Mack for taking time off?"

"I told Dad something came up that Catharine and I wanted to check out."

"What will you tell them when you go home?"

"I haven't decided. Do you have any suggestions?"

Jennifer nodded. "You could tell them, but only them, the truth."

"And break their hearts because you didn't try to see them? I don't think so. Besides, I doubt they'd believe me. They'd probably think their only son had gone bonkers."

"Perhaps," Catharine suggested, "we could say I wanted to travel to England to do some research for the novels I wish to write, and I didn't want to travel alone."

"You've decided to write Kacy's story?" Jennifer asked, having suggested that months ago when she and Catharine lived together.

Catharine nodded. "I'd like to write yours as well. I enrolled in a writing class last fall after you left Denver."

"Good for you." Jennifer grinned. "I have Kacy's journal for you, and while we're together I'll tell you all about my adventure to the past."

"I would appreciate that." Catharine smiled, and tried to calm her racing heart. "Do you know if Kacy saw my mother?"

"She wasn't in Kent when Kacy went there. Apparently her guardian angel said you would see your mother in this time."

A bolt of happiness jolted through Catharine and the loud booming of her heart echoed in her ears. "That gives me food for fodder," she repeated something she'd heard on TV; although she thought it should be the other way round.

"What do you want to see and do while you're here?" Drake asked then.

Tyler massaged his temple. "I never thought beyond seeing the two of you."

"I'd like to visit the West End," Catharine ventured, not nearly as bashful as she had expected to feel around Jennifer's husband. "Perhaps we could take in the theater as well."

Jennifer's eyes sparkled. "We'll do that, and Harrods is a must."

Catharine arched her brow, puzzled. "What is Harrods?"

"A department store. It was built near the end of the nineteenth century, and it's unlike any store you've ever seen. It has everything."

"Everything?" Catharine repeated, doubtful.

Jennifer nodded, her speckled green eyes bright with silent mirth. "I understand a young boy was having lunch with his mother in one of Harrods' restaurants, and he ordered an elephant sandwich. The waiter took the order without batting an eye, but he returned a few minutes later and said, "I'm sorry, young man, we're out of bread. Would you care to order something else?"

Everyone laughed.

Then Jennifer said, "We've got a ton of things to see and do."

Catharine grinned. "I'm certain we'll have a whacking good time."

"Me, too. And I want to hear how you've gotten along without me, Catharine."

As she had when they lived together, Catharine caught Jennifer's enthusiasm. "I managed just fine. However, I have missed you."

"I've missed you, too."

"I want to hear about your adventure to the past," Tyler said.

Jennifer chuckled. "Don't worry. You will."

"And I want to hear about your career," Drake told Tyler. "How does it feel to be a practicing attorney?"

"You know our firm specializes in real estate, so it's rather calm and mundane. Nothing like you see on TV."

"I never imagined it would be," Drake said.

"I'm interested in politics though. "I'm considering tossing my name in the ring and attempting to run for the state legislature in the fall."

Drake grinned. "That's great."

Tyler grinned as well. "Mom and Dad think so, too. But we'll probably have to hire another lawyer. The firm already has more business than the three of us can handle."

"How's your job?" Jennifer asked Catharine.

The word job always sounded strange to Catharine's ears. In her world *job* had sexual connotations. She swallowed and Tyler answered for her.

"At the moment she's unemployed."

"I am?" Catharine asked, astonished.

"Yeah. I called and resigned for you. I don't want you working with Dillon McKenzie anymore."

Tyler had a pack of nerve, resigning for her without even consulting her. But she decided to let the discussion be until they returned to Denver. No need to spoil their time in London exchanging cross words over his high-handedness.

"I must work," she said. "However will I pay my rent and buy food if I don't?"

"You have Kacy's trust fund. I'm sure that will cover your expenses until you find another job."

Job. Catharine blinked at *that* word. She would sooner starve than get involved in anything that had to do with sexual relations. And she couldn't spend Kacy's trust. That would be like stealing.

"Why did you resign for her?" Jennifer jarred Catharine's disturbing thoughts back to the conversation.

Tyler explained, then said, "I'm sure you won't have any trouble finding work, Catharine. Receptionists are in big demand right now.

We hired a new one in November, but she got engaged on Christmas day so she might leave. If she does, you could work for us."

Catharine forced a smile. Engaged was another word that sounded strange. One engaged in conversation. When one intended to get married, one became betrothed.

Although the thought of working for Tyler's family appealed to her, as did seeing him every day, it also befuddled her. "I would like that very much," she said, still a bit perturbed that he had resigned for her without first consulting her.

Anxious to change subjects because he didn't like the tempest gathering in Catharine's eyes, Ty glanced at Drake. "Do you miss this century?"

"To be honest, I didn't remember this time until a couple of weeks ago. Just before I left the past, my guardian angel opened my mind and all the memories returned big time."

Ty studied the man he had known as Dirk for half of his life. They'd been buddies since they were twelve. When Dirk's family had moved in next door, his attraction to Jennifer had been instant. In spite of their youth and three-year age difference, the two had fallen for each other the day they met.

Ty had been as besotted by Kacy as Dirk was by Jennifer. The four had practically been hooked at the elbows for years. Funny how fate had a way of stepping in and changing the future he and Dirk had planned.

A few days after Dirk eloped with Jennifer, he'd been killed in a car crash. Ty felt as though he'd lost a brother. Seeing Dirk again now was like seeing somebody who had risen from the dead. "What's it like, living in the past?"

"Quite different from living in this time."

"I imagine transportation and communication leave a lot to be desired."

"But there's a lot to say for the slower pace of life," Jennifer piped in, startling Ty when she announced, "Drake's a duke. A Peer of the Realm."

"And Jennifer's my duchess," Drake added, a proud gleam in his eyes.

"He's needed in the past," Jennifer said. "That's why we've decided to return, Ty."

"What year will you return to?"

"Eighteen fifty-six."

"Will your lives be filled with hardships?" Ty asked, recalling previous lives and searching his memory bank for scenes of what life had been like a hundred and fifty years ago.

Jennifer shook her head. "Drake's a wealthy duke, Ty. A male secretary helps with business matters. A valet helps him dress and sees to all his personal needs. Servants clean and take care of his homes. Grooms and stable boys care for his horses and carriages, and drivers take him wherever he wishes to go."

"What about you? What will you do to keep busy if he has all those people to see to his needs?"

"Jennifer will share in the decisions that are to be made," Drake said. "She already knows how to run my homes and she gets on remarkably well with both housekeepers and all our servants. We hope to have children who will keep her as busy as she wishes to be. And we have each other. We'll never be lonely, nor bored."

"Then I have only one thing more to say."

"What is it?" Drake asked.

"I hope you're as happy twenty or thirty years from now as you are today."

"Thanks, Ty. That means a lot," Drake said. "Now tell me about the Bronco's. Have they made it back to the Super Bowl?"

Ty laughed, and while they discussed sports, Jennifer and Catharine got caught up on each other's questions.

~ * ~

That evening, after a full day, they dined on a boat cruising the Thames. Jennifer and Drake were dancing to the live music. Seated across from Catharine, Tyler moved the candle aside and reached for her hand. "What did you most enjoy today?"

Her mind whirled and her pulse raced. She liked having her hand in Tyler's. His felt so strong and capable, and his touch didn't give her the creeps. It actually felt quite smashing. Very, very, deliciously good.

"I liked our visit to Harrods. What did you like?"

"Being with you."

She smiled and admitted, "I liked that, too. Modern day London is all that I anticipated and more. And thank you for agreeing to fly here with me, Tyler."

"You're welcome."

As the dinner boat sailed in front of the Houses of Parliament, tears sprang to Catharine's eyes.

Tyler squeezed her hands. "Are you all right?"

She nodded, a little surprised by her emotions. "Seeing Parliament all lit up at night gives me gooseflesh."

"I know." Tyler offered his handkerchief. "It's quite a sight."

Catharine used the handkerchief to dab her tears and when the music changed, he said, "Dance with me."

"I've never danced the way you dance. I might embarrass you."

"You won't. It's easy. Come, I'll show you."

On the small dance floor, he held her rather close which made her heart flutter and her nerves twitter. They moved slowly with the music, their bodies swaying in unison. Catharine's thoughts strayed to another time, another life. Tyler had been just as tender and understanding then, but his intended's father had forced him to make a choice between his friendship with her and her family, and his position of wealth and great renown.

The change in the music drew Catharine's attention back to the present. When Tyler pulled her so close their bodies touched, she jerked away.

"In my own time dancing this way is considered indecent," she whispered, her face heating.

"But you're not in your time, you're in mine, and this is the way we dance." His voice was calm, his penetrating gaze unwavering, but a muscle twitched in his jaw before he tightened his mouth in a straight seam.

A sense of unease scooted up Catharine's spine. Still, she let him draw her back into his arms. He didn't hold her as close, and although she appreciated that, her heart sank. She had thought he was different. *Please,* she silently pleaded, *don't behave like the men who frighten me. Don't destroy my trust.*

Back at the table, Jennifer said, "I need to tell you both something, before I forget."

Tyler hiked a brow. "What?"

"I left my trust to the two of you. Jointly. But I made that decision long ago, and now I've decided I'd really like it split three ways."

"Who do you want to have the other third?"

Jennifer smiled. "Your parents. I owe them something for all they did while I was growing up. I made the legal changes for you and Catharine to be joint beneficiaries when she and I lived together. But she has Kacy's trust, so I don't think she will object to sharing part of my trust with your parents. Would you?"

"No. Of course not," Catharine hastily assured her. "Actually, Tyler and his parents can have it all. It needn't be split three ways."

Jennifer shook her head. "I'll feel better if I know you have some of my money to tide you over if things get tight."

"That's very generous."

Tyler smiled at Jennifer. "Yes, it is."

"Will you take care of my trust when you return, Ty? Turn it into cash, and see that it's split three ways?"

"Yes. Certainly."

Catharine wondered if Jennifer's trust had been greatly diminished by Miranda's spendthrift ways. If so, Catharine would have to find a way to replenish it, because she felt responsible for Miranda.

During the ride back to the Grosvenor, Catharine and Tyler didn't talk to each other. Jennifer and Drake didn't seem to notice. Afraid Tyler was angry with her, Catharine sucked her bottom lip in to keep it from quivering.

The awkward silence continued after they entered the hotel. On the tenth floor, they left Jennifer and Drake. Moment's later, Tyler unlocked Catharine's door, then handed her the big key.

"Good night," he said in a curt tone before he turned.

On the verge of tears, Catharine blurted an apology. "I'm sorry if I upset you while we were dancing."

Tyler turned back. His facial features softened, matching the sudden tender look in his gray-green eyes. "I'm not upset. At least not with you."

"But you are upset."

"Only with myself."

"Why?"

"Because I have no right to have any expectations. But I can't seem to help myself. Every time I look at you I have glimpses of what might have been, but never was."

Excitement mingled with trepidation. *Did he feel it, too? That sense of having known and cared about each other before?* She swallowed the question; not sure she wanted to hear the answer. If their thoughts were in tune, that would form a commitment of sorts, a commitment she didn't feel equipped to deal with right now. "I'm afraid I don't understand."

"No. I don't guess you do. Perhaps we can discuss it sometime. At the moment, you look tired. I know I am. We didn't get much sleep last night." He reached out to touch her arm, but she stepped back, so he caught her hand. Barely. Tension mounted between them. Regret filled his eyes. "Do I scare you that much?"

She shook her head. "No. You don't frighten me, it's just that..."

"What?"

"I don't know how not to flinch when a man reaches for me."

Tyler raised her hand to his lips, kissed her fingers, holding her gaze with hypnotic intensity. "You're not flinching now." Then he smiled. "Good night, Cath. Pleasant dreams."

"Thank you."

Tyler's touch had created a warm fuzzy feeling inside her. She floated inside her room on feet that barely touched the floor, her hand tingling from his kiss. Her blood heated from the tender expression in his eyes. And her heart danced a slow, sensuous waltz, with him as her invisible partner. In truth, she had jerked away when he pulled her closer, more from habit than from fear of him.

After a while she found the strength to change from her long-sleeved black cocktail dress to a modest pale blue nightgown. She climbed beneath the bed covers, and murmured, "Fey, are you with me?"

No answer came. Catharine assumed she was alone, and turned the lamp off before she lay down. Feeling lonely and wishing she had someone to talk to, she whispered, "I wish I weren't such a ninny." A bit frustrated, she raised her head and pounded a dent in her huge pillow for a spot to rest her head.

"You aren't a ninny," Fey said.

Catharine blinked as the bedside lamp appeared to turn itself back on. "I offended Tyler tonight when we were dancing."

Fey folded her wings and plunked down in the center of the other pillow.

"Your emotions are what make you unique."

"But I have displeased Tyler."

"Perhaps. Then again, perhaps not. After years of believing he loved Kacy, she rejected him. I imagine that still rankles. Now tell me what is really troubling you."

Catharine sighed. "I guess I'm just lonely and wanted someone to talk to. Do you think I'll ever get over being afraid of men? Will I ever yearn for one to touch me? Hold me? Kiss me?"

"You yearn for all that now. You're just too stubborn to admit it. As to whether you'll get over your fear, only you can answer that. Humans possess the capacity to do whatever they decide."

Fey reclined on her side and waved her tiny silver wand at the lamp to turn it off again. "Let's get some sleep. Tomorrow is going to be another big day."

"Thank you for being here, Fey."

"You're most welcome, Catharine."

She fell asleep, and dreamed about Tyler in another life. A life where she had been forced to choose between her friendship with him and her father's wrath. Unhappy and upset after she had given in to her father's demands, she refused to marry the man he had chosen. Enraged, the man murdered her while she slept.

Catharine awakened bathed in perspiration. She kicked the covers off and immediately felt cold. But the cold stemmed more from her heart than the moisture on her skin.

Murdered. She'd been murdered in her sleep.

No wonder she was such a timid milquetoast who hated being alone at night.

Seven

"A week seemed a long time when we first arrived," Catharine said six days later. She looked sad. Ty felt sad himself. "Now it's our last night, and I wish our visit were just beginning."

Ty heard the tremor in Catharine's voice, and saw a suspicious sheen in Jennifer's eyes. They were dining in the Grosvenor's finest restaurant and Jennifer dropped a disquieting bombshell into the conversation. "I think you should marry Catharine, Ty. I'd feel a lot better if I knew she wasn't living alone."

"What?" He arched his brow, his heart thudding, and saw Catharine duck her head as her cheeks turned bright pink.

"That would put my mind at rest," Jennifer continued. "It's obvious you like each other, and you're the only man she isn't afraid of. Besides, I think she's the girl in that recurring dream you've always had."

Ty suspected that too, but he didn't intend to discuss it right now. Catharine sometimes responded to him as Kacy never had. But Catharine was also as timid as the shy Koala bears the early British explorers hadn't known existed until ten years after they reached Australia's shores.

"If you married Catharine, that might make this impromptu trip easier to explain to your parents," Drake offered.

Ty had an urge to grit his teeth. He'd like nothing more than to marry Catharine although he suspected she had enough hang-ups to scare off even the most dedicated man. "I'm not going to elope just because the two of you did."

When Jennifer and Drake both laughed, Ty relaxed and grinned. He had enjoyed hearing about the five months they'd shared in the past, and their elopement to Gretna Green prior to the huge formal wedding it had taken Drake's grandmother six months to plan. Ty envied them for being at ease with each other now and so darn happy.

"You couldn't elope here in England anyway," Jennifer said. "There's too much red tape."

"How do you know?"

She smiled. "We checked into it when we first arrived."

"Why?"

"Because we're so delighted to be together, we decided to get married again in Vegas, New York, and here."

"How could you marry in this time when you don't belong here? Aren't you afraid of screwing things up?"

Drake and Jennifer laughed again. "We doubt anyone will figure out we got married in this century then went to live in another. Nobody tracks that kind of thing."

Ty frowned. "What kind of ID did you use?"

"Our passports."

"Where did you get them?"

"From our guardian angel. The same place Catharine obtained hers when she first came to this time. The same place we got current money to enjoy ourselves while we're here. And stop frowning, Ty. Drake would never do anything illegal. Getting married in Vegas and New York was fun. It'll give us something to discuss in secret when we go back. Besides, we did it for another reason."

"What reason?" Ty felt like an interrogator at a trial, yet part of his foggy mind remained glued on Jennifer's suggestion that he marry Catharine.

"Someday we might wind up in this century again," Jennifer said, "and we want to be prepared, and pledged, just in case." With a wave of her hand, she dismissed that topic. "Now about my suggestion…"

"When I marry," Ty interrupted, "Mom and Dad will expect a big wedding. Actually, I want one, too. And if I were to marry Catharine, Kacy's grandparents would expect a big wedding as well. Porter would want to give her away, walk her down the aisle."

"So plan a big wedding, and make everybody happy, including me," Jennifer advised.

Very aware that Catharine hadn't said a word, Ty turned his gaze to her. "What do you think about this conversation?"

"I think you would be foolish even to consider marriage to me."

"Why?"

"Because I don't believe arranged marriages are best for the two people involved. I think a bride and groom should love each other. And in any event, I don't intend to wed."

Ignoring her last comment, Ty asked, "How do you feel about me, Catharine?"

"I'm not—not exactly sure."

"Yes, you are," Jennifer contradicted. "You love Ty. I see it every time you look at him, even if he doesn't."

"Sometimes you see too much," he said, accustomed to Jennifer's gift of sight, and the visions she'd always had.

"Will you at least think about it?" she asked.

Ty refrained from admitting he had thought of little else during the past week, but he didn't think Catharine would even consider marriage. Not to him. Not to any man. At least not until she learned not to be afraid.

"I have a feeling that whatever I do or don't do, you'll see it, Jennifer," he said.

"I hope that's true." She smiled with rueful acceptance. "I do have that one consolation. Prior to Miranda's car accident, my gift allowed me to see her and Catharine's activities. I'm confident I'll continue to see Catharine and know what's going on in her life, if not often, at least occasionally."

"I wish I shared your gift of sight, cousin," Ty said. "It would be marvelous to see parts of your lives and know you and Drake are okay."

"Maybe we could communicate using mental telepathy," Jennifer suggested with her usual enthusiasm.

"It's worth a try," Ty said, wondering why she hadn't suggested that earlier. "How do you suggest we go about it?"

"I've discovered the days are the same in both centuries. How about if we concentrate at the same time on the last day of every month?"

"At midnight?" Ty suggested.

"Midnight Denver time would be seven a.m. in the U.K. That would work for me, except that it would be the next day here, the first day of each month."

"If it's going to work, that shouldn't make a difference. I wish we'd thought of this sooner so we could try it out while we're together now."

"We still have tonight." More of Jennifer's enthusiasm rubbed off on him. "It worked when we were growing up. Every time I needed you, I telepathed a message and you got it and came."

Ty grinned, remembering the times he'd heard her voice in his head, known exactly where she was and gone to her rescue. He'd felt like a hero afterwards, every single time, especially when Kacy had been there, too.

"Half an hour after we go to our rooms, I'll send a message," Jennifer said. "Relax and give yourself time to receive it. If you do, call me."

"I will."

~ * ~

A couple of hours later, Ty laid on his bed, arms propped behind his head, while he waited for Jennifer's thoughts to penetrate his. The message came over loud and clear.

::*If you don't marry Catharine, you'll be making the biggest mistake of your life.*::

Grinning, he picked the phone up and called Jennifer. "I think you're right, but I have to convince Catharine that we're meant to be together."

"I don't think that'll be as hard as you might imagine."

"Maybe not. Do you think this telepathy will work across time, through centuries, Jen?"

"I don't know. Neither of us will until we try it."

"All right. Maybe if we concentrate hard enough I can send one back."

"Let's practice that now. Hang up and send a mental message. I'll call if I get it."

"Will do."

Tyler tried to think what to send, then grinned and concentrated, blanking his mind of every other thought.

::*Name your first son after me, Jennifer, and your first daughter after Catharine.*::

He waited. The phone didn't ring. He tried again, concentrated even more deeply, feeling a little like a conduit.

The phone rang. He snatched it.

"I got your message. Twice. I had to consult with Drake before I could call you. We've agreed. We'll name our first son Tyler and our first daughter Catharine."

"We did it, Jen," Tyler said, amazed. "We actually did it."

"We did it while we were growing up too, Ty."

"Why didn't you ever tell me?"

"Because I wanted you to discover your gift on your own, the way I did."

"Well if that doesn't beat all." Tyler vowed that he would never close his mind to any possibility. The universe was full of them.

~ * ~

The next morning Jennifer and Drake stood in the hall near Catharine and Tyler's rooms while they waited for the bellboy to come collect their luggage.

"It's time to say goodbye," Catharine said, a tremor in her voice.

Jennifer smiled. "We've seen and done so much, there hasn't been a moment to spare, but I'm going to miss you both."

"Yes. It's been great to see you again, Ty," Drake said, "and you too, Catharine."

Tears brimmed Catharine's eyes. "The pleasure has been mine."

"I can't tell you how good it's been to see both of you." Ty forced a grin, attempting to be cheerful, even though he hated the thought of leaving.

If he and his parents hadn't already taken time off when they buried the girl they believed to be Jennifer, he would have stayed in England another week just to be with Jennifer and Drake. Part of Tyler felt guilty for being here now and enjoying them, when his parent's and Dirk's both believed them dead. But everyone agreed that if they told their parents, they might want to tell someone else, and where would it end?

Ty squashed the urge to say what he knew was in the back of all their minds. *::They would miss each other a hell of a lot. But they were lucky to have shared this week, and had the opportunity to say goodbye.::*

Jennifer nodded and repeated his thoughts out loud for Drake and Catharine.

Ty smiled. He *could* send telepathic messages. And he would go home with peace in his heart, knowing Jennifer and Drake were together, as they had always wanted to be.

Would he ever find the same kind of happiness? Was he destined to live alone? Or always marry the wrong woman? Was Catharine the right woman? Or Kacy, who was already lost to him? He suspected the answer was Catharine. Still, it wasn't easy to forget Kacy. For years, she had meant the world to him.

~ * ~

The flight back was uneventful. Having spoken to the tiny fairy godmother every day while they were in London, Catharine felt confident Fey was still with her. As Tyler hailed a cab at the Denver airport, she said, "I'd like to go home."

So he instructed the cab driver to take them directly there.

"What are you planning to do tomorrow?" he asked while they rode side by side in the back seat.

"Call the office and find out whether they've issued my marching papers, or if I'm still employed."

"I don't want you to go back there."

"I must work. I need the money."

"I'll help you find another position."

"What am I to live on in the meantime?"

"Use Kacy's trust. Or stay with me."

Catharine gave up arguing. How could she explain that it would feel like stealing Kacy's inheritance when Miranda had spent Jennifer's money as though it belonged to her? And how could she make him understand that she valued her independence? That living with him would make her feel beholden? Also, as though she were doing something wrong.

Still, she hated the thought of living alone for the rest of her life. The fairy Fey might be with her now and then, but she couldn't count on her all the time.

When they reached her small house on Pearl, located a few blocks from Denver University, Tyler carried her luggage up the snow-covered walk. After she unlocked the door, he asked, "Are you sure you want to stay here alone?"

"I'll be fine," she said, avoiding a direct answer.

"You'll call me if you're not?"

"Yes."

Inside, he set her suitcase on the sand colored living room carpet. "You have my cell phone number?"

"Yes, thank you."

Ty wanted to say more, but didn't. They'd had a very long day, and Catharine might need time by herself after spending more than a week in his near-constant presence. Besides, he had a cab waiting with the meter running.

"Good night then."

"Good night, Tyler. And thank you for everything."

"You're more than welcome." He bent his head and kissed her on the mouth, careful not to touch her with his hands. But that didn't stop him from kissing her thoroughly. When her lips parted in slight invitation, he deepened the kiss. Inhaling her faint almond and cherry scent made him feel heady and needy, but he tamped down the desire to gather her close.

He'd wanted to kiss her all week, but had held himself in check. She needed time to adjust to the attraction between them. And he needed to decide how to help her overcome her fear of men.

When the kiss ended, he saw a question in her eyes. He grinned, nodding up at the light fixture above her entry. "Your Christmas mistletoe is still there. I couldn't think up an excuse to kiss you in England, but that gives me one."

She blushed, and he left before giving in to the temptation to wrap his arms around her and kiss her again, all over. During the long flight, he had concluded Jennifer must be right. Catharine was the girl connected to the never-ending love that had haunted his soul in every life. All of a sudden he had a premonition that if he didn't marry her, and soon, they might lose each other in this life, too, and if they did, they'd never have another chance to share their love.

The cab was more than half way to his home, but Tyler grabbed his cell phone and called Catharine. "Are you okay?"

"Yes. I'm fine," she said. "How are you?"

"Miserable."

"Why?"

"I'm worried about you.

"I see no need for—"

"What makes you think Dillon McKenzie won't attempt to break in?" Ty wasn't proud of himself for using that scare tactic, but he wanted to be with her. Still, he silently cursed himself for the fear he imagined in her lovely eyes.

"You don't think he—Mr. McKenzie will come by just on the off-chance that I might be home, do you?"

"No telling what a pervert might do. Why don't you come and stay with me? That way we'll both get more sleep."

"If I stayed with you tonight, would you suggest that I stay with you again tomorrow night?"

"Yes," Tyler answered with blunt honesty.

"And the next night?"

"Yes."

"I cannot stay with you indefinitely. That would not be at all proper."

"Then marry me."

"Wh—what did you say?"

"You heard me."

"Are you suggesting marriage because Jennifer brought it up?"

"No."

"Then why?"

"You want the truth?"

"Of course."

"Think you can handle it?"

"Certainly."

"I'll call back in a few minutes. We've reached my apartment. I need to carry my bags inside."

Tyler paid the cab driver, and hurried up to his unit. As soon as he closed the door, he called Catharine again.

"Hello."

"Hi. It's me, Ty. And the truth is, I think I've known you in other lives. I should have married you then. I never did. Now I want to marry you to protect you. I also want to teach you to be unafraid. I believe we could have a good life together." He hesitated, then plunged on. "I loved you in those other lives, and I have a feeling, a very strong premonition, that if we don't marry and consummate our love in this life, we may never meet again." He knew he sounded breathless when he finished. But he felt more than breathless. He felt desperate, driven by a strong compulsion to bind her to him and the sooner the better.

After a lengthy silence, Catharine said, "Perhaps I should hang up now and ponder what you have just said."

"Good night then."

"Good night, Tyler."

He hung up and paced his living room like a caged lion. Why did he have a premonition that she wasn't going to be all right by herself? Maybe he should go back and spend the night with her. He'd give her ten minutes max. If she didn't call back by then, he'd call again. Maybe he should just get in his car and drive back to her house. He didn't like the idea of her staying alone with nobody close enough to hear if she needed help. Dillon McKenzie had threatened to break in once. That fact worried Ty. The bastard might do it any time.

The minutes ticked by slowly. Ty's gut tied itself in knots. He picked up the phone, punched in Catharine's number and cursed when the line was busy. Stalking to his bedroom he seized his car keys off the dresser. When his phone rang he considered not answering it, and letting the machine record a message. Instead he yanked the phone off its cradle. "Hullo."

"Tyler?"

"Catharine." Relief flooded him. "I just tried to call. Your line was busy."

"I was trying to call you."

"Why? Are you all right? Has that bastard tried..."

"No. I called for another reason."

"What is it?"

"I—that is, before we went to England, I bought a lottery ticket, and I just checked it and I think I've won. All the numbers match those in the newspaper. But if I have won, I don't know what to do. Can you help me?"

"Yeah." A warm feeling replaced the cold in Tyler's gut and the worry in his brain. "I'll drive down. Shouldn't take me more than twenty minutes."

"Thank you, Tyler. And would you mind staying over? I've decided you're right. I don't wish to be alone tonight. I have two bedrooms. If you stay here, we'll both have a bed to sleep in, and I won't have to feel guilty for depriving you of your bed, or your room."

"I'll grab my shaving kit," he said. "Keep the door locked until I get there."

"I always keep the door locked, even when I am not alone."

"Smart girl."

Eight

When Catharine heard a car pull up and stop out front, she thought Tyler had arrived in record time. She headed for the front door before the doorbell rang, clutching her backpack where she had just stored her lottery ticket.

Ever cautious, she raised the shade covering the window on the top half of the door. When she saw Dillon McKenzie, she dropped her backpack. Unable to stifle a scream, she pressed her hands against her lips and backed away, her scream echoing through the small house, and eerily through her own ears.

To her horror Dillon raised a hammer and smashed the window. Sheer terror froze her to the spot. She watched as he reached inside and unlocked the deadbolt.

Panic struck. She dashed for the hall. In her haste she stumbled over her backpack and overturned an end table and a lamp. Hoping that would deter Dillon, she raced down the hall, intending to lock herself inside the bathroom.

But Dillon crashed through the living room like a frenzied demon. Afraid he'd reach her before she could lock the bathroom, she ran to her bedroom, slamming the door behind her. She tried to turn the lock, but he got there too soon. He pushed the door open, grabbed her arms, and shoved her against the wall.

Catharine squirmed, trying to get free. She hated feeling trapped, hated Dillon McKenzie too.

He pinched her arms.

Pain made her scream, and brought tears to her eyes.

"I've been watching yer place," he growled through gritted teeth. "Every day and night I've driven by and tonight I intend to get what I want. I'm gonna screw your head off..."

Catharine screamed again, drowning out the rest of his words. Twisting and squirming, she fought and fought, but his brutal hold was too strong. She couldn't get free.

"Stop fighting me!" he yelled, his red face contorted with rage. "I only want to screw you. I need to. I need you. I've needed this for so long."

The lust in his eyes turned her stomach. His sour breath made her want to retch. It would serve him right. When she didn't, she did the only other thing she could think of to do. She leaned forward and bit him on the chest.

"You little bitch," he yelled. His brutal hold on her arms tightened. He shook her... hard. She felt like her brain was rattling inside her head.

The fury in his eyes truly scared her. Maybe she shouldn't have bitten him. But she'd do anything to get free. She tried to kick him. He stood so close she couldn't raise her foot.

"Stop fighting!" he yelled.

She screamed again. Where was Fey when she needed her? How long before Tyler would arrive? Please get here soon, she prayed. Oh Tyler, I wish you were here right now.

And suddenly he was.

Weak with relief, Catharine went limp.

"Get your hands off her!" Tyler shouted.

Dillon turned his head and glared at Tyler.

Catharine used the respite to slam her knee into Dillon's groin. Yelping like a dog, he released her and doubled over, holding himself.

In one quick move Tyler shoved him to the floor and dropped a knee on Dillon's chest, pinning his arms above his head.

"Call 9-1-1," he said, "and tell the dispatcher to send the police for attempted rape.

Shaken, Catharine nodded as she reached for the bedside phone. As she dialed, Dillon kneed Tyler in the back. To her relief, Tyler punched Dillon and bloodied his lip.

Dillon fought back. Apparently Tyler's rage gave him the strength of two, maybe three. Finally Dillon gave up. He lay dazed and spread eagle on the carpet until Tyler dragged him to his feet and forced him down the hall to the living room.

The police arrived in record time.

"Do you know this man?" one police officer asked while the other handcuffed Dillon.

"Yes," Catharine nodded. "His name is Dillon McKenzie. He works at the company I used to work for."

"What's the name of the company?"

"Wyze Oil and Gas."

"When did you quit?"

"I—ah—"

"She didn't actually quit," Tyler cut in. "I did it for her. A week ago Saturday I left a message on the office recording machine stating she wouldn't be back and they should hire a replacement."

"Why didn't she resign herself?" the second police officer asked, his attention focused on Tyler.

"Because he... Dillon McKenzie, threatened to break in and rape her."

"I didn't threaten to rape her," Dillon snarled, his swollen lip still bleeding and marking a thin red trail down his puffy, pointed chin.

"You said you intended to sleep with her whether she was willing or not. What do you call forcing yourself on a woman who doesn't want anything to do with you, if not rape?" Tyler demanded, his anger sparked anew.

"She never indicated she didn't want anything to do with me. She flirted with me at the office. All the time."

"That isn't true," Catharine said, her face flaming. The tears puddled in her eyes overflowed, forming a steady stream down her cheeks. "I never encouraged you. I tried, always, to resist your touch, but you were persistent."

"Catharine doesn't flirt," Tyler said. "That's not her style."

"Do you wish to press charges, Miss Rose?"

Catharine looked at Tyler, her eyes imploring, *'Please help me.'*

"Of course she does," he said. "Why wouldn't she?"

The police officer had the decency to look uncomfortable. "This type of charge can get ugly."

"Catharine has done nothing wrong. Her reputation is beyond reproach. I'm sure she wants Dillon McKenzie behind bars where he can't harm or threaten anyone else."

"Is that true, Miss Rose?"

Catharine nodded.

"What do you want him charged with?"

"Breaking and entering to begin with," Tyler said, "with the intent to do bodily harm. Attempted rape."

"I didn't attempt to rape her," Dillon denied the accusation again.

"Then why did you knock furniture and lamps over trying to catch her?" Tyler demanded.

Dillon didn't answer, but he glared.

"I heard her screaming, and you had her pinned against the wall in her bedroom when I arrived. You were threatening to screw her head off, and she'll have bruises on her arms because you were holding her against her will."

Dillon hung his head.

"Get your camera," Tyler instructed Catharine. "We'll take photos of him and the broken window for evidence at the trial."

Catharine unzipped her suitcase and found the digital camera she'd taken to England.

When Tyler finished snapping shots, he looked at the policeman holding Dillon by the arm. "Take him away," Tyler said in disgust.

"I'm an attorney. Sexual harassment and stalking charges will be filed tomorrow."

The two policemen escorted Dillon out of the house.

Tyler shut the door behind them. More loose glass from the shattered window fell on the carpet.

Watching him, Catharine saw a cut in the knee of his trousers. He must have slipped and fallen on the broken glass when he first arrived. "Your knee's bleeding," she said shakily. "So are your hands. We should tend your wounds."

"Later," Tyler said. "Where's your phone book? We need to call someone to replace the door window."

"Should we call my landlord first?"

"Yes."

Tyler called him and explained while Catharine fetched the yellow pages. Then Tyler found a company that advertised twenty-four hour window and glass repair. After he made arrangements, he said, "Do you still want to stay here tonight? Or would you prefer to stay at my apartment?"

"I—I don't know."

Tyler stepped closer. Wary and frightened, Catharine backed away.

"I won't hurt you." He took another step.

She shriveled inside, knowing fear filled her eyes as she backed farther away. At the moment she couldn't bear to be touched. Not by anyone. Not even Tyler, even though she admired and respected him above all men.

Tyler dropped his arms to his sides. "I won't let Dillon hurt you again, I promise. And if you need a reason to marry me, that's as good as any."

"But we hardly know one another," she protested.

"We knew each other in previous lives."

She stared up at him. Fear still churned inside her. "I believe that too," she admitted. Images of past lives were usually sketchy and always left her wondering what she was missing. What she might have blocked from her mind. "However, never in any of those lives were we betrothed or wed to each other. I'm not at all sure we should consider marriage now. I fear intimacy, and that will undoubtedly create insurmountable problems."

"Your fear isn't unreasonable. We'll have to learn how to deal with it, but we'll learn together."

"I cannot condemn you to a life without the physical side of marriage. Before I commit to marriage, I must find a way to make myself a whole woman."

That thought reminded her she hadn't talked to Fey since before they left England. She didn't sense the fairy's presence now either, and that worried her. Would she ever see Fey again?

Looking around, hoping to see the tiny fairy perched somewhere, Catharine said, "I—I feel so out of place, like I'm in uncharted waters." Her voice quivered with uncertainty.

"If it makes you feel any better," Tyler said, his voice deep and husky, "we're both in uncharted waters, Catharine."

He stepped closer. She forced herself not to back away, but she breathed a sigh of relief when the doorbell rang.

"That must be the repairman."

Catharine drew in a grateful breath. She didn't mind Tyler's touch. Actually, most of the time she liked it. Right now though, she couldn't handle any kind of contact. Not after Dillon's mauling. His manhandling reminded her too much of her step-papa's thwarted attempts to bed her. Those memories made her shiver and she felt cold. Would she ever feel warm and safe again?

While two repairmen prepared to replace the door window, Catharine led Tyler down the hall to the bathroom. "We need to clean your cuts and make sure they're not deep."

"They're only scratches," he said.

"Nevertheless, we'll wash the blood off and apply an antiseptic."

Very aware of his closeness in the confines of the small bathroom, she used a soft flannel to carefully clean the cuts and scratches on his hands. Then she spread first-aid cream over them and applied bandages. At the same time she took care not to touch him except when and where absolutely necessary.

"Can you roll your trousers up?" Ready to tackle the cut on his knee, she prayed he wouldn't have to remove his trousers. That would be too embarrassing, and probably render her useless.

Tyler nodded, and rolled his pant leg up. Although the bunched fabric fit tight above his knee, he didn't complain. As fast as possible she cleaned his wound, made sure there was no embedded glass, and applied salve and three plastic Band-Aids.

"Now about that lottery ticket," Tyler said when she finished fussing over him.

"It's in my backpack. I had just put it away when Mr. McKenzie broke in."

Back in the living room Catharine and Tyler straightened furniture and overturned lamps before she picked her backpack up off the floor where she'd dropped it when Dillon arrived. She rummaged inside until she found the ticket. Then she handed it, along with the newspaper section containing the winning numbers to Tyler.

"They match, don't they? Did I see straight? I was so excited I might have been cross-eyed in my delirium."

Ty drew her to the kitchen, away from the repairmen where it was quiet and they could talk in private.

"Is money what it takes to excite you, Catharine, to make you deliriously happy?"

"No, but what money can buy excites me."

He gave her a searching look. "Is there something in particular that you want?"

She nodded. "I'd like to buy a house."

"You want to own a house?"

"No." She shook her head. "The house would be for my, or rather Kacy's grandparents, Eileen and Porter Rose."

"They have a house, an extremely nice one in an excellent neighborhood. It's only a few blocks from Mom and Dad's."

"I know. However, they might sell it in order to buy one in Arizona. If I've won the lottery, I could purchase a house for them there, and they can also keep the one they own here. That way they may spend their winters in Arizona where it's warm, and their summers here in Denver, when Arizona is hot."

Tyler smiled. "That's very generous."

"Not unless I've won. Have I?"

He checked the numbers. "They match. Looks like Eileen and Porter are in for a wonderful surprise, Catharine."

"I'm glad you think so."

"Do you have any other plans?" Ty asked.

She glanced around the small kitchen. "I don't want to live here any longer. Not without Jennifer or Miranda, and not now that Mr. McKenzie has broken in. I'd like to terminate the lease, or pay it off and live somewhere else."

"Do you have anyplace in mind?"

"With you," she said without blinking.

Ty rarely found himself speechless, but his breath got trapped in the back of his throat. For a few seconds he couldn't say a word. "Is that an offhand way of saying you'll marry me?"

She sucked her bottom lip in, once again reminding him of a shy, uncertain girl when she stared down at her feet

"Couldn't we just be flatmates or something?"

"Flatmates?" A little confused, he was still frowning when one of the repairmen, standing in the kitchen archway, cleared his throat.

"We're finished. Here's the bill."

"Should I write a check?" Catharine asked, looking at Ty instead of the repairman.

"No. We'll send it to your landlord. He said he has insurance that'll cover it. He'll need the receipt for a claim. You can wait for payment for a couple of days, can't you?" Tyler asked the repairman.

"Yeah. Sure. I'll tell the boss."

After the repairmen left, Catharine said, "I don't want to stay here tonight. I'm afraid I might not be able to sleep."

"I understand," Ty said. "I know a number of people whose homes have been broken into. They all felt violated, and it took several weeks, sometimes months before the feeling eased."

She curved her lips, a feeble attempt to smile. "I'm glad you understand."

"We'll stay at my place." Ty glanced at her suitcase, still in the living room where he'd parked it. "Do you need anything else?"

"Yes. A few things." She hurried to her bedroom, and returned minutes later, carrying a garment bag. "I'm ready."

Ty grinned, feeling like a schoolboy. Also like a hero. Catharine had agreed to live with him. Soon she would agree to marry him. He would find a way to convince her and help her overcome her fear.

And not for an instant did he doubt that he could.

Nine

Early the next morning Tyler called to claim Catharine's lottery winnings. Then he insisted on taking her to the doctor to get a written medical report on her bruised arms that could be used at the trial. It was almost noon before he left for work.

Alone in his apartment, Catharine looked around, calling, "Fey, are you here?"

When only silence answered, Catharine called her office and discovered her marching papers were in the mail. Wyze Oil had already hired a replacement.

She made the bed, tidied the kitchen, then sat down and read a portion of Kacy's journal.

Feeling a bit guilty for being idle, she finally loaded Tyler's washer with water and detergent and started to unpack.

If Tyler hadn't taken it upon himself to resign for her without first discussing it, she wouldn't have had the nerve to tackle his luggage. But as long as she was doing the laundry, she might as well do his, too.

While she sorted soiled clothes into neat piles by color, she hummed, thinking this is how it must feel to be a charwoman... or a wife. Still humming, she carried a stack of clothes to the utility room and dumped them in the full washer. To her astonishment soapy suds overflowed.

She slammed the lid down.

More suds worked their way through the crevices, slid over the edges, down the sides of the washer, all the way to the floor. Bewildered, she pressed her hand against her mouth. What had she done wrong? Although she took her laundry out because she didn't have a washing machine at the small house,
she had gone to a Laundromat once.

Suds began to creep across the linoleum floor. She fled to the bathroom and grabbed an armload of towels. By the time she returned half the floor was covered with bubbles. She kicked her shoes off, sank to her knees and mopped frantically. Barely half-finished, she heard the front door open and close. Had Tyler returned? Or was it someone else?

A huge chill crawled down her back. If only Fey was here, she wouldn't be afraid. Tyler hadn't been gone much more than an hour. Did anyone besides him have a key to his apartment?

Then she heard him call, "Catharine, where are you?"

Relieved, she called back. "In the utility room."

She was still on her knees when he poked his head through the doorway.

"What are you doing here?" she asked, staring up at him.

She could tell he was fighting the urge to laugh. "I was about to ask you the same thing."

"I'm pretending I'm Mrs. Mop," she teased in an attempt to calm her racing heart. "I guess I should have put the clothes in the washing machine before I filled it with water and detergent. Or maybe it wanted less water."

Stilling looking as though he was fighting a grin, he said, "I brought the newspaper. Thought you might want to read about Dillon McKenzie."

Catharine surged to her feet, leaving the towels in a heap at her wet feet. Wiping her hands on her damp denim skirt, she reached for the

Denver Post in Tyler's hands. Her heart thumped as she hesitantly asked, "Is my name in the article?"

Tyler nodded, all traces of humor gone.

"It's all right," she assured him. "I don't mind."

"Are you sure?" He looked concerned. "I don't want this incident to upset you any more than it already has."

"It won't." She smiled. "Actually, in spite of the mess I've made in here, I'm happier than I've been for a very long time, Tyler."

"You couldn't have said anything that would please me more."

He glanced at the suds on the floor, then at the washer. To Catharine's relief, suds were no longer oozing out from the lid or sliding down the sides.

"I hope I haven't damaged the floor," she said.

Tyler grinned. "I'm sure it'll take more than a few suds to do that." He stuck his hands in his tan overcoat pockets and cleared his throat. "Do you want me to help you mop up the suds?"

"No. I can manage. Besides, I wouldn't want you to muss up your suit." He looked so handsome, she was tempted to say she wanted to marry him. But that would only lead to folly.

"I'd better get back to work. Just wanted to make sure you're all right."

She smiled up at him. "I'm as right as rain."

He smiled, too. "You'll be here when I get home from work, won't you?"

"Yes, of course. I haven't anywhere else to go."

After he left, she finished mopping, then changed her wet skirt before she sat down and read the newspaper.

Shivers trailed through her as she relived Dillon's break-in last night. She'd been so confident Fey was with her and more than a little frightened when she discovered she wasn't, and that she was all alone.

Her heart had stopped when he smashed the window with a hammer. Now she quivered as she touched her bruised arms. She didn't want to think about what might have happened if Tyler hadn't arrived when he did.

Forcing her thoughts off Dillon and last night, she put the newspaper down and went to check the washer.

In between batches of washing, she read more of Kacy's journal. Mesmerized, Catharine had a hard time putting it down. Kacy had done a fine job expressing her emotions. Catharine hoped she could do a credible job when she wrote the story.

~ * ~

That evening when Tyler came home, Catharine said, "I called my landlord. He asked for another month's rent to break the lease."

Tyler took a few minutes to read the lease, then said, "The lease ran out more than a year ago, so you've been on a month to month. Giving your land lord thirty days notice is fair and adequate."

While they were watching the Monday night news, the phone rang. Tyler picked it up. "Hello." Then he mouthed to Catharine, "It's your grandparents."

To them he said, "Yes, she's here. Just a minute. I'll get her." He handed her the phone.

"Hello."

"How are you?" Eileen Rose asked.

"I want to know too," Porter Rose said, apparently on an extension. Still marveling that such things were possible, Catharine heard their anxiety. Sudden guilt bogged her down.

"I'm fine," she said. How had they known where to find her?

"I just talked to Rachel," Eileen announced. "She said a man broke into your house last night. Did he harm you?"

"No." Rachel was Tyler's mother, also Eileen's good friend. Catharine cleared her throat, silently berating herself for not calling and telling them about Dillon's assault. "Tyler arrived shortly after he—Mr. McKenzie broke in."

"Rachel said you're staying with Tyler."

"I am," Catharine said cautiously. Would Eileen and Porter condemn her?

Neither one did. "Rachel also said you flew to England with Tyler and spent a week there."

"I did," Catharine admitted, feeling guilty for not calling to tell them that either.

"You had our phone number down here, didn't you? Or did you lose it?"

"Yes. I have it. Sorry. I should have called to tell you we were going to England, but it happened so fast, I barely had time to pack."

"Well, you're back safe and sound. That's what matters," Porter said.

But Catharine knew it wasn't all that mattered. She had to start treating them like they truly were her grandparents. She had promised Kacy she would, just as Kacy had promised to treat her mother like her own, even though she apparently hadn't seen her.

"We'll be home day after tomorrow," Eileen said. "The drive is too long for old people like us to make in one day. We want you to move back in with us when we get there. We don't think you should live alone anymore."

"You need not return to Colorado," Catharine objected. "The weather here is terribly cold. I'm sure it's much warmer in Arizona. Tyler said I can stay with him, so I won't be alone."

"We'll be home," Porter said, a note of finality in his voice.

Resigned, Catharine said, "I miss you and I'm anxious to see you both. Please drive safely."

"We will, dear."

When they hung up, Tyler said, "I talked to the District Attorney this afternoon. After the article in the Post this morning, three other women filed sexual harassment complaints against Dillon."

Rather than the elation she expected to feel at such news, a shiver traced down Catharine's spine. Although he had been arrested, Dillon really worried her. "Has a date for the trial been set?"

"Not yet. I imagine it'll be sometime in the fall, eight or nine months down the road. Bail has been set though, and I'm afraid Dillon will be out of jail soon."

Catharine shivered, and frowned. "I'm afraid he might try to harm you. Or me."

"Don't worry," Tyler said. "I'll get a restraining order and Dillon will have to be on his best behavior. Another complaint will look very bad."

"I'll try to keep that in mind."

Seated beside her on the couch, Tyler fished in his pocket, and pulled out a small box. "I have something for you."

"A surprise." Catharine smiled. "How lovely." She opened it and gasped when she saw a beautiful diamond betrothal ring.

"May I put it on your finger?" Tyler asked.

Her heart thumped. Dread mixed with elation. But good sense prevailed. "I can't marry you, Tyler. I wouldn't be doing you a favor." She closed the box and handed it back.

"I don't intend to give up." He stuck the ring in his pocket, slid his arms around her, then kissed her.

To her surprise, she responded. But when the kiss ended, fear coiled around her heart. If she agreed to marry him, he would own the right to do whatever he wished with her. She mustn't encourage him.

Her fear vanished the instant Tyler released her.

"We should probably discuss your lottery winnings," he said.

She forced a smile. "I can hardly wait to share my wonderful surprise with Kacy's grandparents."

"Your grandparents," Tyler corrected gently.

She nodded. "I'm certain they'll be pleased with my news."

"I have a suggestion."

"What is it?"

"I'd like us to take my parents and your grandparents out to dinner on Friday night."

"That's a wonderful idea. Friday is Valentine's day."

"A perfect day to have dinner with those we love."

Smiling again, Catharine nodded agreement.

~ * ~

True to their word, Eileen and Porter Rose arrived home on Wednesday afternoon. After they called her, Catharine called Tyler at his office.

"I can leave work now and drive you over to see them if you'd like," he said.

"I'd be ever so grateful," Catharine said, twisting the phone cord.

"I'll be home in about thirty minutes."

"I'll wait for you down by the front door."

About an hour later, after she embraced Eileen and Porter, Catharine said, "I have two marvelous surprises."

"What are they?"

"I won the lottery. And I want to buy a house for you in Arizona. If you want one there, that is."

"Those certainly are wonderful surprises," Eileen said.

"But," Porter added, "you don't need to buy us a house. If we want one, we'll buy it ourselves."

"No, please. Not if you must sell your home here to do so. I want you to spend your summers in Colorado and I've won ten million dollars. Therefore, I can afford to buy a second house for you. And I really want to. Please don't stop me from doing something nice for you."

They were both speechless, she could tell, but pleased, too.

"And now that you're home," she added, "Tyler and I would like to take you and his parents to dinner on Friday night. Are you free then?"

"Yes. But it's Valentine's day," Eileen said. "Are you sure you want to spend it with us old folks?"

Catharine smiled. "Certainly."

Porter looked at Tyler. "We'd like to thank you for being here when Catharine needed you."

Tyler smiled. "Consider it my pleasure."

Catharine glanced up at Tyler. She was extremely happy to have him at her side. But sometimes she feared something awful would happen to spoil their friendship. It always had in the past. Could they somehow break the cycle? If they failed to get things right in this life, were they destined never to meet again, as he had suggested? The mere thought made her want to cry.

"Do you want to move back here with us?" Eileen asked, jarring her thoughts.

Catharine shook her head. "I prefer to stay with Tyler. He says he doesn't mind."

Porter and Eileen eyed them both. Catharine suspected they were wondering if they slept together. Since they weren't and hadn't done anything untoward, she didn't know what to say. In the past merely being alone with a man would have destroyed her reputation.

"Her virtue's safe with me," Tyler said. "So please don't worry about her. I won't do anything to compromise her in your eyes, or hers."

Eileen and Porter both looked relieved. "You're a good young man," Porter said.

Tyler grinned. "Mom and Dad would be proud to hear you say that."

~ * ~

Later, back at his apartment, Catharine looked around at the walls that now seemed more familiar than the small house where she had lived for twenty months. "This feels more like home than anyplace else."

"I'm glad you think so." Tyler wrapped his arms around her and kissed her forehead, her cheek, her mouth. She responded, up to a point, but was relieved when he released her.

By mutual agreement, Tyler continued to sleep on the couch and she slept in his bed.

He never attempted to do more than kiss her good night on the cheek or forehead. Each time he touched her, Catharine's heart quaked. She hoped and prayed he could help her overcome her fear. But she couldn't make herself believe that he could. If only the fairy godmother were here. Maybe she could help.

~ * ~

Knowing he had to break off with Sloan, Ty called and invited her to lunch on Thursday. They agreed to meet downtown at Marlo's, on the Sixteenth Street Mall.

"I was beginning to think you were avoiding me." Sloan plopped a wet kiss on his cheek before he realized her intent.

"I've been out of town."

"To England. I know." Sloan smiled. "I called your office and the receptionist told me. Was it business or pleasure?"

"Some of both."

When he didn't explain, she hiked her perfectly penciled eyebrows, and reached for his hand with one of her fake fingernailed hands. "Are you taking me out to dinner tomorrow night to celebrate Valentine's day?"

"I have other plans."

"Are you trying to give me a message, Ty?"

He nodded. "I've asked someone else to marry me."

A combination of hurt and fury flashed in her amber eyes. "You've been seeing someone else while you were seeing me?"

"No. I've known Catharine for—years. He'd almost said for infinity. "We hadn't seen much of each other until Jennifer's funeral. Then, when we did, I realized I've always loved her," he surprised himself by saying. Did he love Catharine? In past lives they'd been close friends but he'd always been committed to someone else, and never free to express his love. Only once had he admitted he loved her. But that love and their mutual demise now haunted his dreams.

"Is Catharine that little mouse I saw clinging to your arm at the cemetery?" Sloan asked.

Ty resisted the urge to snap a curt reply. He hadn't realized how possessive Sloan had become, or how catty she could sound. "That remark doesn't deserve a comment."

"Sorry," Sloan said, but he doubted she meant it. "Have you set a date?"

"Not yet." He didn't intend to elaborate. It wasn't any of her business. Eventually Catharine would marry him. He wasn't going to take 'no' for an answer. Whether they loved each other yet or not, they belonged together. He felt that in his head, his heart and his soul.

"Is your engagement a secret?" Sloan asked.

She was an attorney too and Ty didn't appreciate her grilling him, so he hedged, "We haven't told Mom and Dad yet. I think they should be told before we announce it."

"Well if this is to be our last lunch, we might as well enjoy it. I'd like a glass of wine. How about you?"

Feeling a little like a cad, Tyler indulged her. But he also felt guilty, as though he was somehow betraying Catharine. Because of that he barely sipped his wine, and when his food arrived he ate fast.

"Sorry I have to rush." He set his napkin back on the table and stood. "I have a lot of work to get caught up on."

"No problem," Sloan said, her bold gaze turning sultry and inappropriately seductive. "Are you still interested in running for the state legislature?"

"Yes."

"Will this Catharine you've decided to marry be an asset to your political career, Ty?"

Irritated by Sloan's snide innuendoes, he stood. "Catharine is an asset all by herself."

"Well, if you change your mind, I'm sure you won't have any trouble finding me."

He didn't reply. Why hadn't he ever realized how manipulative and domineering Sloan could be? "Goodbye, Sloan."

"Not goodbye, Ty. Only so long."

His lunch turned sour in his stomach as he strode away. But he was relieved he hadn't picked Sloan up and didn't have to drive her back to work, or endure her company any longer.

Grateful he'd had enough sense not to sleep with her, he dismissed Sloan from his thoughts and stopped at a corner flower stand to buy a bouquet for Catharine.

Ten

When Ty arrived home with the flowers that evening, Catharine's whole face lit up. "Are those for me?"

He smiled. "Yes."

"Is there a special occasion?"

Not about to tell her he'd met Sloan for lunch and these were an attempt to salve his conscience, he said, "Consider them an early Valentine's gift."

Catharine accepted the flowers carefully, as though they were worth a million dollars. "No one's ever given me flowers before. They're beautiful. Thank you ever so much."

Ty suspected there were a lot of things she had missed and decided to try to rectify that. Although he knew very little about her life in the nineteenth century, he knew a great deal about previous lives. None of them had ever been easy. He intended to change that.

The next morning while they were eating breakfast, Ty stuck a Valentine gift on the table in front of Catharine. Wrapped in pink paper with small red hearts, she smiled while she opened it. "A cell phone."

Ty nodded. "You should take it with you wherever you go."

"Okay. But I don't know how to use it."

"I'll show you."

After he did, she said, "Thank you, Tyler. I'm sure it will come in handy."

He smiled. "I think so, too." He set another gift, a smaller box in front of her.

As Catharine unwrapped, her eyes sparkled. The glow amplified when she saw the double string of pearls. She lifted them gently, almost reverently, as though they were priceless.

"They're gorgeous."

"For a gorgeous lady."

She swallowed, and Ty detected a suspicious sheen in her luminous eyes. "I really shouldn't accept them."

"Nonsense. You'll spoil my day if you don't." Pleased with his surprise, he grinned. "Should I fasten them for you? I'd like to see how they look around your lovely neck."

She nodded. And when he finished, he kissed her cheek.

Catharine then extended a gift wrapped in bright red paper with small pink hearts. When he unwrapped it, he grinned again. "The latest *Harry Potter*." He'd mentioned he hadn't yet read it. "When did you buy this?"

"I rode the bus to the Tattered Cover yesterday. I hope you enjoy it."

"I'm sure I will."

She offered another gift, wrapped in the same red and pink paper. He unwrapped a huge jar of chocolate covered cashews, then looked up. "You didn't buy this at the Tattered Cover."

"No. I found it in a sweet shop nearby."

"Thanks. Cashews are one of my favorites."

When Tyler stood to leave for work, Catharine realized how much she had to learn about him and the things he liked and disliked. It might take a lifetime. She hoped nothing would prevent them from sharing it. But often when she thought about the future, a foreboding sensation descended. Dillon McKenzie worried her. So did something else... a vague sense of unease. Day and night, the disturbance hovered in her mind. She could neither describe nor explain the reason why. If she saw the fairy again, maybe she could tell her what she feared.

As soon as Tyler left, Catharine muttered, "I wonder if I'll ever see Fey again."

"Is now too soon?" Flying close, the tiny fairy winked. "Have you missed me?"

"Terribly," Catharine admitted, smiling. "Where have you been?"

"When you left England I took the opportunity to travel back in time to see Kacy."

"How is she?"

"Very well. Happy as a meadow lark. How about yourself? Are you happy?"

"Yes," Catharine said, "yet I'm worried, too."

"What about?"

"A number of things. Dillon McKenzie. Something I can't explain. My fear of intimacy. Tyler's proposal."

Fey blinked. "Tyler's proposal? I seem to have missed something important."

"I said, 'no'." Catharine explained what had happened since their return.

When she finished, Fey said, "Have you considered seeking help to overcome your fear of marriage?"

"What kind of help?"

The fairy shrugged and her tiny wings wiggled. "Medical. Psychiatric. Or perhaps hypnotherapy."

"I doubt a medical doctor or a psychiatrist could help me, and I don't have the foggiest notion where to look for a hypnotherapist."

"Perhaps you could ask your adopted grandmother for guidance."

Catharine nodded thoughtfully. "Yes. Perhaps I could. Thank you for suggesting it, Fey."

"You're most welcome, sweetling."

"Could I ask some other questions?"

"Certainly."

"I seem to be afraid of something I can't see or explain. I hold the fear at bay when I'm awake, but it attacks my consciousness when I sleep, invades my dreams, turns them into nightmares."

"Don't borrow trouble," Fey said, her expression sympathetic. "At the moment you're in no danger. DillonMcKenzie is still behind bars."

"Thanks for putting my mind at rest."

"You said questions. Do you have another?"

Catharine nodded. "Jennifer seemed to think my mother is in this time. Do you know if she is?"

The fairy nodded, but her eyes took on a shuttered look.

"Does she remember me?"

"Yes."

"Do you know where she is?"

Once again Fey nodded. "I cannot tell you. You must find her on your own." Raising her wand, Fey said, "I must go now. Time travel wears me out and I must seek rest with my own kind to restore my energy." With a quick wave she disappeared.

Alone again, Catharine grinned. The fairy had not forsaken her. She would see her from time to time.

~ * ~

That evening at the Wellshire Inn on south Colorado Boulevard, Catharine squinted, trying to adjust her eyes to the muted interior. The delicious aroma of well-prepared food almost made her drool as Tyler guided her across the foyer to greet his brown-haired parents and Kacy's gray-haired grandparents.

After the hostess showed them to their reserved table, Tyler kissed his mother's smooth cheek and gave her a heart-shaped box of chocolates.

"Thanks, Ty." Tall and reed-thin, Rachel's green eyes gleamed with maternal pride. "You've always been such a thoughtful son."

Smiling, he repeated the process with Catharine and Eileen.

Not to be outdone, Catharine distributed the Valentine cards and books she had selected for each person, including Tyler.

"You already gave me two gifts this morning," he whispered, while the others examined and exclaimed their appreciation.

She smiled and whispered back, "I bought three for you."

His gaze softened. "Thank you."

A few moments later a waiter struck a match and lit the candle on their table while another popped the cork on a bottle of champagne. After he filled six tall champagne glasses, Tyler raised his. "I have an announcement."

"What is it, son?" His gray-eyed father, Mack, grinned, exposing twin dimples on his smoothly shaven cheeks.

Tyler grinned, too. "I've asked Catharine to marry me."

"'Bout time," Porter said.

Catharine gasped, unable to believe Tyler had said that. She had turned him down! Didn't he remember?

She tried to swallow. The champagne fizzed up instead of going down. Her eyes watered. Too stunned to speak, she gaped at Tyler as though he had two heads.

Still grinning, he asked his mother and Eileen, "What do you think?"

"It's wonderful news." Eileen's blue eyes sparkled like small twin peaks of light. "I'm so happy for you."

"Me, too." Rachel turned her smile to Catharine.

She squirmed as Mack raised his champagne glass.

"I'd like to propose a toast."

The others raised their champagne. Catharine clutched her water glass.

"To your marriage. May it be long, and as filled with happiness as ours and the Rose's have been."

"That's a great toast, Dad," Tyler said.

"Have you set a date?" His mother asked.

Catharine sipped water in an attempt to unclog her throat. "No," she said, in spite of her wildly pounding heart and half clenched teeth. "I said, 'no'. I haven't agreed to marry him."

"Why the hell not?" Porter asked, frowning.

"Because I don't think I'd make a very good wife," she hedged, too embarrassed to explain her fear of intimacy and men.

"You'll be an exceptional wife," Tyler said, his full attention on her. "You don't want people to think we're living in sin, do you?"

Catharine pursed her lips. How unfair to mention the one thing that most bothered her. *Living in sin.*

"But we're not," she sputtered. "We're not sleeping together or anything like that." She looked at the others. "He sleeps on the sofa. We're merely sharing his flat."

"You've always been extremely fond of each other." Rachel smiled indulgently, an expectant gleam in her green eyes. "And I think your birthday in April would make a wonderful wedding day, Kacy, I mean Catharine."

"I think so too," Tyler agreed.

"Perhaps we should order dinner," Eileen said, and Catharine silently blessed her for changing the subject.

When their salads arrived, they discussed their trip to England, but avoided mentioning their reason for going.

Then Catharine took a deep breath and announced, "I no longer work at Wyze Oil and Gas."

Everyone stared at her.

"Why?" Eileen's warm blue eyes filled with concern.

"Because of Dillon McKenzie," Catharine said, unwilling to publicly blame Tyler for resigning for her without first consulting her. That would be bad form. Make her sound ungrateful.

"Tell us about Dillon McKenzie," Eileen urged as the waiter cleared their salad plates away.

Haltingly, Catharine explained how Dillon had touched her at work when no one else could see him. How he had threatened to force himself on her. And then broken into her rented home.

"How terrible," Eileen sympathized, her concern evident.

"Aren't there laws to protect women from sexual harassment?" Porter asked, his round ruddy cheeks redder than usual.

Mack nodded. "Dillon McKenzie has been arrested."

Catharine shivered. The memories of that night still gave her the jitters and nightmares.

"And he'll stand trial." Tyler closed his hand over Catharine's. She knew he was trying to calm her and looked up. His smile seemed to say everything would be all right. And to her surprise, his expression and his touch did make her feel better.

The waiter brought the main course. While they ate, Tyler's mother said, "The new receptionist we hired to replace Gert when she retired gave notice last week. She's getting married and her future husband has accepted a job out of state. I've interviewed a number of candidates. The woman I'd like to hire has two small children and would like to work half days, afternoons. Would you be interested in working the other half, Kacy? I mean Catharine? In the mornings?"

"I'd love to work for you and your family," she said, delighted by Rachel's suggestion.

"Work with us, not for us," Tyler said gently. "You'll soon be part of the family, too."

Unwilling to argue about that just yet, she said, "If I work half a day, I can spend the rest of the time writing."

"What do you want to write?" Rachel asked, her eyes bright with interest. And curiosity.

"Women's fiction," Catharine said.

"Romance," Tyler added with a smile.

"I'd love to read whatever you write," Eileen said, also smiling.

"Me, too." Although Porter's voice sounded gruff, the warmth in his eyes radiated pride.

"I'll be happy to share it with you." She knew she'd have to explain she and Kacy had switched places and identities before that happened though.

"Nice pearls," Mack complimented.

"Yes," Porter agreed.

Smiling, Catharine fingered the pearls at her throat. "Tyler gave them to me."

Rachel and Eileen exchanged knowing looks. Catharine didn't have it in her to tell them that accepting the pearls didn't mean she intended to marry Tyler.

During the drive home Catharine frowned at Tyler in the near dark. "I think it was a bit cheeky to announce your proposal tonight. You can't have forgotten that I said no."

Ty shifted behind the steering wheel. He had ordered the champagne ahead of time to celebrate Valentine's day. Once it arrived, he'd let the occasion and enthusiasm carry him away. But he didn't regret what he'd done. Catharine needed someone to look out for her, take care of her. He couldn't think of anyone better suited than him. And that nagging premonition that this was their last chance to get things right, to consummate their love prevailed.

"Have you no comment to make?" she asked. "No words to defend yourself?"

He shook his head, knowing she watched him intently. "No. I apologize if I upset you."

She looked so much like Kacy he had to keep reminding himself they weren't the same person. When he'd first met Kacy he'd felt certain he had known her in prior lives. At the time he had nothing concrete to base that belief on. Nothing except the repetition of a dream that for years had never faded. A dream that depicted them together, living that myth of happily ever after and all that stuff. Sometime during the last two weeks he had transferred all those emotions to Catharine. Would he regret it?

There was one thing he couldn't deny. Deep inside he carried the memory of their never-ending love. That's why he hadn't been able to get serious with Sloan or any other woman. Now he had a strong, almost desperate feeling time was running out for him and Catharine, and if he didn't act quickly, he'd lose an opportunity that might never be presented again. How could he make her understand?

He cleared his throat, glanced at Catharine, then pulled over to the side of the road and parked. Turning sideways to face her, he said with grim determination, "I think we should have married in other lives but we never did. We're not going to make that same mistake again. We're closer to fulfilling a love relationship than we've ever been before. Surely you understand the importance of the chance we've been given now?"

When she didn't comment, he continued. "You seem to have two choices." He raised his hands and ticked them off on his fingers. "Live with me and marry me, or move in with your adopted grandparents. Surely you don't want to live alone again. Even if you did, none of us who care about you will let that happen." He dropped his hands to his lap. "You don't have to make your decision right away, but you should give your future careful consideration."

Catharine frowned. Although Tyler had raised her dander, she squashed the urge to make a few tart retorts. She didn't want any man controlling her life again.

Even so, she felt her resistance weakening. Tyler might be a bit high-handed, but he was also a dear man. If she married him, he would take care of her as he had always taken care of those he had been responsible for in prior lives. If she didn't marry him, she could go through life unhappy and unfulfilled, as she always had before.

Tyler's friendship meant the world to her. If he truly wanted to marry her, she should feel flattered. A small part of her longed to be his wife. Another stronger part yearned for things to remain as they were. The thought of intimacy terrified her. What if he forced himself on her like Dillon and her step-papa had tried to do? Weren't all men like that? Fear clutched at her heart. *Please,* she silently pleaded, *don't behave like other men, Tyler. Be special; someone I can admire and trust.*

Tyler shifted gears and pulled back onto the road.

Much later, Catharine changed to her high-necked, long-sleeved nightgown, preparing to sleep in Tyler's bed again. This had been an eventful week. Even more hectic than the one in England. Her head had spun from one event to the next.

Every time she thought about Dillon McKenzie, she cringed and shook inside. As long as he posed a threat, she was in no condition to surrender her heart or her body to any man.

Catharine climbed in bed and stared up at the dark ceiling. As she did every night, she thought about her fairy godmother. Perhaps Fey's suggestion would work. Not the medical profession or psychiatrists, but hypnotherapy.

Or, maybe if she found her mother, she could help her remember *why* she was afraid. Catharine's heart began to pound. How could she find her mother? Did she have the same name? *Does she know I'm in this time, too? If so, why hasn't she contacted me?*

Unable to calm down enough to sleep, Catharine racked her brain for solutions. But it didn't help. She couldn't come up with a single idea how to look for her mother or find a hypnotherapist.

A crushing weight settled in her chest. If only she knew more about living in this time. If only she weren't such a wimpish timid soul. If only she possessed more courage. More confidence. If only she weren't afraid of marriage. Afraid Tyler would change, if they married.

Eleven

"Reorganizing my life is taking more time than I anticipated," Catharine said while Tyler drove her home from the office after she'd been working there a week. "I love working with you and your parents. Actually, I consider it a pleasure. But I've been so busy I haven't moved everything from the rented house. I don't know what to do with Jennifer's things."

"Mom might want to sort through them and see if there's anything she'd like to keep," Tyler said. "We can donate the furniture to charity. You might want to keep Jennifer's clothes. They should fit, since you're five feet tall and only weigh about a hundred pounds."

"Good idea." Catharine stared outside, delighted with the sunshiny blue sky, and exhaled a quiet sigh. "My life is ever so much more exciting now, even if it isn't organized yet."

Tyler grinned as he signaled to change lanes. "How so?"

"Before we went to England I rode the bus to and from work every day, ate dinner at home and watched TV. On Saturday I picked up the laundry and shopped for groceries, and on Sunday, I stayed home and read."

His chuckle surprised her. "Now I know why you overloaded my washer. You took your laundry out."

She nodded. "We didn't have a washing machine, and that's what Jennifer taught me to do. In any event, my life was mundane and rather boring. Now I do something different every day, even if it's only eating lunch at a new restaurant on our way home, or writing another chapter of Kacy's story. The excitement of living with you is smashing, Tyler."

Tyler smiled. "I like sharing our lives, too."

Catharine changed the subject before he mentioned marriage again, something he did almost every day, as though repetition would wear her down.

"We must decide what to do with the money I will receive from the lottery. In the eighteen fifties people spoke in denominations that were less than a hundred. Before I came here I had never even heard the word thousand. Millions and billions are far beyond my comprehension." She shook her head in bafflement, then had to shove her long blond hair back behind her shoulders. "What does one do with ten million dollars?"

"Invest a good portion of it," Tyler suggested.

"I'd like a new computer. Do you think I can afford one after I buy a house for the Rose's?"

Tyler grinned. "With ten million dollars, even discounted for taking it in cash, you can afford several houses and as many computers as you'd like."

"One will be sufficient. Unless you'd like a new one, too. Would you?"

"No. My laptop—notebook's fine, but thanks anyway. By the way, I've checked into Jennifer's trust. It's worth about a million dollars. It'll take some time to turn it all into cash. Then I'll divide it three ways, like she asked me to do."

"I really think you should split it between you and your parents, Tyler. I don't need it, and I'll have to pay more taxes if I accept it."

"We'll worry about that next year. I doubt it'll be liquid before then."

Catharine folded her arms, and continued to watch Tyler. Would she ever tire of looking at him? She doubted it. She never had in past lives.

He was so clever, charming and compelling. But he *was* a man, and undoubtedly he would eventually want what all the others did.

Ty parked in front of the apartment complex, switched the engine off and pulled the key out of the ignition. "Do you have plans for this afternoon?"

Catharine nodded, smiling in anticipation as she collected her backpack and gloves. "Eileen invited me to go shopping with her."

"Good. Then you won't mind that I'll be home late tonight. I have a cocktail party after work."

A little surprised he hadn't mentioned it before, Catharine swallowed. "Do you usually have a lot of those?"

"Yeah." Tyler nodded. "Two or three a week. If I run for state senator, there'll be more. There's a cocktail party Friday night at the governor's mansion. I'd like you to go with me."

Catharine took great care not to let Tyler see her trepidation before he got out of the car and walked around to open her door. She wasn't comfortable in crowds.

Even though she had attended her share of soirees and balls in the past, she hadn't enjoyed them. She'd always felt as though she were on display. And her step-papa had watched her like a hawk. If she said or did something Wilbur disapproved of, he scolded her for days afterwards and used whatever impropriety she was guilty of as an excuse to keep her from doing the things she really wanted to do. For that reason, she had been delighted to escape to the haven of Miss Treacher's Finishing Academy when she was sixteen, after her coming out season.

Catharine truly doubted she would enjoy the cocktail party at the governor's mansion, but she kept her misgivings to herself. That uncomfortable sense of unease, that Fey had helped her shed, returned.

"How about a kiss?" Tyler startled Catharine after he walked her to the front door of his apartment building. "To send me back to the office with a smile on my face?"

She looked up, her drumming heart gaining momentum as they stared. *Was he teasing? Flirting? Or serious?* She didn't want to appear a flirt, yet part of her wanted to kiss him, to see how it affected her. To see if she was still afraid.

"By all means," she heard herself say, in spite of her better judgment.

Grinning, Tyler brushed her long hair away from her cheeks. She summoned her courage a moment before his lips found hers.

It shouldn't have surprised her that his kiss stirred her senses and aroused her emotions. If only she didn't fear where his kisses would lead, if they got married.

He smelled divine. Like a mixture of exotic spices. And his arms around her waist made her feel safe and secure. But then she had always trusted him. In every life.

With his overcoat unbuttoned, and her hands splayed on the white shirt covering his chest, she felt his muscles tense as he deepened the kiss. Her last thought before she lost all of them was what would people think to see them kissing so passionately outdoors?

When the kiss ended, she said dazedly, "Your kisses drive all else from my mind."

"Good. That's how they affect me, too. You're delightfully refreshing. Brave and honest. You don't have a coy thought in your head."

He opened the lobby door with his security card and waited until she went inside before he said, "Have fun shopping with Eileen. Buy something pretty to wear to the governor's party."

"I shall," Catharine said, but the joyful anticipation of shopping faded when she remembered the governor's party. How could she get out of going?

~ * ~

At the Cherry Creek Mall on First Avenue Eileen and Catharine looked in several department stores before Catharine found some gowns that appealed to her.

"This one is perfect," she said, staring at herself in the wall of mirrors at Neiman Marcus.

"You look lovely," Eileen said.

Catharine twirled, delighted with the backless black gown, and the way it made her feel. Special. And beautiful. "I like the other one, too."

"Buy them both," Eileen advised. "You can afford to splurge now that you've won the lottery and embarked on two new careers."

Catharine held up the other gown, a long-sleeved, turtleneck made of soft, navy blue knit, and lined with silk. "I think I *will* purchase both."

"You look happier than you have for years," Eileen said while Catharine changed back to her own clothes.

She smiled. "I am."

"You've been different since the accident."

Catharine's smile froze. Did Eileen suspect she wasn't Kacy? "In what way?"

"You picked up a British accent while you were in England. I thought it might go away after a while, but you still have it."

Panic sizzled down Catharine's spine. The elocution lessons hadn't worked. Sometimes her accent slipped back in. Probably far more often than she realized. Tyler had mentioned it, too.

"Does my accent bother you?"

"Goodness no. Port and I like it. You've always been good at mimicking." Eileen smiled. "You act more timid than you used to. But there's one thing that hasn't changed. You've always said you wouldn't marry Tyler. I hope you change your mind about that. He's right, you know. Some people do think you're living in sin."

A slice of guilt knifed through Catharine, but she said, "He and I know we're not. And if I change my mind, you'll be one of the first to know." The thought of marriage terrorized her heart. Something else she could neither name, nor explain, fluttered inside too. Giddiness? Excitement? Hope?

From Neiman Marcus they went to Lord & Taylor where they made more purchases. As they wandered through the mall, their arms laden with packages, a tall robust man who seemed to appear from nowhere blocked their path.

Catharine stopped in her tracks, stifling the scream that erupted inside her head.

"Hello, Catharine," Dillon McKenzie said, his tone mild, but his eyes blazing with fury. "I got fired because of you, and I intend to make you pay."

Stark terror rippled through her. She stared up at him, speechless. Would he harm her? Abduct her? Force himself on her?

Finally she found her gumption. And stepped around him. Her frightened heart beat double time. Her knees shook so badly she could hardly walk. *Be brave,* she admonished herself. *Tyler thinks you're brave. Act as though you are.*

After Dillon was some distance behind them, Eileen nudged Catharine with her elbow. "Who was that man?"

"Dillon McKenzie." The words gushed out in a breathless rush. "The man who broke into my home the night Tyler and I returned from England."

"I thought he'd been arrested."

"He must be out on bail. Tyler said he would be."

"Meeting him in the mall seems an odd coincidence."

Catharine's knees still wobbled and her terror-filled heart pounded. "It probably wasn't a coincidence. He might be following me be—because he wants to scare me. You heard what he said, didn't you?"

"Yes, and I'll be happy to testify that he threatened you."

"Th—thank you. I'll tell my attorney."

"You're going to be all right," Eileen sympathized.

"I hope so." But Catharine couldn't make herself believe that. Dillon's fury had turned her heart ice cold. She was beginning to feel numb, and afraid her brain might stop functioning. She had to force her feet to keep walking.

Outside, they found Eileen's car in the parking lot, deposited their packages on the back seat and climbed in front.

Eileen touched Catharine's arm. "Dillon wouldn't dare hurt you again."

"I'm sure you're right." But a heavy weight crushed down upon her, adding to Catharine's host of doubts.

"Actually, most of the time I feel terribly overwhelmed," she changed subjects after Eileen started the engine. "A few weeks ago I was living alone, contemplating my future, gloomy and bleak. Now I live and work with Tyler. Our friendship both excites and frightens me. Sometimes I wonder how so much happened in such a short time."

Eileen patted her shoulder. "That's how I felt before I married Porter. You sound just like me. A nervous bride-to-be."

"I'm not a bride-to-be. But if I were, can you tell me when the nervousness, well, when it might end?"

"Probably sometime after the ceremony, while you're on your honeymoon."

Honeymoon. The mere word made Catharine shiver and shake. "I'm nervous about being intimate with Tyler, and I can't seem to shed my fear. I like his kisses," she admitted, "however, the thought of a—um—sharing the other is more than a bit daunting… Actually, it's terrifying."

"The only thing to fear is fear itself." Eileen clapped her hand over her mouth. "Forgive me for spouting such a platitude. Why don't you tell Tyler how you feel? Perhaps he can ease your fear somewhat."

As Eileen drove out of the parking lot, Catharine considered mentioning hypnotherapy, and asking if Eileen could recommend a therapist. But she hesitated. If hypnotherapists were men, she'd be too frightened to visit one.

As she had done all her life, Catharine tried to shove her worry to the back of her mind. A solution would come eventually. It must. In the meantime, fretting wouldn't solve a thing.

She fretted and stewed and worried anyway.

~ * ~

On Thursday Tyler called Catharine around four o'clock. "I left the office early. I'll be home in about fifteen minutes."

"I'm ready." Butterflies flitted around in her stomach like a swarm of bees searching for nectar. A few days earlier Tyler had invited her to have dinner in Breckenridge, and said it would take more than an hour to drive there. She was both elated and nervous. Although she had gone out with him in England, they had always been with Jennifer and Drake, and Catharine hadn't considered those outings real dates.

"I'll meet you downstairs, near the front door," she said.

"Good. I'll stop at the curb."

Dressed in her new navy blue turtle-necked gown and white winter coat, she waited on the sidewalk. A black sporty car drove by her. She recognized Dillon McKenzie behind the wheel. When he yelled an obscenity, and raised his fist through his open window, her stomach knotted and her legs nearly buckled.

112

She half turned, intending to dash back inside the safety of the lobby, but somebody tooted a car horn. She saw Tyler's gray Mercedes approaching. As soon as he stopped, she jumped in and slammed the door.

"What's wrong?" he asked, his hand still on the door handle. He always got out to open her door for her, but today she hadn't given him a chance. "You look as though you've see the devil."

"I have," she gushed in a breathless gasp. "Dillon McKenzie just drove by. He glared and yelled at me. I'm beginning to feel as though he's stalking me."

"Why? This is the first time you've seen him, isn't it?"

"No. On Monday when I was shopping with Eileen, Dillon stopped us in the mall and said he'd been fired because of me and he intends to make me pay for that."

"Why didn't you tell me before?" Tyler's tone sounded harsh.

Catharine tried to swallow and found it difficult. "I wanted to handle this without bothering you."

"I want to be bothered. We need to tell your attorney."

"I called him Tuesday. Eileen said she would testify that she heard Dillon threaten me."

Tyler frowned. "I don't think he's very bright."

Catharine cleared her throat. "Why?"

"Dillon flunked out of law school. Flunked out of the Colorado School of Mines, too. He isn't a petroleum engineer. He lied. Faked his resume. That's why he got fired. Not because of you." Tyler shot her a quick glance, his gaze barely leaving the windshield. "I don't want you to go anywhere alone."

"I won't." Catharine stuck her cold clenched hands inside her new satin coat pockets. "I've no desire to go out alone."

"Good."

During the drive she did her best to put Dillon out of her mind, and finally leaned back and gazed out the window. Although the sky was peacock blue, the temperature outside was too cold to melt any of the frosty snow. The ground was covered with white and snow glistened on bare-branched trees as well. Luckily the clear sky prevailed, and the plowed roads were dry or cindered all the way to the small mountain town of Breckenridge.

"This little town declared itself a kingdom when they were left off the map during Civil War times," Tyler said, slowing his speed as small buildings appeared on both sides of the road. "They also changed the spelling from Breckinridge, with an i in the middle, named after the then Vice President of the United States, to Breckenridge with an e."

Enchanted by the small town built at the base of tall, snow-covered mountain peaks and ski slopes, Catharine smiled as she looked around.

"I've never seen anything like this before. It's lovely. Actually it reminds me of a village."

Tyler smiled. "I'm glad you like it. By decree from the town council, every building is painted a different color."

Catharine nodded, admiring the atmosphere as well as the hustle and bustle of skiers and tourists mucking about her. Even though it was now dark, a multitude of lights showed off each building's uniqueness. All were painted and trimmed with bright colors; blue, lavender, yellow, red, lime-green.

Dazzled by the colorful environment, Catharine smiled. "Where are we eating?"

"At the Hearthstone. It's located one street east of the main road. I reserved a table on the second floor, which I suppose you consider the first because you British people call the first the ground floor."

Catharine grinned. He really was making an effort to understand her.

As they walked up the stairs a little later, her pulse picked up speed. The dim intimate setting was romantic and this was her first real date. The first time she had ever truly gone out with a man alone for the purpose of enjoying herself. Always before she'd been chaperoned, as well as apprehensive. But with Tyler she felt safe.

In the center of their table a lighted candle floated in a glass container of clear water. She looked around at the other diners and couples. A few ladies wore skirts and baggy, long-sleeved sweaters, but most wore trousers or ski clothes. Catharine was the only one in a dress. She felt a little out of place, especially when strange men smiled at her.

Tyler must have sensed her discomfort because he said, "You look lovely. Actually, you're the prettiest woman in here. That's why the men are looking at us. They envy me."

She forced a smile, glad she hadn't worn the backless gown. That would surely have caught attention in the casual atmosphere. Besides, she was saving that gown to wear tomorrow night to the governor's party. Since she hadn't figured out an excuse not to go, she'd have to drum up some enthusiasm.

"Do you like burgundy wine?" Tyler asked while he studied the wine list.

Catharine nodded, thinking wine might put her at ease.

Tyler ordered a bottle.

A few minutes later the waiter made a show of removing the cork and filling their glasses.

Tyler tipped his glass to Catharine's. "To us."

"To us," she repeated before she sipped.

She nibbled on a buttered roll while they chatted. When they finished their wine, Tyler refilled their glasses.

The more Catharine drank the more she relaxed. By the time their salads arrived, she had consumed two full glasses and Tyler had ordered another bottle in spite of her protests.

They dined at a leisurely pace. Catharine kept sipping her wine. Tyler kept topping her glass, more often than he topped his own.

After they finished eating, he said, "I brought you here for a reason."

Catharine's heart started to race. Suddenly she felt overly warm and woozy.

"Don't look so frightened," he admonished in a gentle tone. "I'm not going to hurt you, or suggest something bizarre."

She relaxed a little. "Why did you bring me here?"

"I'd like to discuss marriage, and I wanted to do it in a neutral place, not at home."

"I appreciate your thoughtfulness." She summoned a smile and waited for him to continue.

"In a few weeks you could be walking down the aisle to become my wife."

Catharine shook her head no, although her fickle heart was nodding yes inside her chest. "I can't marry you, Tyler. I wouldn't be doing you a favor."

"I think you would."

"Wouldn't it be easier to get a larger flat so we could each have a bedroom, and possibly our own bathroom?" she attempted to reason despite her spasmodic thoughts to the contrary.

"We could do that even if we marry."

She felt her eyes widen in astonishment. "You'd be willing to have separate bedrooms?"

"If that's what it takes."

Her unruly heart reacted with a resoundingly loud thud. *Would he really marry her without any intention of bedding her?* The thought created goose bumps on her neck and arms, sent them skipping up the back of her head. *She could be Mrs. Quinlane and safe at the same time.* It seemed too incredible to believe.

She stared dreamily at Tyler. Part of her would love to be his wife. Why did he have to be so handsome? So masculine? Why did his shiny black hair, silvery-green eyes, aristocratic nose and that determined chin, create such conflict inside her? Make her pulse race at such an alarming speed? She knew the reason why. Because she loved him. Just as she had loved him in past lives.

"Memories of past lives tell me I loved you in secret, but spoke the words very rarely," he said. "I think if we give ourselves a chance, we might both discover we're in love now."

"But what if that doesn't happen? What if you meet someone else and wish you had married her?"

"I'm quite sure I won't, and I'm willing to gamble on us because my brain tells me I'll be sorry if I don't."

Catharine didn't dare admit that part of her fuzzy brain felt the same way.

"At least think about it," he suggested.

"I will," she promised, doubting she'd think of little else.

"I suppose we should also discuss our current living arrangement."

Her heart fell. So did her gaze. Did he intend to suggest a change?

"Most people these days don't give a rip about couples living together without being married, but the Republican party is made up of a network of good old boys with old-fashioned ideas. I can't toss my name in the ring to run for a political office if we're just living together. It might never be stated as a reason to preclude me, but it could be an obstacle."

Catharine sighed. To her horror it sounded like an inelegant snort. Embarrassed heat crawled up her throat. Part of her agreed with Tyler's assessment of the political party he favored. Living together without marriage was wrong. But in their case, they weren't living in sin. They were merely sharing his flat.

"You're very interested in politics, aren't you?" she asked, hoping the heat would crawl back down her throat and disappear before it covered her face.

Tyler nodded. "Yes. Very."

"If we married and it didn't work out, how much trouble would it be to obtain an annulment?"

"There's always a way to get out of any contract, but I don't think we should go into this with that in mind. I want you. This time for keeps."

Her heart gave a sudden crazy lurch. *He really did fancy her.* What strange luck. In spite of her fuzzy state, the mere thought felt like a compliment of the highest order. On a par with a compliment from the Queen.

"I have something for you," he surprised her.

A thrill ripped through her. *The betrothal ring? Would he suggest she accept it now?*

He set a box in front of her. Her heart plummeted. Too big to be the diamond ring box. Cautiously, she opened the lid. A colorful circle of strung beads rested on a bed of black velvet. "It looks like a bracelet?"

"It is. A worry bead bracelet. Whenever you're worried about something, anything, you stroke them, and poof, your worry disappears. Just like magic."

Catharine laughed. "You're joshing, aren't you?"

"Nope. I'm a believer in magic, and they're magic." He winked, and reached for the bracelet. "Let me put this on your wrist so all your worries will vanish."

She extended her arm, fascinated by him, his whimsy, and his smile. Did he really believe in magic? A wonderful warmth spread through her veins as he slid the beaded bracelet over her right hand. His touch was gentle. His gaze tender. He truly was a magnificent man.

Should she give his suggestion a go? Trust instinct instead of backing down from a challenge, as she had done in so many other lives? After all, if she could agree to time travel and live in a different century than the one she'd been born into, she could surely handle marriage to a man she admired, revered and respected, couldn't she?

Deep in thought, she sipped the last of her wine.

Tyler paid the check.

Outside the restaurant when they reached his car in the snow-packed parking lot, he kissed her chastely on the mouth. Having enjoyed herself more tonight than she dreamed possible, Catharine was thrilled by every gentle touch. While he unlocked the car, she rubbed the worry beads and made a wish that those feelings would never go away.

~ * ~

Back at his apartment a couple of hours later Catharine looked around, feeling pensive, unsure and still a bit inebriated in spite of the coffee they had stopped for during the drive home.

"Is something wrong?" Tyler asked.

"No. Not at all." She smiled up at him. "I've been trying to remember what life was like without you. And I remember. Dismal. Desolate."

Tyler stepped closer. "You're a joy, Catharine."

Lowering his head, he cupped her cheek. She lifted her lips slowly to his. The kiss tasted perfect. As perfect as any girl could wish for.

Testing her feelings, she let her hands creep up to his neck. He felt strong. Solid. And his spicy cologne smelled wonderful. She raised her hands to his nape.

The kiss changed. Tyler's mouth claimed more of hers as he tightened his arms around her. His tongue delved inside. She didn't resist. Couldn't resist. Surrounded by his wonderful spicy masculine scent, she kissed him back until she felt breathless. She loved the way his kisses made her feel. Desired. Wanted. Needed. Also a little afraid.

When his fingers wandered to her breasts, alarm bells rang in her head. She wrenched her mouth from his and broke free. "We need to stop," she gasped, her body shaky, her voice ragged.

Tyler shook his head, as though to clear it, but he didn't say a word. Visibly, he slowed his breathing, staring at the wall behind her.

Still standing close, but no longer touching, she said, "Tyler?"

"Yes?"

"Will being together be this exciting if we are married?"

"Yes," he promised. "We'll make it this exciting... or more."

Neither said another word, but both knew a commitment of sorts had been made.

He reached inside his suit coat breast pocket and removed the betrothal ring. "You'll let me know when you're ready to wear this, won't you?"

She nodded, staring at the huge diamond solitaire sparkling up at her. Then she extended her left hand, feeling as though someone else had taken over her body and her actions. Her heart drummed as Tyler slipped the ring onto her fourth finger.

She was wearing the pearls he'd given her on Valentine's day, the worry bead bracelet, and now the betrothal ring, too. She felt all dolled up, decked out in jewels given to her by the most wonderful man she'd ever known.

Tyler smiled, looking from the pearls to the worry beads, then at the diamond ring. "I liked Mother's suggestion to get married on your birthday. What do you think?"

"Isn't that a bit soon?" Catharine asked, unable to believe she'd just committed herself to marry him. If she backed out now, would he rescind his friendship? Send her packing? Force her to live alone again?

"We can do anything we want to do, Catharine. I've already checked into getting a larger apartment in this complex. One should be available next month. We could move before we get married."

"All right," she whispered. Everything seemed unreal. Like she was dreaming and would wake up any moment. Since she had nothing else to blame, she blamed her reaction to his kisses and accepting his proposal, on the alcohol. Why oh why, had she consumed so much wine? Goodness knew she would never have agreed to wed him if she'd been in her right frame of mind. Would she?

~ * ~

At the office the next day, Tyler's parents were ecstatic when they saw the ring on her finger. "I'm so happy for you." Rachel beamed a smile of approval.

"I am, too." Mack slapped Tyler on the back, while Rachel drew Catharine into a warm embrace. "As I said before, I hope you'll be as happy as your mother and I have been."

After the excitement died down, Catharine sat down at the reception station. Every little while she gazed at the betrothal ring. Dozens of doubts assaulted her. Should she tell Tyler how she felt? Would that bruise his ego? Or should she keep her doubts to herself?

She hated her wishy-washy thoughts as much as she disliked her doubt and fear. As the morning progressed, sketchy images of past lives flickered through her mind. Each one left her wondering what she was missing, what she couldn't recall.

In the end she decided not to tell Tyler how she felt. One of her greatest desires in life now was to stay with him, be near him, try to make him happy. If only she knew how. When had things changed? When had he become necessary? She didn't have a clue.

Twelve

During the drive to the political cocktail party, Catharine twisted her hands on her lap. In the dim dashboard light, the betrothal ring glittered. Every time she looked at it, her heart quivered, and a spurt of happiness spiraled through her. Tyler truly wanted to marry her. She could hardly believe her good fortune.

"I'm so afraid I might say or do something that will embarrass you tonight."

Tyler smiled, but kept his gaze trained on the road. "You won't. Relax. My colleagues are friendly and they'll like you. Besides, I promise to stay at your side all night."

Catharine folded her hands in a pose of tranquility, but her insides still roiled with uncertainty.

Shortly after they arrived at the governor's mansion and greeted the governor and his wife, a tall, willowy lady, with very short-cropped dark brown hair and amber eyes approached.

"Catharine, this is Sloan Cole," Tyler introduced them.

When they shook hands, Sloan's felt as limp as moldy pudding. She let go and glanced at the diamond solitaire on Catharine's hand.

"So, you went through with it. I thought you might change your mind, Tyler."

When he didn't comment, merely eyed her without emotion, Sloan placed her hand on his arm. Catharine disliked the bold, proprietary gesture. She disliked Sloan Cole, too. The woman acted as though she owned some part of Tyler, a secret part that might always preclude her.

"Have you set a date yet?" Sloan asked. "Or is that still top secret?"

"We've set a date."

Catharine was glad Tyler didn't divulge more. And proud when he took a step backwards, dislodging Sloan's hand in the process. "If you'll excuse us," he said coldly, "I see some people I'd like Catharine to meet."

"Of course," Sloan said, but her mouth turned down in a frown. Except for the too short hairstyle, Catharine had thought Sloan quite beautiful. Until she frowned. Now she not only looked unattractive, she looked mean.

Standing at the far end of the ladies powder room some time later, Catharine overheard two other women chatting as they entered.

"I wish Fey were here, and would make me invisible," Catharine muttered, fingering the worry beads, and pressing her back against the wall when she recognized Sloan's voice. Something small fluttered a few feet away. Fey. The fairy winked, waved her silver wand, then vanished as Sloan's voice intruded.

"Did you meet that little mouse Tyler's engaged to?"

"Yes, but that's a catty remark," the other lady said. "Sounds like you're jealous, Sloan."

"Of her? Never. I'm sure Ty will realize he made a big mistake before he marries her."

Catharine gasped. Clapped her hand to her mouth. Then cringed when Sloan looked her way. But Sloan's expression didn't so much as change. Catharine stuck her hand in front of her face. And gasped again when she didn't see anything. Not even the worry bead bracelet. *I'm invisible. But how could that be? Was Fey responsible? Is that why she had winked before she waved her wand?*

With her heart pounding in frantic speed, Catharine remained absolutely still while she listened to Sloan rattle on.

"Ty's fiancée can't possibly be an asset to a politician. He has great ambition and even greater potential. He needs someone stronger than that timid girl who acts like she can't say a word without first consulting him. Did you notice how protective Ty acts? I haven't had a chance to talk to him alone, not even one word."

"Maybe you've forgotten that men like to protect women," her companion said. "It makes them feel like heroes."

Sloan applied purple lipstick and smacked her greasy lips together. "You're just as aggressive as I am."

"But I have a husband because I know how to act when I'm around him. Chuck never would have married me if he'd thought I was manipulative."

"You make it sound like a game."

"It's more than a game, Sloan. It's a battle. The battle of the sexes. Where would men be without women behind them? Pushing them? Pampering them? Bowing to their supposed superiority? Feeding their egos? Letting them believe we buy into all that crap?"

"Nowhere. And I aim to make Ty see that marrying someone else isn't in his best interest."

"You can't fault his fiancée's figure or her taste in clothes. That backless designer dress must have cost a mint. Those pearls look real, too. And her body looks like she spends all her time exercising at the athletic club."

"I wouldn't be surprised if Ty or someone else picked the dress out. I doubt she has such good taste."

The other lady smiled and changed the subject. "What do you think of that chartreuse dress the governor's wife is wearing?"

"It's truly awful. I can't believe she has the nerve to wear something like that in public."

Her heart racing and her lips pressed together as tight as a sealed tin, Catharine turned toward the door and inched her way out of the ladies room, careful not to make a sound. *Did all women talk about others behind their backs like that?*

Her fear mounted. Now that she'd agreed to marry Tyler, she desperately wanted to be his wife. Would he change his mind? Decide not to wed her? Dare she ask? Or would that plant an idea in his mind that might split them apart? Would he tell her to move out if they didn't get married?

She saw him and started toward him. When he seemed to stare right through her, she realized she was still invisible. Although a bit frightened by her invisibility, Fey motioned her to take advantage of it, so Catharine ambled around, listening to people gossip. While she wandered, Fey flitted around, smiling and making gestures at one group or another, all without making a sound or uttering a single word. The fairy's presence kept Catharine from panicking, but just barely.

A good portion of the men discussed Tyler and said he would make a great addition to the state senate. After a while, wanting to tell Tyler all the good things she'd heard, she stroked the worry beads, wishing she hadn't somehow become invisible.

Suddenly Tyler smiled at her. Catharine looked down. She wasn't invisible anymore. Puzzled and frightfully upset, she wondered again if Fey was responsible.

Catharine licked her lips, drew in a deep breath, and walked toward Tyler. As soon as her fingers touched the warmth of his hand she felt safe. Safe from the strange men, as well as from Sloan and her aggressive friend and their vicious tongues. Safe from the invisibility.

It had upset her and left her shaken. Would it happen again? If so, when? What had triggered it? Fey waving her wand? Would her invisibility upset Tyler if she told him about it? Unable to find answers, Catharine couldn't control the jerky spasms in her hands and fingers, or arms and legs.

"Are you okay?" Tyler asked.

"Yes." She tried to fake a calm she couldn't force herself to feel. "Why did you ask?"

"You're shaking." He caressed her arm. The shaking calmed slightly, but her heart raced, and nearly shot through the ceiling when Tyler continued to stroke her arm.

"I saw Sloan follow you into the ladies room. I thought she might have said something unpleasant, especially when she came out before you did."

"She didn't talk to me."

"Good." Tyler pulled Catharine to a secluded corner, all the time caressing her arm, her shoulder, her waist. Her insides were melting, turning to jelly.

"Sometimes Sloan can be rather—a—snide," he said.

More like lethal, Catharine thought, vowing to keep her eyes on Tyler whenever Sloan was around him. But that meant she would have to attend more cocktail parties. The very thought made her feel ill. What if she turned invisible again right in front of a crowd? How would she explain when she didn't know what caused it? And how would Tyler react? With understanding, or revulsion?

The sick feeling skyrocketed as Catharine glanced around at the noisy crowd. She preferred quiet nights at home. The smiles pasted on so many wives faces seemed false. Their glamorous clothes were not nearly enough reward for the price of giving up the privacy they might have shared at home with their husbands.

Is this what her future would be if she married Tyler? More parties where people pretended to be friends, yet gossiped like magpies?

Catharine's qualms regarding marriage increased tenfold. Not only because she might embarrass Tyler. But also because she might detest the life he had mapped out for his future.

What a wanker she'd gotten herself into now.

~ * ~

In the days that followed Catharine couldn't believe how fast time passed. She finished moving out of her old rented house. Every morning she worked at the law firm. She spent her afternoons working on Kacy's story at home. Two or three evenings a week she went to cocktails parties with Tyler. She kept so busy she fell asleep as soon as she hit the bed each night.

"Now that we've set our wedding date," he said one morning while they were driving to work, "maybe we should hire a wedding consultant."

Any mention of the wedding gave Catharine the jitters. The inside of the car felt close, stifling, yet her hands felt cold and clammy. "April sixteenth is only six weeks away. Will a consulting firm have time to do everything by then?"

"Sure, if we pay them enough." Tyler winked. "And by the way, I've arranged for a two bedroom apartment across the courtyard. We'll move in at the beginning of April."

"That's terrific." Catharine grinned, glad she could show true enthusiasm for something. "What's the new flat like?"

Tyler flashed a grin. "It's a near replica of the one we're in except it has another bedroom and bath and two more closets. I'm sure the extra closets will come in handy."

"I'm sure they will." Catharine exhaled, only then realizing she was having difficulty breathing. The last time she felt her life was out of control, she had run away. That wasn't an option now. She loved Tyler too much to leave.

~ * ~

On the first Saturday in April, they moved across the courtyard to the new flat. "Every room smells of fresh paint," Catharine said, following Tyler down the hall, their arms laden with clothes they didn't think needed packing. "Even the cupboards," she added as Tyler hung her clothes in a closet in one of the bedrooms. "The carpet looks new, too."

"It is."

Her spirits buoyed by the move, she smiled. "The apartment is quite spacious. And very lovely."

Tyler chuckled. "I'm glad you approve."

After the movers transferred their furniture, Catharine and Tyler unpacked. At the end of the day, she heaved a sigh of relief. Now that Tyler had his own bedroom and bathroom, she felt less guilty. He had assured her they could continue living together as friends until she felt ready for more. Even so, he kissed her before they went to bed. Of course, she responded.

One part of her wanted Tyler to kiss her passionately, while another part warred against it. He deepened the kiss and wound his fingers through her long hair. She anchored her hands on his shoulders to steady her wobbly knees while he kissed her breathless. And still he kissed her. Her heart cried out for him to stop, and not to stop both at the same time.

Finally, when she felt dazed and light-headed, Tyler pulled away, his features taut. "Catharine," he whispered, and that one word spoke volumes.

He slid his fingers to the back of her nape.

Chills or thrills, she didn't know which, sizzled down her spine. Tyler trailed his fingers around to her cheek, his gaze never leaving hers.

He wanted her. She saw the desire in his eyes. The knowledge should have terrified her. But it didn't. She wanted to please him. That thought startled her.

Dazed by his kiss and his touch, all she could do was stare. Would he renege on his promise not to expect intimacy?

That fear put her on edge. Would he want more as soon as they wed? Why oh why, was she so afraid of something everyone else seemed to enjoy?

With a gentle smile, he turned her and guided her to her new bedroom. At the door, he let go. "Good night, Catharine."

"Good night." In a stupor, she walked inside, undressed and climbed in bed. Worries about her own hidden passion kept her wide-awake. Every time she closed her eyes, they popped right back open. Shivers of apprehension wiggled up and down her spine.

She didn't recall when the niggling fear that Dillon might ruin their future had begun, but she could no longer shove the fear to the back of her mind. She didn't fall asleep till dawn.

~ * ~

Ten days before the wedding, while Catharine was busy working at her computer in her new bedroom, the telephone rang. Expecting Tyler, she grinned as she answered it.

"Don't get married," a female voice said. "You'll regret it if you do."

Before Catharine could reply, the caller hung up.

Stunned, she sat there trying to calm the rapid beat of her frantic heart. Her stomach knotted. *Who would make such a call?* Two people came to mind. Sloan and Dillon. Had he asked some woman to call for him?

When Tyler came home, Catharine hurriedly explained the call while he took his overcoat off.

He frowned. "Have you used the phone since that call?"

She shook her head. The knots in her stomach cramped, making her uncomfortably aware that they hadn't gone away.

"We have caller ID." He flung his coat over a chair back, then tramped to the phone in the kitchen. Catharine followed.

"I don't recognize the number. If it was Sloan, she didn't make the call from her home or her office."

"I wouldn't expect her to make that kind of call from either of those places," Catharine said, disturbed that Tyler apparently knew Sloan's phone numbers by heart. "She's too smart to be foolish and careless."

He rubbed his temple, as though deep in thought. "Did the voice sound like Sloan's?"

"No," Catharine admitted. "She didn't sound like anyone I've ever heard before. But that's the sort of thing a jealous, vindictive woman might do. Sloan might have had someone else call to brew mischief."

"That's true of Dillon McKenzie, too."

"I know," Catharine conceded.

A muscle twitched in Tyler's jaw. He looked both aggravated and concerned. "Don't answer the phone anymore when you're home alone, unless you recognize the number. If I need to talk to you, I'll call your cell phone."

Catharine offered a feeble smile. "Good plan." But her uneasiness grew. What if the caller decided to do more than call? What if he or she tried to break in when Catharine was alone? What would she do? The apartment complex had a security system but she knew how easily it could be breached.

Fear kept her thoughts in constant turmoil and her stomach upset. At dinner she ate only a few bites. Would she ever feel hungry again?

~ * ~

The next morning at the office, Ty made a few phone calls. Then he walked out to the lobby where Catharine worked. "I checked out that phone number from yesterday's caller. It's a pay phone."

Catharine pursed her lips, her eyes troubled.

Willing to do just about anything to erase that fearful look, Ty said, "Don't worry. It might have been a prankster."

He stuck his hands in his pockets. He wasn't proud of plying her with wine back in February and using her weakened state to coerce her into agreeing to marriage. He knew she wanted to back out. But a desperate premonition plagued him. *If they didn't marry soon, they never would in this lifetime.* The voice in his head backed up the dream that now repeated itself nightly. Their never-ending love would continue, but this was their last chance to get things right. He didn't doubt that. If they failed, they might not meet in another life, ever again. That premonition was so strong, Ty felt desperate. Pressured. Because without Catharine, an essential part of him would be missing.

When Ty went home that evening, he found Catharine in front of her computer. "Did you have any calls today?"

She nodded, her eyes loaded with strain. "Three. They were all made from the pay phone. I didn't answer them. After the first three calls, I unplugged all the phones. We should probably plug them back in now. You may get calls you'll want to answer tonight."

A quick spurt of anger ripped through Ty. He wanted to smash the phones to smithereens. Controlling the urge, he helped plug them back in. Then he headed for the shower. He and Catharine had another cocktail party to attend. Although he generally enjoyed them, he knew she preferred to stay home.

If he went into politics, she would be required to go with him. This was a good way to get her used to them. And he liked seeing her in something other than the long voluminous skirts she wore every day. The skirts hid her figure. Even so, they couldn't camouflage her appeal. Still, he'd like to see her in a pair of slacks. Or shorts. He'd bet she would look great.

Whenever he worried about her fear of sex, he relied on his memories of her responses in other lifetimes. Fear must have blocked her memories. He felt confident he could help her overcome her fear once they were married. He refused to dwell on the worry that he might fail. Their love would prevail in the end. He had to believe that or go mad.

~ * ~

At the office the next morning, the phone rang out in the lobby. Ty heard Catharine answer it in a gentle, pleasant voice. "Good morning. Quinlane Law Firm."

A few seconds later, she dashed into his office, her face a mask of fear. "A man just called. He asked if I wanted to..." Her cheeks flamed a bright pink.

"To what?" Ty's irritation rose to heights he'd never known before.

"He used that four letter 'f' word and suggested that I have—uh—sex with him before I get married so he can teach me how to please you."

Beyond furious, Ty growled, "This harassment must stop." He grabbed his phone and called Dillon's attorney, venting on the only person he thought might be able to do something about it.

After a heated exchange Ty said, "I suggest you inform your client that Colorado has some of the most severe laws in the country to punish sex offenders. If Dillon is convicted, he could go to prison, and if he's ever released, he may have to undergo a plethysmograph to determine what stimulates him. From what I understand, that's not a pleasant experience. He could even be banned from talking to his own children."

"My client doesn't have children and he didn't make any foolish telephone calls to your fiancée or anyone else," Jack Slater, the other attorney, said. "Dillon hasn't been convicted of committing a sex offense, and I'm confident he won't be."

Ty hung up and looked at Catharine. Jack Slater sounded a mite too confident. Ty kept that disturbing thought to himself. "Dillon's attorney swears he didn't make those calls."

"I can't think of anyone else who might." Catharine's whole body shook and the fear in her eyes raised Ty's protective instinct. He walked close and put his arm around her shoulders.

"He won't hurt you. I won't let him hurt you."

But even as he said the words, Ty knew he couldn't protect her all the time. It wasn't possible for them to spend every minute together. Thankfully it was Friday, and he wouldn't have to let her out of his sight much during the weekend.

Thirteen

Catharine couldn't relax. Tyler kept her too busy to allow time to express her worry, but it lived inside her just the same. Although she didn't receive anymore weird or obscene phone calls, she had a feeling whoever was responsible might be biding his or her time.

Monday morning, frustrated and filled with unspeakable fear, she stared out the office window. Located east of downtown in an old-fashioned two-story house that had been magnificently refurbished, the Quinlane Law Office looked out upon a shaded section of Grant Street. While she studied the newly leafed tree branches swaying in the spring breeze, she clenched her hands into tight fists.

Maybe she couldn't do anything about the phone calls, but she must get to the root of her other problem. In five days she would be married. But her fear was spoiling everything.

She drew in a deep breath and blew it out slowly, relaxing her fists in the process. Her mind needed to be calm, her thoughts clear.

Inner strength had driven her from her home in Kent and propelled her forward into this century. Therefore, she had enough gumption to figure out how to find help now. She gritted her teeth. Somehow she must. Feeling like a frightened ninny was intolerable.

If she could find her mother, she might help. Catharine's thoughts took a nosedive. Would she ever find her mother?

Think positive, Catharine admonished herself. *Who else could help? Fey, possibly.* But she hadn't seen the fairy for weeks.

Catharine folded her arms and pursed her lips. Her outlook brightened as she decided that a hypnotherapist might help. One of the things she had learned when she worked at Wyze Oil was how to surf the Internet. Maybe she could find a therapist online.

Inspired by that idea, Catharine turned back to the reception station to answer an incoming call. As soon as she got home from work, she would start searching.

After a quick lunch of canned soup and crackers, Catherine turned her computer on, went online and typed in hypnotherapy. When the first screen came up, she typed in Denver, Colorado and her zip code. The search found two offices, one located on Yale, the other on Bellaire.

Buoyed up when she realized one of the therapists was a woman, Catharine kept searching. She narrowed her search to include only women hypnotherapists in Colorado. A site named ELIZA PAICE caught her attention. Catharine's heart banged against her chest. *Her mother's name before she married Wilbur was Eliza Paice.* Could there be a connection? Could her mother be in this century working as a hypnotherapist?

With shaky hands and excitement bubbling inside, Catharine composed an email, telling as much about herself as she dared without actually admitting she had traveled through time. She proofread her message and clicked on send, hoping with all her heart that she had stumbled upon her mother.

Then she studied Eliza's web site. The office was located in Boulder, Colorado. Not all that far from Denver. Hope fluttered inside Catharine. Maybe, after almost two years, she would see her mother again.

As nervous as a skittish kitten, Catharine checked her email frequently throughout the afternoon to see if she had received a reply.

Finally, to her overwhelming glee she did. With her heart thumping like a drum, Catharine opened it and read:

Dearest Catharine,

You cannot imagine how happy I was to hear from you. I, too, am from England, and like you, I lived there long ago. Now I live in Boulder, close to my office, which is near downtown. Both of my telephone numbers are listed below. In England, my second husband's name was Wilbur. I understand he's now deceased. Could you be my daughter?

Tears blurred Catharine's vision. She couldn't read the rest of the message. She wanted to call Tyler. Or Eliza. But emotion made it impossible to move.

Finally she calmed down and reached for the phone. With trembling hands, she punched in the numbers for Eliza's office.

"Dr. Paice's office," a young sounding female voice answered.

"Hello. My name is Catharine Paice. I think I might be related to Dr. Paice. May I speak with her?"

"Just a moment please."

Moments later Catharine heard a very dear and familiar female voice say, "Hello, Catharine. I've been expecting to hear from you. How are you?"

"In a bit of a shock just now," Catharine managed, her heart swelling with joy. "Is it really you, Mother?"

"Yes, 'tis truly me. I'd like to see you. Where are you?"

"In Denver. I live here. And I want to see you, too. Oh, Mum, I've missed you so."

"I've missed you too, darling, and I can hardly wait to see you. I want to hear all about your experiences. The angel who brought me to this time explained, but I'm anxious to hear the details from you."

"Do you have time now? Or do you have patients waiting?"

"At the moment, I'm free, so tell me everything."

Catharine didn't hesitate. She ploughed through the last two years, leaving nothing out, pausing now and then to give her mother a chance to ask questions.

About an hour later, Catharine finished. "Now tell me about yourself, and the angel who brought you to this century."

"He's the same angel who brought you. He set me up as a hypnotherapist and gave me the knowledge and tools to help people. Since you're getting married on Saturday, perhaps I can help you overcome your fear of intimacy."

"Oh, Mum, if only you could."

"Before we try hypnotherapy, I may already know why you're afraid."

"Why?" Sitting on the edge of her chair, Catharine's heart began to pound. She clutched the phone with both hands while her mother explained.

By the time she finished, Catharine remembered everything. Some of the fear inside her dissolved, some of it remained.

"I can hardly wait to see you, Mum."

"I'm as anxious as you are."

"Maybe Tyler could drive me to Boulder when he gets home from work."

"That would be wonderful." Catharine sensed a sigh in her mother's voice when she added, "I hate to hang up, but I have a patient waiting to see me now."

"I'll call you if Tyler agrees."

"Why not call me one way or the other and let me know?"

"I will."

After they hung up, Catharine sat for a long time, reminiscing, and marveling at all she had experienced since she'd left her mother. The single most important event had been meeting Tyler.

When he arrived home, she met him at the door. Her skin felt warm, her face hot. So excited she could barely contain herself, she wanted to hug him fiercely. Would that be unsuitable behavior?

"You'll never guess what happened."

Ty studied her flushed face. She looked ready to burst with some kind of marvelous news. "You're right. I can't even hazard a guess. "What?"

"I've found my mother. She's in Boulder, and she's helped me understand my fear of men."

"She has?"

Catharine nodded, her eyes brimming with emotion. "Could we drive to Boulder tonight and go see her?"

Ty's mind whirled. *Her mother was in this time.* "I have a cocktail party, but I won't go." He was as anxious to see Catharine's mother as she was, and he wanted Catharine to know she could count on him. He also wanted to witness her reunion with her mother.

"We'll go as soon as I change clothes."

"Wonderful. I'll call mother and tell her we're on our way."

Less than ten minutes later, as soon as he changed from his suit to blue jeans and a chestnut sweater, Tyler ushered Catharine down to his gray Mercedes in the parking garage.

During the drive to Boulder she talked in a nervous rush, faster than he'd ever heard her talk previously. "Mother explained what happened to me after Papa died."

Tyler forced himself to keep his gaze trained on the busy street. "What did?"

"After she told me, I remembered, so I can tell you with my own words."

He flicked a quick glance at Catharine. He'd never seen her this animated. Not in any life. "Please do."

"I was alone in the garden one day after Papa died, grieving because Mother said he would never come home again. The church gardener saw me and invited me to go with him to Papa's grave. He said we could stop at his cottage and pick flowers to put by Papa's headstone. Of course I thought he meant exactly what he said."

Catharine cleared her throat and clasped her hands on her lap. "When we reached his cottage, he urged me inside, saying he wanted a cup of tea. Then he bolted the door and took his clothes off. I was so shocked I didn't know what to do. He asked me to touch him. Fondle him. But I couldn't." Her voice had taken on a note of hysteria and Ty reached over and took hold of her trembling hands.

"You don't have to go on, if you'd rather not."

"I must. I need you to understand."

"All right. What else happened?"

"When I refused, he grabbed my hand and forced my fingers around his—his private parts. Then he started stroking, and his eyes glazed over. Before I could stop him he ripped my clothes off, touching me everywhere." She shuddered, and Ty squeezed her hands again, understanding how difficult this must be for her. It was just as he had envisioned. Some sicko had used her as a child to satisfy his lust.

Catharine blinked. Tears spiked her long lashes. "He dragged me to his cot and laid on top of me. He was so heavy, I thought I might suffocate. I was so scared I started to cry. When he rubbed that part of himself against my—my privates, I knew I had to fight. I kicked and screamed and scratched and bucked, and finally slid out from under him. He came after me, but he tripped over a chair and I managed to get the door unbolted. I ran all the way home without a stitch on," she finished on a sob.

Ty found a spot to pull over, thankful he hadn't reached the freeway yet. He shifted into park, slid out from under the steering wheel, and drew Catharine into his arms.

When she stopped shaking, he used his handkerchief to mop her tears. Smiling tenderly, he asked, "Do you want to continue?"

She nodded. "Mother surmised what happened when she saw me without clothes. She held me and comforted me and told me to try to forget it. After I stopped crying, she made sweet cream tea and put me to bed. During our talk today she said she put a draught in the tea to help me sleep. It must have worked because I slept the rest of the afternoon and all night. The next morning the experience seemed like a bad dream, and eventually I did forget. Maybe because I never saw the man again."

More tears filled Catharine's eyes. She swiped at them with her fists. "On the phone today, Mother said she told the vicar what happened while I slept and he sent the man packing."

Ty found his handkerchief again and dried the new tears trickling down Catharine's cheeks. "I'm glad we know what caused your fear," he said, his protective instinct raised to the hilt. "You're not afraid of me, are you?"

"No. Not you, Tyler. Never you." She smiled through her tears. "I've known and loved you too many times to fear you. The intimacy thing worries me, still scares me even, but Mother thinks she can help me overcome my fear by talking about it. I want that, Tyler. More than anything. I want to come to you as a whole woman."

"You are whole, Catharine. And I'm very proud you've agreed to share my life."

"Please don't be disappointed if I can't..."

"I won't be disappointed. I promise. Now give me a smile so I know you believe me."

She did... a weak smile, but a smile nevertheless.

~ * ~

About an hour later, Catharine's mother opened the door of her small home with a bright smile and warmth in her blue eyes. The instant she saw Catharine, she spread her arms.

Catharine flung herself into her embrace. "Oh, Mum, I've missed you so!"

"I've missed you, too." Eliza squeezed Catharine once more, then looked up at Tyler, and offered her slender hand. "I'm Eliza Paice. Catharine's mother. You must be Tyler."

He nodded, shaking her hand. Her grasp was firm and businesslike. Ty judged her to be about forty, maybe even younger. "Pleased to meet you."

Eliza smiled. "The pleasure is mine, please believe me."

Staring at her was like staring at an older version of Catharine. Beautiful and elegant, Eliza was dignified, too. Watching them together made his heart swell with quiet pride.

"How did you get here, to this time?" Ty asked.

Eliza smiled. "A guardian angel brought me."

Ty nodded. Her story was consistent with Catharine's and how she had gotten here, too.

After much hugging and talking, catching up on each other's lives, Catharine leaned back in her beige wing chair and grinned again. "I told you about our wedding on Saturday."

Eliza nodded. "That's your birthday."

"It's also Kacy's, the girl I switched places with. Her grandparents think I'm her." Catharine's expression turned pensive. "You'll come to our wedding, of course?"

"Yes. I wouldn't miss it." Eliza glanced from Catharine to Tyler.

"How will we introduce her?" he asked. All kinds of problems flashed through his mind. "What will we tell your ah... grandparents? And my parents?"

Catharine met his gaze with a steady stare. "I'd like to tell them the truth."

Part of him thought that best too, but when he hesitated, Eliza said, "Perhaps someday we can tell them, but I don't want to spoil your special day by creating any kind of problems. I'll attend the wedding and share as much as I can, hopefully without disturbing anyone."

Catharine smiled and nodded.

Knowing that was enough to satisfy her for a while when she smiled, Ty heaved a quiet sigh of relief. Then he doused the beginning of a frown. If word leaked out that he'd married a time traveler, he'd be made a laughingstock, and his involvement in politics would be doomed. Even if the news didn't leak, and he got elected, he would always be in jeopardy of having the information exposed. For the first time since he had considered entering politics, doubt crept in. Maybe he should give the race up. He and Catharine belonged together. They had loved each other for centuries.

He looked at her and smiled. She smiled back. Contentment stole through him. For the first time in any of their lives, they were on the right track, headed in the right direction. Nothing must be allowed to spoil it.

Fourteen

Although Catharine talked at length with her mother about her fear, the obscene phone calls added to her dilemma. Could she respond to Tyler with such worry hovering over her?

Part of her didn't want their relationship to change. She loved kissing him good night. And sleeping under the same roof.

But he might not get all he wanted in a wife. Maybe they should wait. Stay single until she had more to offer. Until she knew she could bear the endless cocktail parties and dinners that took up so much of his time.

Yet, in spite of her trepidation, she thought Tyler was top drawer. He had such a clever, brilliant mind, she couldn't find it in her heart to tell him how afraid she still was to be his wife in every way.

The night before the wedding arrived. Catharine's dicey doubts increased as she rode with Tyler to his parent's church for the rehearsal. Upset that her mother wouldn't be sharing any part of the wedding except on the periphery, Catharine fretted and stewed in private.

The rehearsal went off without a hitch, as did the dinner party afterwards at Footer's, Tyler's favorite restaurant. His friends and relatives smiled throughout dinner. Many teased. Their provocative suggestions embarrassed Catharine, but Tyler only grinned.

"Kiss the bride," his cousin, Bob, egged as they left the restaurant and headed for their cars in the crowded parking lot.

Tyler didn't hesitate. Holding Catharine's hand, he turned her into his arms. She lowered her gaze, feeling shy and more than a little inept.

He wrapped his arms around her, and his mouth closed over hers in fierce possession. Neither gentle nor harsh, but rather needy, greedy, and demanding. He took her breath, robbed her thoughts, stirred her hidden passion.

The sound of his cousin's clapping ended the kiss. Catharine didn't have time to feel relieved or disappointed.

"Come," Kacy's grandmother said, taking Catharine's arm, reminding her she had agreed to stay with Eileen and Porter tonight. "It's bad luck for the groom to see the bride before the ceremony on their wedding day."

Catharine waved goodbye to Tyler, and left with the Rose's. The feel of his lips still lingered on hers, but worry sprinkled her mind with more doubts.

Alone in the pink bedroom where Kacy had grown up, Catharine shivered, even though the room was warm. Not only fear, but a terrible tension bogged her down, and she couldn't shake it. If only her mother could be part of this, she might not be so nervous.

In an attempt to settle her nerves, Catharine studied the photographs on the white French provincial dresser. The photo of Kacy's mother resembled hers. A wave of loneliness struck.

Catharine walked to the second-story window and pushed the lacy curtains aside, staring out at the clear, dark sky. Could her mother be looking at the stars and moon, too? Or was she already in bed?

Aching to talk to her and share her woes, Catharine twisted her hands together. The betrothal ring slid around on her finger. Turning it, she stared down at the sparkling diamond. Never had she owned such an exquisite piece of jewelry. Not in any life. That Tyler had given it to her made it all the more special. He was such an incredibly wonderful man.

She touched the worry beads. Every day she wore them. Even on weekends when they stayed at home. Unable to shed her doubts, she faced them head on. If she didn't marry Tyler, she could go through life unhappy and unfulfilled. Worse, she might never meet him again in a future life. But she didn't want to drag him down with her in this one.

When her cell phone rang, she jumped, then dashed across the bedroom and snatched it off the dresser. "Hello."

"Hi. It's me... Ty. I miss you and I thought you might be nervous. Are you?"

"Yes. Aren't you?"

"Not at all." He paused a moment. "You're not afraid, are you?"

She considered her reply before she answered. "I'm not afraid of you."

"If you're afraid of being intimate, don't be. I won't push. I promise. We have the rest of our lives to make love."

"Oh, Tyler, I don't deserve you," she said, trying not to sound as relieved as she felt.

"Of course you do. And I want you to know the apartment feels bare-naked without you."

An image of them both naked flashed through her mind. Was that his intent? If so, he'd succeeded. Heat spiraled through her whole body. She swept her gaze around the frilly room and said the only thing she could think of, "Being here feels strange. Kacy apparently likes pink. The walls, the bed coverings, even the carpet are that color."

"I know," Tyler said. "She wore pink all the time when she was little." He cleared his throat. "You said the story you're writing about Kacy is titled *Glimpse of Eternity,* and the one you intend to write about Jennifer will be *Glimpse of Forever.* If you were to write our story, what would you name it?"

"I—I don't know. I haven't given it any thought."

"I have. I think you should title it *Glimpse of Never-Ending Love.*"

"Why?"

"Because that's what we've always shared."

His husky declaration touched her deeply. Flooded by a wonderful warmth, Catharine coiled the pink phone cord around her fingers, and spoke quietly. "I'll give some thought to writing our story, Tyler."

"Good. That means I'll have to make sure we have a happy ending."

A cold chill demolished the warmth of moments earlier. She wanted a happy ending with Tyler, but that might not happen in this life. Not if history repeated itself. She'd had happiness snatched out from under her so many times, she now lived with constant doubt. No wonder she was so afraid. She toyed with the worry beads until they said goodbye.

After they hung up, Catharine knew she should get ready for bed. But she felt too keyed up to sleep. Fear of something unknown, the demon she had tried to ignore, billowed within her. She fought it, recalling Fey's words. *"Do not borrow trouble."*

Feeling a little better, Catharine walked back to the window, rubbing the worry beads, and murmuring, "I wish I weren't alone."

And then she wasn't. Fey fluttered her tiny wings. The fairy flew down from the ceiling and landed feet first on the pink windowsill. "I sensed your desire to see me," she said, grinning.

Catharine laughed. "How did you know where I am?"

"You're my charge. I most always know where you are." Fey folded her silver-tipped wings and crossed her arms. "Tell me what troubles you."

"I'm nervous about getting married and I miss Mother. If only I could see her, I'm sure I'd be all right."

"Seeing her tonight is a simple matter. Come, give me your hand."

Catharine's heart brimmed with exhilaration. "Can you take me to Mother?"

"Certainly." The fairy raised her small arm and curled her hand around Catharine's pointer finger. Then she waved her glittering silver wand.

The next thing Catharine knew they were in the living room of her mother's small home in Boulder. Catharine blinked in astonishment. Twice.

Her mother didn't look the least bit surprised. "I was hoping you would come." Eliza smiled. "Thanks for bringing her, Fey. You will stay while we visit, won't you?"

"Certainly. I must return Catharine before she's missed."

Eliza turned her smile back to Catharine. "We had a nice visit when Tyler drove you here at the beginning of the week, and on the telephone every day, but I'm glad to have time together now."

"Me, too." Catharine grinned. "For girl talk. It's been so long. Oh Mother, I'm so afraid I'll disappoint Tyler."

"All virgin brides are nervous on the eve of their wedding, dear one." Eliza spread her arms.

Catharine stepped into her warm embrace and closed her eyes, savoring her mother's touch. "I'm so glad you're here. So grateful you're going to be part of my life from now on."

"I'm happy about that, too. We have a guardian angel and a fairy godmother to thank for bringing us both to this time."

"We're very fortunate," Catharine agreed.

Her mother pulled back to look at her. "Yes, we are."

"But you must beware," Fey announced from her perch on the TV. "Wilbur Lugamon is also in this time."

Catharine gasped, "I thought he was dead."

"He is in the past, but before he died, he made a bargain with an evil wizard who promised to let him live until he had his way with you. That may be why he's in this century."

Rattled by sheer terror, Catharine stared mutely at the fairy. *Wilbur. Her stepfather was here. The man who had tried to defile her. The man who had magnified her fear of men. The reason she had left the nineteenth century.*

Icy cold chills shivered through her. Now she had more to worry about than Dillon McKenzie. And then it hit her, like an avalanche of snow falling, surrounding her, burying her beneath its wet heavy weight. Wilbur being in this time must be the other thing that had bothered her. The reason for the nagging fear that invaded her sleep, and turned her dreams to nightmares.

She moved back into her mother's open arms.

"We can't let Wilbur ruin our lives," her mother said.

"I know," Catharine mumbled. "I know."

~ * ~

The moment Tyler climbed in bed, his phone rang. Expecting it to be Catharine, he grinned as he grabbed the phone off its cradle. "Hello."

"Tyler, it's me, Porter. Catharine's gone."

Tyler bolted upright so fast he smacked his head on the headboard. Rubbing the sore spot, he repeated, "Gone?"

"Yes. When Eileen knocked on her door to tell her good night, Catharine didn't answer. Her bed hasn't been touched. Not even sat on. Is Catharine with you?"

"No. I talked to her about an hour ago. She didn't say anything about going anywhere. Are you sure she's not somewhere in your house?"

"Yes. But it doesn't make sense." Tyler could imagine Porter shaking his gray-haired head in bewilderment. "Eileen has radar hearing and she didn't hear Catharine leave. Didn't hear a single sound. But the kitchen door is unlocked."

Dread skittered through Tyler's brain as he recalled the disturbing phone calls Catharine had received last week. Maybe he should have taken them more seriously. "I'll be there as soon as I can."

Bolting off the bed, he jammed his legs into a pair of Levi's, grabbed a shirt, jacket and shoes. As he sprinted out of his apartment, it dawned on him to call Catharine on her cell phone. While he rode the elevator down to the parking garage, he punched in her number. She didn't answer. His pulse kicked into overdrive. He considered calling the police. But what would he tell them?

A hundred thoughts slammed through his mind while he drove. Could she be gone for good? Back to the past? Were they destined always to meet but never marry? Never fulfill their love? Surely fate wouldn't be cruel enough to make him suffer through another lifetime without her, would it?

Could Dillon have abducted her somehow? Again Tyler considered calling the police. But something held him back—a strong premonition that she wasn't in danger. And then he heard Jennifer's voice in his head. They telecommunicated more often than they had originally discussed. Apparently they shared some kind of mental bond that made it easy to link thoughts.

::Ty, I sense your worry. But you needn't be upset. Catharine's safe.::

He eased his foot on the gas pedal and sent a mental message back to Jennifer in the nineteenth century. *::Thanks, Jen. Do you know where Catharine is?::*

::Yes. But she should be the one to tell you. I've gotta go now. I'm pregnant, and I feel a desperate need to heave.::

::Sorry you're having morning sickness.::

::Don't be. I'm not. I'm delighted.::

::Me, too. Good luck.::

Passing his parent's dark Cherry Hills' home, Ty drove two more blocks, turned a corner and parked in the Rose's driveway. It looked as though every light in their big two-story house had been turned on. All the other houses on the block were pitch black.

Porter opened the door before Tyler rang the bell.

"Have you found her?"

Porter shook his head. His thinning silver-hair looked as if he'd raked his fingers through it a dozen times.

"The bathroom door's locked," Eileen said, joining them in the kitchen. "I knocked but Catharine didn't answer. I wonder if she's sick, or fell asleep in there." Eileen looked from Tyler to Porter. "Did you find that key?"

"No. I thought it was right here." He stared at the open drawer. "This is where we always keep it."

"Maybe I can open the bathroom door with a hairpin," Tyler suggested, heading for the stairway.

"If she's not there, I suggest we call the police," Porter said.

"I agree," Eileen nodded.

But then they spotted Catharine, standing at the top of the stairs.

Dressed in a long pink robe that Ty didn't recognize, she rubbed her eyes as though she'd been asleep. "What's all the fuss about?"

"Where have you been?" Eileen asked.

"I must have fallen asleep while I was soaking in the bath." Catharine's eyes telecast another message to Ty as he ran up the steps and grasped her arm. She leaned close and whispered for his ears alone, "Fey took me to see Mother."

Fey? Who the hell is Fey? "I'd like to talk to Catharine alone for a few minutes, if you don't mind," he said to Porter and Eileen, who still stood at the bottom of the staircase staring up at them.

"I'm sorry we disturbed you, Tyler," Eileen apologized. "It's just that we were so afraid someone might have abducted Catharine when we found the door unlocked."

"I'm sorry I worried you," Catharine said, her blue eyes full of apology.

She looked truly repentant, Tyler thought, but she had scared the hell out of him. *Gone to see her mother?* He didn't think so. But he had to impress the importance of never hiding again. And he had to discover who Fey was, too.

"I thought you had retired for the night," Catharine said to Eileen and Porter. "It didn't occur to me that you might check on me again."

"Well, all's well that ends well." Eileen reached for Porter's arm. "Come, they want a few minutes alone."

Porter stood his ground, his arms folded across his robust chest, his forehead wrinkled in a frown. "I have to lock up when Tyler leaves."

"I'll make sure the door's locked," Catharine said, smiling.

"And we'll turn all the lights off, too," Tyler added.

Eileen latched onto Porter's arm and urged him up the stairs. "Good night then."

As Eileen ushered Porter past them, she said, "Just a few minutes mind you. It's almost tomorrow—your wedding day."

"We won't be long," Catharine promised.

Ty led her down to the brightly-lit family room. Inside he folded his arms and mimicked Porter's wide stance of moments earlier. "Who the heck is Fey?"

"My fairy godmother."

Ty had accepted that Catharine had come from the past. But a fairy godmother? No way. "You don't have to pretend with me."

"I'm not pretending." Catharine's eyes twinkled as she smiled up at him. "I truly do have a fairy godmother. She went to England with us, but when we returned she traveled back to eighteen fifty-six to see Kacy. I haven't seen much of Fey lately, and I was delighted to see her tonight. I know you don't want to believe this, but Fey really did take me to see Mother."

Ty recalled Jennifer's stories about Kacy's fairy godmother and gave up arguing about her existence. "You weren't gone long enough to travel to Boulder and back."

Catharine's long, unbound hair billowed as she shook her head. "Fairies travel very differently than humans. Fey simply flicked her wand and we were there. Then she flicked it again when she realized you were here, and croikey, we were back."

Ty rubbed the sore lump on his head, not about to argue the night before their wedding. "Maybe we'd better talk about something else."

"Very well." Catharine licked her lips and folded her arms. "I'd like Mother to be part of our day tomorrow."

"I know you would." Tempted to draw her close, Ty stuck his hands in his pockets. "However, your mother's suggestion to share our wedding from the periphery is best."

"I suppose that's true, but it seems so unfair."

"Life isn't always fair." Ty wished he hadn't said that the instant the words left his mouth. A frown replaced Catharine's smile and the twinkle in her eyes.

He reached for her arms, and held them gently to soften his reprimand. "I want you to promise you'll never go off anywhere without first telling or calling me."

"All right. I guess I lived on my own long enough to get used to a bit of freedom."

Taking her chastisement in stride, Ty grinned. "I don't want you to feel as though you're going to prison just because we're getting married."

"Oh, Tyler, I could never feel that way. And I don't wish to keep secrets from you either."

Startled, he tilted her chin higher, holding her gaze. "Are you keeping one from me?"

"Not for long. Fey and I brought Mother back with us."

"Your mother's here? Isn't that dangerous? I mean, what if Eileen or Porter sees her? How will you explain?"

"They won't. We'll make sure. I just wanted you to know. This way she can help me get ready tomorrow."

"I think Eileen expects to do that."

"And she will, but Mother deserves to share part of it too, doesn't she? Besides, I haven't spent a night with her for two years. I don't know when, or if, I'll ever get another chance."

Catharine looked so hopeful Tyler couldn't find it in his heart to disagree. Would he ever be able to refuse anything she asked for? Or disagree with anything she did? Disappearing from his life maybe, but he couldn't think of anything else. That never-ending-love stuff had hit him where he was most vulnerable. In the heart.

"All right." He kissed her forehead and her cheek gently, murmuring, "Good night, Cath. Sweet dreams."

"If I dream, I hope it will be of you."

Satisfied, he headed for the door. He was marrying a time traveler who claimed she had a fairy godmother. It could be worse. He could be marrying someone who had no imagination at all. Someone like Sloan.

As he stepped outside, a blast of frigid air hit him in the face. An icy chill slithered down his spine as he remembered Jennifer's stories about Kacy's fairy godmother named Fey. A second chill followed the first. Who the hell was he about to marry? Kacy? Or Catharine?

He massaged the sore bump on his head. It didn't matter. He loved her, whoever she was. Yep, he'd fallen hard. He loved her deeply. Profoundly. Unquestionably. Never-endingly.

Fifteen

Catharine locked the door behind Tyler, turned the lights off and scurried back up the stairs. In the bedroom, she found her mother staring at the photographs on Kacy's dresser. Fey was sitting beside the one of Kacy's mother.

"You look so much alike, you could be the Rose's daughter," Catharine said.

Eliza smiled. "That's true of you and Kacy as well."

Catharine stared in wide-eyed amazement. "You've seen Kacy? Met her?"

"Seen her, yes," her mother said. "At the earl's trial. But I haven't met her. The angel was anxious to get me away from that time period."

"I asked her to go see you in Kent and tell you where I was."

"I know. The angel told me."

"Did he bring you here to get you away from Wilbur?"

"Perhaps." Eliza pursed her lips and folded her arms, her gaze thoughtful. "He also brought me here so that I could be near you."

"And yet all this time I didn't know you were nearby."

"The angel and fairy both thought it best for you to adjust to this century before you found me."

"Do you think Wilbur will find us?"

"I don't know." Her mother sat down on the queen-sized bed and patted the spot next to her. Catharine sat beside her.

"Tis inevitable." Fey jumped to her tiny feet on the white dresser, drawing their attention.

"I know." Eliza winced at her admission. "He has already called me."

Catharine flinched, and her question came out in a dry gasp. "Have you actually talked to him?"

"No. But his phone messages left me with little doubt that he intends to see both of us."

Catharine pressed a hand to her hot forehead. "I had some weird phone calls last week. I wonder if they might have been instigated by Wilbur."

Eliza wrung her hands, her eyes and voice laced with worry. "I wouldn't be surprised."

"I shall protect both of you from Wilbur," the fairy said.

"How can you make such a promise?" Catharine asked. "You can't be with both, or even one of us all the time."

"No, I cannot. However, I can give you these." Fey extended two tiny, thin, stick-like wands.

As soon as they took them in hand, the wands grew in size and turned to shiny gold. Fingering the four-inch wand in wonder, Catharine asked, "Will this protect us from everything?"

"No," Fey said. "I cannot give unlimited power to any human. Those wands were conjured for the specific purpose of protecting you from Wilbur Lugamon."

"What about Dillon McKenzie?" Catharine asked. "Could I use it if he tries to harm me?"

Fey nodded, and waved her small silver wand over the bigger gold wand in Catharine's hand. "It will have no other power. If you should feel threatened by anyone other than Wilbur and Dillon, you have but to tell me. I shall see that no harm befalls you."

"Thank you, ever so much." Eliza smiled. "You have taken a great deal of worry off my mind, Fey."

Catharine furrowed her brow in a frown.

"What's wrong?" Fey asked.

"I'm still worried."

"What about?"

"Lots of things. Wilbur. Dillon. Tyler. Sloan. My upcoming marriage. Disappointing Tyler."

"Perhaps talking will ease your worries," her mother suggested.

Catharine settled back against the headboard, her back cushioned by a pillow, while her mother did the same.

They talked until the wee hours of the morning.

Even after they changed to their nightclothes and climbed in on opposite sides of the bed, they talked.

Sleep came in patches, if at all. Although she discussed getting married at length with her mother and Fey, Catharine continued to worry about being Tyler's wife. She kept reminding herself they had known and loved before, and this might be their last chance to fulfill their love. Even with that reminder, her nerves were stretched to their limit by morning.

Lying on her back, staring at the frilly pink canopy above the white-framed bed, Catharine's thoughts roved. This was her wedding day. She should be happy and excited. Instead she was nervous, distraught. By nightfall the waiting would be over.

When her mother stretched, Catharine rolled onto her side to face her, resting her arm on the pillow to help cushion her head. "It's so nice to be together."

Eliza smiled. "Yes, it is, darling, and you must put your fear behind you. Tyler's a good man. I'm sure he won't force you to do anything you don't want to do."

Her doubt and fear somewhat assuaged, Catharine rolled out of bed to face perhaps the biggest day of her life, in any of her lives.

After eating breakfast with Eileen and Porter, Catharine scurried back up to the bedroom. Fey had provided food and new clothes for her mother.

Thankful she wasn't alone, Catharine spent most of the day talking with her mother in hushed tones while Fey watched, listened, and made comments from time to time.

When a brisk knock sounded on the door, Eliza said, "I think it's time for you to prepare for your wedding."

"That will be Eileen," Fey confirmed Eliza's conjecture. "She has come to help you dress." Fey aimed her wand at Catharine's mother.

"Are you leaving?" Catharine's voice wavered. They'd had a wonderful visit, but time had run out.

Fey nodded her tiny head. "Not to worry, sweetling. Your mother and I shall see you at the church."

With that she waved her wand and they both disappeared.

Catharine opened the door, stroking the worry beads, wishing her worry would disappear. And then it did. Her heart needed no help for her to act cheerful. She truly wanted to wed Tyler. She smiled at Eileen. "I'm so excited I can't stop trembling."

Eileen returned her smile. "I understand."

~ * ~

Dressed in the exquisite white wedding gown Eileen had helped her purchase, Catharine rode to the chapel with the Rose's in their tan Lincoln Town Car.

Made of white satin and yards of frothy net, with long sleeves, and a low scalloped neckline, the full-skirted gown covered most of the back seat. Catharine was glad she had that part of the car all to herself. She didn't want any unnecessary wrinkles to spoil the way she looked before Tyler saw her.

Rachel and Mack greeted them at the front door of the small church where they worshiped every Sunday. Her expression warm with approval, Rachel smiled. "You look radiant, Catharine."

"Yes," Mack added, a gleam in his eyes. "Beautiful."

Catharine smiled at their compliments, but her insides quivered. *Was Tyler here?* She forced herself to say, "You look very elegant, and Mack looks dashing."

In keeping with the color scheme they had selected, Eileen and Rachel wore long pink gowns. Mack and Porter were dressed in burgundy tuxedos, with matching bow ties and frilly-fronted white shirts.

"Is Tyler here?" Catharine asked, afraid he might not be, and nervous that something might have detained him.

Mack nodded. "Porter and I will go wait with him." Mack opened the door.

As Rachel escorted them inside, uncertainty reared its ugly head again. Catharine frowned. In previous lives Tyler had always been wonderful. Sometimes she thought he was too good to be true. Would he change once they married? That thought frightened her. Wilbur, her stepfather, had been kind and considerate before her mother married him, but cruel, stroppy and vulgar afterwards. Catharine trembled with the knowledge that the crass disagreeable sod was now in this time. Suddenly she felt ill, like she might swoon. She drew in a long, slow, calming breath. This was not the time for vapors.

Rachel led her and Eileen to a small room where Catharine could primp and repair her makeup while they waited for the ceremony to begin. She walked inside and sat gingerly on a wooden chair, mindful not to crush her beautiful gown. With clenched hands, she struggled to breathe normally. She mustn't allow fear to control her. She had to forget Wilbur and think only about Tyler. He was waiting for her to join him in the chapel. To walk down the aisle on Porter's arm.

Thinking about Tyler calmed her a little bit. He had been so kind. Somehow she must reciprocate. Find a way to repay him for all he had done. Perhaps she could do so with love.

Love. She loved Tyler as she could never love another. As she had loved him in all their other lives. A calm that had escaped her before descended, her fear as forgotten as last week's rain.

While Eileen and Rachel pinned corsages to their gowns, Catharine primped in front of the full-length mirror provided by *Weddings For You*, the wedding consulting firm she and Tyler had hired weeks ago.

She stared at the double strand of pearls. They looked exquisite. A perfect compliment to her white wedding gown. She still could hardly believe Tyler had given her such an extravagant gift on Valentine's day. Some day she hoped to surprise him with something equally as valuable. Or wonderful.

After rearranging her veil, she applied fresh lipstick and lowered her gaze. "The neckline is too low," she complained. "It exposes too much cleavage." She pulled a face and tried to raise the gown.

Eileen and Rachel both laughed.

"Tyler will adore your gown," Rachel said.

Catharine hoped that was true. That he wouldn't find her lacking.

Eileen glanced at her watch. "It's time." She extended a beautiful bouquet made of orchids, pink and burgundy roses, and baby's breath.

Catharine raised the bouquet and inhaled the lovely, combined fragrances. Trust Tyler to select the finest flowers.

Without quite knowing how, she found herself at the entrance to the chapel, standing beside Porter. Sparkling glass chandeliers and soft candlelight filled the small interior.

Catharine loved the warm waxy candle scent. She looked at Tyler, waiting near the altar. Her mouth went dry when their gazes met. His blazing eyes telecast his approval of her long white wedding gown.

She licked her lips. Tyler looked spectacular in a white tuxedo, ruffled white shirt, burgundy cummerbund and bow tie. Every inch of him was flawless. Even the burgundy rose boutonniere pinned to his lapel.

Porter offered his arm. Anxiety got the best of Catharine, and she started to shake—all over. More questions attacked her brain. Was she making a mistake? One that would hurt Tyler?

He smiled.

Unable to finger the worry beads concealed beneath the long sleeve of her wedding gown, she bottled her courage and returned Tyler's smile. When she saw her smiling mother standing beside a human-size wingless Fey near the back of the chapel, more of her qualms faded.

Barely registering her footsteps, she floated toward Tyler on a cloud of wonder. His smile grew when Porter placed her hand on his arm and stepped away.

"Please face each other," the clergyman said.

Rachel stepped up and took the bridal bouquet as Tyler reached for Catharine's hands. His palms felt cool. So did her fingers.

She raised her eyes to his. Flickering candlelight accentuated his straight nose and sensitive lips, slightly parted and somber. A pulse beat above his high, tight collar and the dark burgundy bow tie. Awed by the seriousness in his gaze, she trembled. He tightened his fingers around hers. Never in any of their other lives had they reached this stage. She uttered a silent prayer of thanks that they had found each other again. And that their love had endured throughout time.

Tyler flashed a smile. Catharine wasn't afraid when he smiled at her with such tender warmth. Not only did she love him, in a few short weeks he had become her life.

The ceremony began. Combined scents of candle wax, flowers, and Tyler's cologne filled Catharine's senses. Her heart thumped while she listened to Tyler pledge his troth. Then it was her turn. To her surprise, her voice sounded normal when she spoke.

Tyler slid a clustered diamond ring, that matched the betrothal ring, onto her finger. In a hazy daze she slipped a gold wedding band on his, and smiled up at him. "We're married," she whispered, trying to make herself believe she wasn't dreaming, trying to shake the feeling of impending dread.

He smiled back. "Yes, we are." Very gently he squeezed her hand.

The clergyman closed his hands around their joined ones. "May your marriage be blessed," he said benevolently.

A huge lump formed in Catharine's throat.

The cleric smiled. "You may seal your vows with a kiss."

Catharine's breath got trapped in her lungs as Tyler reached for her. She lost her thoughts when he folded her into his arms and brought her against the starched ruffles of his elegant shirtfront.

Mesmerized, she closed her eyes, and lost herself in the magic of him and his kiss. A hundred thrills danced along her nerve endings and for those brief moments she feared nothing.

"Congratulations," the clergyman said, while she struggled to recapture her breath and her composure.

"Thank you." Tyler's husky voice sent shivers down her sensitive spine.

Eileen, Porter, Rachel and Mack rushed forward.

"Congratulations," everyone said, almost in unison.

Catharine smiled. "Thank you." Now she was Mrs. Tyler Quinlane. She didn't think she could be happier. Looking around she saw her mother in the crowd. Her smile grew when her mother winked and smiled.

Tyler took Catharine's hand and led her from the chapel.

Outside they posed for photos with Rachel, Mack, Eileen and Porter. The weather cooperated, as though blessing their day. Not a cloud in the April sky, nor even a whisper of a breeze.

"You look gorgeous." Tyler's husky compliment made her insides quake.

She smiled up at him. "You look rather splendid yourself." She squeezed his hand, and he smiled.

After the photo shoot, Eileen announced, "It's time to drive to the reception center."

"We'll meet you there," Catharine said, hanging onto Tyler's arm to detain him.

As soon as his parents and the Rose's were out of earshot, Catharine turned to the photographer. "I'd like you to take a few more photographs, please."

"Certainly. Of you and the groom?"

"Not only us." Catharine motioned at her mother, standing alone except for Fey, now that the crowd had dispersed. "We'd like our special guest included this time as well."

Smiling, Eliza embraced Catharine then Tyler. "I'm so happy for you. I pray you'll be happy always."

"Thank you. That means a lot." Tyler slipped his arm around Catharine's waist and grinned at the photographer. "Where do you want us?"

"How about right there?"

When he finished snapping photos, Eliza said, "You'll be sure to have copies made for me, won't you?"

"Absolutely," Tyler promised. "Would you like to ride with us to the reception center?"

Eliza shook her head. "Fey will take me. We won't go through the formal greeting line, but you'll know we're there, sharing your celebration."

Catharine smiled. "Thanks, Mother."

Eliza smiled, too. "You're more than welcome."

At the reception center, a small band played both classical and modern-day music. Because Catharine didn't have a bridesmaid or a maid of honor, Tyler hadn't asked anyone to be his best man. Standing between Eileen and Porter and Mack and Eileen, they greeted their guests.

A small part of Catharine resented the fact that her mother wasn't part of the wedding party. She supposed that was the price she must pay for impersonating Kacy. Catharine vowed then and there that she would tell the Rose's and the Quinlane's the truth. She must if she wanted to share the book she was writing about Kacy's time travel adventure.

When the formal line broke up, the band continued to play.

"Dance with me," Tyler invited with a warm smile.

Catharine smiled as well. "I'd love to."

He drew her into his arms and waltzed her around the dance floor. Catharine closed her eyes, forgetting they were on display, knowing she would cherish her memories of this day forever. For all time. For infinity.

The fragrance of his boutonniere mingled with the scent of Tyler's spicy cologne while they danced. With her eyes closed, the scents created a world all of their own. She reveled in the pleasant essence, the dance, and Tyler's nearness. While he guided her expertly around the floor, his long, lean legs brushed hers through her full-skirted wedding gown, reminding her that from this night on, she would be a married woman.

As far as she was concerned, the dance ended too soon. Before they pulled apart, the band struck up another tune, *Here Comes the Bride.*

Tears clouded Catharine's vision. *How unutterably, wonderfully appropriate.*

Tyler surprised her by lifting her off her feet and twirling her around while their audience sang and hummed the bridal march.

When the song ended, he set her on her feet, and threaded her arm through his.

"Kiss the bride," a guest yelled.

Tyler obliged.

Catharine's world whirled crazily as he tipped her back over one arm and kissed her soundly, giving the cheering crowd exactly what they wanted. She held nothing back. In those moments she believed she could share the marriage act with Tyler without fear.

Bliss had pushed all fear aside. She couldn't have asked for a more wonderful wedding day. Even her mother had been there to share her happiness.

Tyler's parents drew them aside. "Come see the tables displaying your wedding gifts," Rachel said.

Marveling at the generosity of their guests, and wondering where they would keep such bounty, Catharine said, "It's a good thing we moved to a larger flat."

Tyler nodded. "Yes, it is." Then he bent his head and whispered in her ear. "Let's go."

Catharine blushed. His whisper sent tiny tendrils of excitement trickling down her back and arms.

They headed for the door. No one tried to stop them.

Outside in the cool night air, well-wishers tossed multi-colored rose petals and blew bubbles that floated above their heads as they hurried to the white limo waiting at the curb.

Sixteen

After they checked into the Adams Mark Hotel in downtown Denver, they rode the elevator up to their suite.

"We have a custom I'm not sure you're aware of," Tyler said with a gleam in his grayish-green eyes.

"What is it?"

"This." Their gazes held while he lifted her up in his arms and carried her over the threshold. He eased the door shut with his foot, keeping her nestled against his chest.

"You're a beautiful bride." His tender gaze matched his quiet words.

"And you're a handsome groom." Catharine touched his cheek with the tips of her fingers, tracing a line across his upper lip, then over his lower. He caught her finger between his lips, drew it inside his mouth and slid his tongue around it in an erotic dance. Tingling inside, she felt excited, yet also unsure. What if she disappointed him?

Slowly she pulled her finger out. Then she missed the warm moisture inside his mouth and the contact with his tongue.

"Don't be timid with me," he coaxed as though he knew her thoughts. "I want you so much, you can't disappoint me."

That gave her enough courage to say, "I'm ever so glad I met you in this life."

"So am I."

"Our wedding was the greatest ever."

"I think so too."

"I love you, Tyler."

"I love you, too, Catharine."

He carried her to the couch and sat down with her on his lap. For a few moments all they did was stare at each other in the dim glow of lamplight. Finally he invited, "Kiss me."

With the words love, honor, and cherish lingering in her mind, she cupped his smoothly shaven cheeks and pressed her mouth against his.

The kiss promised more than mere kissing. That frightened her a little, until the memories of kissing him in another life flashed. Emboldened, she threaded her fingers through his shiny clean hair, and gave in to a throaty sigh as he held her tight.

Would they consummate their vows tonight? If they did, they would truly belong to each other... as she had never belonged to another.

Her thoughts scattered as Tyler aroused her with another drugging kiss. Moments later he spread tiny butterfly kisses all over her face, kissing her closed eyes, her temple, the corner of her mouth, her throat, behind her ear.

When he kissed her mouth again, she lost all her thoughts. Captivated by the sensations he alone aroused, her lips clung to his. A wonderful heat sizzled through her veins. Her blood caught on fire. She returned his passion, gasping in shallow, fluttering breaths when his hands delved below her scalloped neckline to cup her full breasts.

His fondling stimulated, excited, aroused. She ran her hands down his frilly shirtfront, fumbling with the buttons.

The shrill ringing of the telephone interrupted their pleasure.

She arched her brows, perplexed. "Who would call us?"

"No one, unless it's something important."

Catharine's mind raced with possibilities. "Maybe there's been an accident. Or Porter or Eileen might have had a heart attack... or a stroke."

Tyler plucked the phone off the table. "Yes?"

"Do you need help fucking your bride tonight?" a crude male voice asked.

Tyler slammed the phone down, but Catharine had heard the loud lewd question.

"Do you know who it was?" Her voice wobbled and her shoulders trembled.

Tyler wrapped his arms back around her. "Some pervert."

"Probably Wilbur," Catharine surmised.

"Who's Wilbur?"

"Mother's second husband. Her bigamist husband. My step-papa. My bigamist step-papa."

"What makes you think he's here in this time?"

"Fey told us last night—Mother and I. She said an evil wizard brought him here."

Tyler ran his hand down Catharine's arm. "Don't think about him."

She shuddered again. "I can't help it."

"The caller could have been Dillon McKenzie."

Catharine nodded. "They remind me of each other. Both he and Wilbur said they would make me pay for rejecting them. Maybe harassing us on our wedding night is their way of doing it."

Tyler grabbed the phone and punched the number for the front desk. "Don't put any more telephone calls through to our room tonight."

"Not even if it's an emergency?"

"No. If anyone needs to contact us, they'll call us on our cell phones."

No sooner had Tyler hung up than Catharine's cell phone rang. She fumbled in her new purse and found it. "Hello."

"Your hubby hung up on me," a nasal voice said. "That wasn't very nice. I asked a simple question. Is he gonna need help screwing you tonight? Maybe I could demonstrate a knee trembler. That's sexual intercourse standing up, in case you don't know."

The blood drained from Catharine's shocked head. "How did you get my cell phone number?"

The caller didn't reply. He laughed. It sounded vile and ugly.

Tyler grabbed her phone and shut it off. "What did he say?"

Catharine repeated what she'd heard. The explicit description played before her eyes. She cringed. Closed her eyes. The caller had turned something beautiful and precious into a base, carnal act.

"Don't think about it." Tyler reached out to draw her close again. "It's not important."

All Catharine's previous doubts and fears flashed through her. She resisted Tyler's attempt to hold her close. Disgust at herself warred with love, but she could no more respond now than fly to the sun. She felt sick to her stomach.

Tyler must have sensed her feelings. "Let's get ready for bed," he suggested, and started to unfasten the back of her wedding gown.

Catharine froze. "Please, no. Don't," she choked out, drawing away, raising her hands to ward him off.

Tyler looked puzzled. "What's wrong?"

"I'm afraid."

He clamped his hands around her arms. "I won't hurt you."

"I can't help it." Hot tears scalded her eyes, spilled over, and rained down her cheeks. "I'm still afraid."

Slowly Tyler gathered her close, little more than an inch at a time. "Hush, Catharine. There's nothing to fear. I won't rush you. I'll give you time to get used to me. We'll sleep in each other's arms. That's all we'll do tonight. I won't even kiss you again."

Catharine hated disappointing him. She loved his kisses. Why couldn't they be enough?

And why couldn't she make herself want more? But more than anything now, she feared how she would feel if he forced her to be intimate. "I'm sorry, Tyler. I'll try to overcome my fear."

"And I'll try to help you. Let's go to bed. We have an early flight in the morning."

In the privacy of the bathroom Catharine changed to the pretty bed gown she had bought for this special night. But it no longer felt special. Now everything felt wrong.

Maybe she should have stayed away from the small chapel today. Wouldn't that have been more kind than hurting Tyler now that they were wed?

She crushed the urge to cry, forced herself to leave the sanctuary of the bathroom, and get in bed with Tyler. He wore nothing except black silk shorts.

Fear resurfaced when he reached for her. "I'll protect you," he vowed. "I'll find a way to keep Wilbur and Dillon from hurting you."

With all her heart, Catharine hoped Tyler could somehow keep that promise. But nagging doubts kept her tense.

"Good night, Catharine." He kissed her temple, gently, and pulled slightly away, his arms relaxing.

All he did was hold her, as he'd promised. A shivery sigh escaped. For a while she found it impossible to relax. It felt too strange to be in bed with someone else. Especially a man. Never before, not in any life, had she slept with a man. She hadn't had a husband either. This life was full of firsts. Not all of them were unpleasant. She vowed to do her best to be a good wife.

Deprived of sleep the night before, she closed her eyes. But she couldn't sleep. All she could do was worry. About Dillon... Wilbur... her honeymoon. Would Tyler expect to make love before she felt ready?

Seventeen

"I'm sorry our wedding night was a failure," Catharine said the next morning. "I'm sorry I failed you, Tyler. Sorry I let those phone calls spoil everything."

Still lying in bed, he drew her close. Although he wore boxer shorts, his bare chest made her self-conscious. She liked being in his arms, though. His powerful body made her feel safe and his masculine scent smelled wonderful.

"As I told you before, we have the rest of our lives to get used to living together, Cath. We sort of rushed into marriage, but I'll try not to rush you into being intimate. Please tell me if I wait too long."

She smiled through the tears puddled in her eyes. "I don't think I deserve you."

"Never say that." He dried her leaky tears with a corner of the white bed sheet. "We've lived through entire lifetimes and never been this close before. We'll make our marriage work."

Her pulse lurched, her blood drumming through her veins. "Do you truly believe we're destined to be together?"

"Absolutely. Even if we hadn't known each other in prior lives, I'm head over heels, crazy in love with you."

Catharine stared. The echo of her thumping heart boomed in her ears. She swallowed to moisten the tightening in her throat. "I love you, too. In those other lives, I loved you secretly. Even when you thought we were only friends, I loved you."

Tyler smiled. "I loved you as well. Unfortunately, our love was either forbidden, or our stations in life so far apart, we couldn't express how we felt."

"How well I know that." Her heart quickened, her pulse raced. They seemed so in tune.

"We can't allow anything, or anyone, to ruin this chance at happiness."

Catharine smiled, this time without tears. "Everything you've said is exactly what I feel. I love you so much, Tyler. I'll always love you."

"The feeling's mutual."

He gave her a quick kiss on the cheek. "Now, we'd better get up and get dressed. We have a plane to catch, wife."

Relieved that he didn't give her time to mope, she said, "I'm excited about flying again."

Tyler tossed the covers aside. "Then get moving, woman."

~ * ~

Their honeymoon in Hawaii, on the big island, was all Catharine could have wished. And more. She loved every minute they spent outdoors. But hated disappointing Tyler when they returned to their room.

He didn't force her. She knew he wouldn't, yet some perverse part of her had to make him prove that.

One night she lay on the bed, flat on her back, as close to the edge as she could get without falling off.

Tyler rolled onto his side, to the middle of the bed. He drew her close and kissed her gently. She did her best to kiss him back. His arousal pressed against her hip. She stiffened, unable to help herself.

"I want you, Catharine," he murmured, caressing her back through the sheer filmy fabric of her new blue bed gown. "And I'll be gentle. I promise. Making love is one of the nicest ways to express our feelings for each another."

"I know," she whispered, not trusting her voice. It would sound terrified, she knew.

He kissed her again. Part of her felt aroused. Part of her wanted passion. Tyler stroked her flesh, nuzzled her ear, lowered his head, and kissed her breasts. Leaving the sheer fabric of her bed gown to cover them, he teased her nipples into hard nubs.

Would he undress her next? Force her into submission? The worry beads pressed against her arm. She'd been so nervous she'd forgotten to take the bracelet off. She tried to respond to Tyler, but wished she could be invisible. Maybe then he wouldn't want her.

"What the hell happened?" He grasped her arms, shaking her.

"What's wrong?" she asked, startled by his question and the shaking.

"I can't see you. You're in—invisible."

"I am?" Confused, she looked from his incredulous expression down at herself. She couldn't see her body.

"How did it happen?"

"I—I don't know."

"One minute I was kissing you, stroking you, and the next you disappeared right before my eyes."

"I'm sorry," was all she could think to say. Stunned herself, she tried to comprehend. But couldn't. Did her invisibility mean she was on the verge of disappearing from this time? Lose her mortality, as Kacy had written about in her journal?

Or was Fey here? Had the fairy granted her secret wish to be invisible?

"Has this ever happened before?"

Catharine's voice went dry, her mind racing with possibilities, none of which appealed to her. She swallowed convulsively before she answered. "Once. Maybe twice."

"When?"

She forced herself to lay her own fears aside and focus on Tyler's concern. "At the governor's cocktail party."

Tyler frowned. "Do you know what caused it?"

"No." *Could a mere thought, a silent, secret wish, make it happen?* Catharine had thought Fey's magic made it possible previously. *Was the fairy here now, watching them?*

Much as Catharine adored Fey, she didn't want an audience when they were in bed.

"I can feel you," Tyler said, his voice tight, "but I can't see any part of you." He gentled his hold, then asked, "Do you feel all right?"

"Yes. Please don't worry. I'm sure I'll be visible again by morning."

"I can't help but worry. I don't relish spending our honeymoon talking to my invisible bride."

"I don't think you have to worry about that." Bad enough that she would worry.

"You said this might have happened twice," Tyler interrupted her morbid thoughts. "When was the other time?"

"About two years ago. In the woods when I ran away from home. And I'm not certain it happened then. It might only have been my imagination. The night was so very dark. I couldn't see my hand in front of my face. At the time I thought perhaps I was invisible and that would protect me from harm."

"How long did it—the invisibility last?"

"I was visible by morning."

"At the governor's mansion. How long did it last that time?"

"Only a few minutes. Well, maybe as long as fifteen. While I was in the ladies powder room. Sloan didn't talk to me because she didn't see me."

Tyler's frown deepened the lines between his eyes. "Can you do something to make the invisibility go away?"

"I don't know what."

"Are you too cold, or too warm, or anything?"

"I'm fine. How do you feel?"

"Like a wretch."

Affected by his deepening concern, Catharine said, "I think it's possible that Fey, my fairy godmother, might be here. She could be responsible for my invisibility."

"Then tell her to make you visible again.

Catharine closed her eyes and mumbled, "Fey, I wish I were no longer invisible."

Leaning close, Catharine kissed Tyler. First on the cheek, then on the forehead as he often kissed her. Then she kissed his chin, and finally his mouth. He didn't tighten his arms, but he kissed her back, gently, almost reverently.

When the kiss ended, he said, "You're visible. That kiss made you visible."

Although puzzled herself, she smiled. "I'm so glad I married you, Tyler. And I'm sorry I'm such a disappointment."

"You're not." He kissed her forehead "Maybe we should go to sleep. You might be fatigued."

Snuggled against Tyler's warm chest, her head nestled in the crook of his shoulder, Catharine closed her eyes, and let out a quiet sigh. In the future she must be careful. If the fairy was nearby, she might grant any wish, whether silent or spoken out loud.

~ * ~

Ty vowed to be patient.

He was very patient. It damn near drove him crazy though. A honeymoon was supposed to be a time of sexual fulfillment, not sexual frustration.

They swam in the ocean; strolled along the beach.

He got turned on.

Catharine got turned off.

He knew she tried to overcome her fear, but couldn't. He sympathized. Lost his patience. Then found it again, which surprised even him. Was the memory of her tears responsible? Or the fact that she had turned invisible? He worried that she might become invisible again. And then he wondered if that had truly happened, or if he'd only imagined it.

Silently he cursed the phone calls on their wedding night. He suspected they had been made by Dillon McKenzie. The one to Catharine's cell phone had been made from a phone booth, thus impossible to prove.

~ * ~

At the end of the week, when they finally boarded the plane to fly home, Ty heaved a sigh of relief. Maybe once his mind wasn't focused on sex all day, they could find a way to solve her problem. And maybe it was going to take months. Maybe he had to back off and give her more time to know him, to feel comfortable with him.

Ty vowed he wouldn't push her. He could wait until she was ready. At least in this life, they'd made it to the altar. They'd never before been this close. He had to believe they would eventually consummate their marriage. Otherwise, he would go mad.

Eighteen

Catharine spent Sunday morning, after their return, doing the laundry and putting their clothes away. The chores helped her feel like a wife. Taking care of Tyler's things gave her great pleasure, more than she could have imagined.

She planned dinner, a simple meal of salad, pork chops, and macaroni and cheese. After she laid the table, Catharine added two tapered blue candles in clear crystal holders, one of their wedding gifts that had been delivered by Tyler's parents while they were gone. Then she selected a bottle of burgundy wine. Tyler's favorite.

"How did you know this is one of my favorite meals?" he asked.

"I didn't. I fixed it because Jennifer taught me how and I didn't think I could do much to ruin anything. But now that I know, I promise to cook this meal whenever you want."

He smiled. With the two top buttons of his polo shirt unbuttoned, he looked sexy. And very desirable.

Catharine smiled dreamily. The music in the background, combined with the soft candlelight created a romantic atmosphere.

Relaxed by the wine, she longed to stand up, walk around the table to Tyler's side, kiss him, and make him forget all about dinner.

Surprised by her thoughts, she frowned. She mustn't give mixed signals. She wasn't yet ready to make love.

~ * ~

Later that evening, seated in front of her computer, Catharine smiled after she answered the phone. "I'm delighted you called, Mother."

"Are you busy?"

"No, not particularly."

"Where's Tyler?"

"In the other room, watching TV and catching up on all the newspapers. Where are you?"

"At home. How was your honeymoon?"

"Wonderful." Catharine's smile faded. "Except for one thing."

"You didn't make love," Eliza said.

"You're right," Catharine gasped. "How did you know?"

"I didn't. I guessed. How's Tyler handling the situation?"

Catharine blew out a breath, fanning her bangs and cooling her overheated forehead. Only then did she realize how warm she felt. She snatched a blank sheet of paper from the printer tray to fan herself. "Actually, he's handling it better than you might imagine. We've a—um—decided to sleep in separate bedrooms."

"Whose idea was that? Yours or his?"

Catharine sucked in her bottom lip. Trust her mother to cut right to the heart of the problem. "Both." She explained the phone calls on their wedding night, ending with, "They spoiled everything. And then on our honeymoon, I think Fey was with us. It felt so odd. I couldn't get in the mood to make love with a fairy nearby."

"I can imagine how intimidating that might be. How long do you expect sleeping apart to last?"

Catharine set her makeshift fan down and twined the coiled phone cord around her fingers. "I don't know. Tomorrow we'll resume our normal routine. I'm hoping that when I adjust to the idea of being married, I'll get over my fear, and want to sleep with Tyler every night."

"Would you like me to work with you on this, Catharine?"

"No. Not yet. I thought a hypnotherapist could help me, and I appreciate your offer and your concern, but I love Tyler and I hope to overcome my problem by myself. And soon."

"What is your normal routine?" Eliza asked then.

"Tyler drives me to the office each weekday morning. I work from eight to twelve-thirty. When the afternoon receptionist arrives, Tyler drives me home. We usually stop for lunch on the way, unless he has something else he has to do. I spend my afternoons writing, working on Kacy's story."

"Who cleans your apartment?"

Catharine's lips curved in another smile as she unwound the phone cord. "Tyler has a cleaning lady who comes twice a week, in the mornings while I'm at the office. It's very nice to come home to a clean flat. I feel spoiled."

"How trustworthy is she?"

The tiny hairs on the back of Catharine's neck stood on end. She'd been concerned about the apartment's security herself, and decided never to answer the door when she was home alone unless she knew for sure who on the other side. "I—I don't know. I've only met Virginia once. Why?"

"You can't be too careful, dear. Anyone who has a key to your home might be persuaded or forced by Wilbur to let him in."

The reminder of her ex-stepfather knotted Catharine's insides. She pressed a hand against her cramped stomach, unable to think of a comment.

"Perhaps you should mention that possibility to Tyler and ask him to talk to the cleaning lady," Eliza said. "Alert her that there could be a problem and she should be on guard."

Catharine let out the breath she'd been holding. "I'll do that, Mother. Thanks for suggesting it."

Shortly after she hung up, Tyler stopped by the door. "Who called?"

"Mother." Catharine repeated their conversation and her concern about the cleaning lady and Wilbur.

"I'll talk with Ginny," Tyler promised. "Explain the possible problem. Tell her not to answer the door when she's here."

"Thanks." Catharine smiled. "That will make me feel ever so much safer."

"I could also come up here with you after I drive you home, to make sure the place is empty before I go back to work."

"I don't think we have to go that far." But Catharine knew she would worry from now on. Her mother's concern had planted a new fear in her head.

She must remember to keep the four inch gold wand with her all the time. In Hawaii, she'd felt safe with Tyler, and she'd been lax. Now she had to be prepared for anything, especially when he wasn't nearby.

Tyler cleared his throat. "Good night." He turned away.

Suddenly Catharine changed her mind about sleeping alone. She loved spending the night beside Tyler. If only they could continue, she felt certain she would overcome her fear. "Are you sure you want separate bedrooms?" she asked.

She saw Tyler's whole body jerk before he turned his startled gaze back to her. "Why? Don't you?"

Catharine shrugged. "It will be lonely without you." Encouraged by his stare, she stood up and started across the room.

He met her halfway. Without a word they wrapped their arms around each other. Her fear forgotten, she arched up to kiss him. Again, Tyler met her halfway, bending his head, claiming her lips.

Her heart pounded with joy. How she loved his kisses, his touch, his scent. He made her feel like a woman. A wanton, desirable woman. The kiss deepened. She felt as though she were floating toward heaven.

Tyler tightened his arms. She tightened hers, too. Pressed against his chest, she felt his heart hammering against hers, proof that they were both aroused.

Tyler finally ended the kiss, but he kept her in his arms. "Which bed do you want to sleep in?" The husky question brought her back down to earth, destroying the euphoria of moments ago.

"I—I don't know." She sucked in her breath, nervous, confused and paranoid. *Was Fey here with them now? Or were they alone?* "Which do you?"

"You've changed your mind." Tyler released her and backed away.

Too flustered to agree to disagree, she asked, "Wh—what makes you ah—think so?"

"I can see it in yours eyes." His didn't condemn, they merely accepted. "Maybe you should seek counseling."

"I don't want to talk about this—my problem with someone I don't know."

"You could talk to your mother."

"I have. It hasn't helped."

He gave a negligent shrug. "Well, good night then. I'll see you in the morning."

Catharine swallowed. She didn't know whether to laugh or cry. She felt like doing both. And she still wanted to spend the night at his side. Why, oh why, did such conflict battle inside her?

~ * ~

At the office the next morning, Rachel and Mack greeted them with warm smiles. While they stood in the photocopy room waiting for the coffee to brew, they discussed their honeymoon. Then Rachel said, "I hired another attorney while you were gone."

Tyler hiked his brow. "Anyone I know?"

Rachel said, "Sloan Cole."

Dismay tumbled through Catharine. *Sloan. Why her?*

She heard the front door open and close. No one spoke again until Sloan, dressed in a pinstriped navy blue pant suit that resembled a man's, walked in. "Good morning." She smiled until she spotted Catharine. "I didn't know you worked here."

The sneer on Sloan's face made Catharine want to retreat to the reception area. She glanced at Tyler. He didn't look any happier than she felt.

"You must only work mornings." Sloan's eyes seemed to say, *'So I'll have Tyler all to myself in the afternoon.'* "It must be nice to have a husband support you."

Catharine didn't bat an eyelash. "He's supporting me because that's his choice. However, I'm perfectly capable of supporting myself."

"She sure is," Mack piped in, looking ready to defend Catharine, which made her grateful. "She has a substantial trust fund, and she won the lottery in February, so she's worth more than Tyler might earn in several years. She's offered to buy a house for her grandparents. I don't imagine very many young women are that generous."

Sloan's black penciled eyebrows steepled at Mack's praise. "Some of us aren't as lucky as others. That's all winning the lottery is, pure dumb luck."

"I'm the lucky one." Tyler also looked as though he had to defend her. "For convincing Catharine to be my wife."

"We're both very lucky." Catharine touched Tyler's arm and smiled up at him. She knew the gesture bothered Sloan more than anything she might have said. And it made her aware that she was probably missing something wonderful by not being intimate.

An hour later, in the privacy of his mom's office with the door closed, Ty asked, "Why did you hire Sloan without consulting with me?"

"I thought you'd be pleased. She said you were great friends, that you dated for six months before you realized you were in love with Catharine. Did I goof? Were you more than friends?"

"If you're wondering if we slept together, the answer is no. Sloan wanted to. I didn't. And she was rather nasty when I told her I intended to marry Catharine."

"Well, if Sloan doesn't work out, we'll let her go."

"We can't fire her without a very good reason unless we want to risk a law suit."

Rachel leaned back in her chair and folded her arms. "Sloan called, said she'd resigned from her old job for personal reasons, and wondered if we could use another attorney for a few months, to tide her over until she finds something else. I told her we'd try it on a trial basis, and I had her sign a contract agreeing to those terms. I don't expect her to stay indefinitely, and we are short-handed at the moment."

Partially pacified, Ty frowned. "Did you see how she glared at Catharine?"

"Yes. I noticed. If Sloan makes Catharine uncomfortable, I'll tell her it isn't working out. She'll have to leave."

"I hope she works out." Ty swiped his hand across his chin before he admitted, "We do need help. We've got more business than the three of us can handle."

Rachel smiled. "Especially now that you've decided to get involved in politics. I'm very proud of you, Ty." She unfolded her arms, bent forward and leaned her elbows on her polished walnut desk. "Let me know if Sloan treats Catharine shabbily."

"Don't worry. I will."

Catharine couldn't ignore Sloan. She seemed to take perverse pleasure making snide comments whenever no one else was within earshot.

"Tyler must have felt sorry for you. That's the only reason he married you," she hissed after she'd made a few other rude remarks.

Catharine held her silence, but she wondered if she was destined to have unpleasant co-workers for the rest of her life.

By the middle of the week, Sloan had formed a nasty habit of slamming Catharine with every derogatory comment imaginable.

"Why don't you give Tyler up?" Her thin face twisted in an unflattering sneer. "You'll never make a politician's wife. You're nothing more than a little mouse of a woman."

Tired of Sloan and her taunts, Catharine retaliated. "Why don't you grow up and act like an adult instead of a poor pouting childish loser?"

In a huff, Sloan squared her shoulders and stalked back to her office. Catharine wondered what the stroppy woman would say the next time she decided to attack.

When she saw Sloan walk down the hall to Tyler's office for the third time in less than an hour, Catharine switched the incoming calls to the answer machine and followed.

In the doorway of Tyler's office, Catharine fumed as she watched Sloan flirt. With her hip on his desk, she bent close, placed her hand on Tyler's chest, curled her fingers around his tie, and pulled him close until their faces were mere inches apart. "Kiss me, Ty."

"No."

Mad enough to choke Sloan, Catharine demanded, "Do you always flirt with other women's husbands, or is mine your prime target?"

Tyler jerked back. Catharine didn't know whether she was angry with him or not. But she was furious with Sloan.

"He's interested in me," Sloan said.

"No, I'm not." Tyler shook his head, denying Sloan's boast.

Both relieved and proud, Catharine winked at him as Sloan straightened and walked toward the door. Catharine rubbed the worry beads. "I wish a pox on your smug, haughty face," she said as Sloan sauntered by.

"You should wish for a husband who really wants you," Sloan said in an undertone that Catharine was sure Tyler didn't hear.

"I have wished that, and I suggest you make yourself scarce when he's around. Otherwise you may find yourself wishing you had never met me."

Sloan raised a hand and scratched her forehead, but didn't utter another word. Catharine saw a red rash appear on her cheeks and chin. Her wish couldn't have caused that, could it?

~ * ~

Determined not to let Sloan upset her any more, Catharine stared out the windshield while Tyler drove her home. Her thoughts reverted to past lives. Her unrequited love, and the pain.

Something clicked in her brain. Were the worry beads magic as Tyler had suggested? She'd thought he was only teasing. But she knew the gold wand was magic. If she could wish herself invisible, and she wasn't sure that's what had happened, maybe she could wish her fear of intimacy away.

Hoping Fey was nearby and would grant the wish, Catharine stroked the worry beads. For added insurance, she slid her hand into her skirt pocket and clasped the four-inch gold wand, too. Then with fervent sincerity, she made her silent wish. *"I wish I could want to make love with Tyler. I wish I won't disappoint him again. I wish that next time he takes me in his arms, I won't want to pull away."*

She let go of the wand and beads, and opened her eyes. Had the wish worked? Could the fear plaguing her be gone?

To her surprise and delight, she wasn't afraid anymore. A sense of wonder and contentment flooded her. Why had it taken so long to discover how easily she could overcome her fear? Was it really gone? Yes!

Ripples of excitement shot through her. She truly wanted to make love to Tyler. More than she had ever wanted anything else. Startled, she tried to examine her feelings. They hadn't changed, just increased. *Their platonic relationship was about to end.* She grinned, her heart humming a merry tune.

The first time had to be perfect. "It will be perfect," she mumbled under her breath. "I'll make it perfect."

"What?" Tyler asked, grinning as he changed lanes.

"I've overcome my fear," she said, startled as much by her admission as she was by the joy and desire racing through her entire body. She no longer feared making love. No. What she feared now was not being intimate.

"Are you trying to entice me to take the afternoon off?"

Realizing that he was flirting with her, and enjoying herself immensely, Catharine smiled and did her best to look seductive. "I'll try to make it worth your while if you do."

Ty couldn't believe he'd heard her correctly. Nor could he believe he had suggested taking the afternoon off. He had piles of work stacked on his desk. And a small mountain of phone calls to make as well. All that paled into insignificance when Catharine smiled at him again. The expectant gleam in her eyes could only be described as seductive. He squelched a groan. *Had she truly said she had overcome her fear? Did she really want to make love?*

He cleared his throat, unsure of himself, and even more unsure of her. "Are we on the same page?"

"I hope so. And I'm hoping that soon we'll be in, or on, the same bed. Unless you'd prefer to make love in the living room. It's your choice, Tyler. I'll need help. I don't know exactly what to do. But I do want to be your wife in every way. And I want that to happen as soon as possible. I don't know how long it will take, but we didn't stop for lunch, so you can spare some time before you have to return to the office. Can't you?"

For a few seconds Ty could only stare at his wife. Finally he asked, "When did you get over being afraid?"

"About thirty seconds ago. I don't know exactly how it happened. I only know that suddenly I want to make love to you more than I've ever wanted anything else. Except maybe being your wife. I wanted that pretty badly, too. But I'm not yet your wife in every way."

"You will be soon," he promised, smiling at the stars twinkling in her eyes before he signaled to turn into the apartment parking garage. All of a sudden he was nervous. Like he had never before made love. Would he rush things too much for her? Could he control himself enough to keep her fear at bay?

More anxious than he ever remembered being about anything, he turned the engine off, and opened the door. Despite his reservations, he jumped out of the car, and dashed around to open her door before she could change her mind.

She smiled up at him, unfastening her seatbelt. Then she got out, flung her arms around him and kissed him passionately... right there in the semi-dark parking garage.

Delighted by her unusual show of affection, his nervousness evaporated, replaced by desire and instant arousal. "Let's go upstairs," he murmured against her lips.

"Yes, let's," she whispered back. She pressed her body against his briefly, then unwound her arms from his neck.

He wrapped his arm around her slender waist and shoved the door closed. As they hurried toward the elevator, Ty felt her tremble. His wariness returned. Would she remain unafraid? Or freeze up the instant they reached their apartment?

Inside the elevator, Catharine recalled wishing that Tyler would always want to kiss her, and no matter what else had happened, he still seemed to enjoy kissing. Emboldened by that knowledge, she reached up and drew his head down to hers. They kissed as the elevator traveled all the way up to their floor and didn't stop until the door opened.

Arms wrapped around each other, they staggered to their door. She fumbled with the keys. He took them from her shaky hands and unlocked the apartment. Catharine half expected stage fright to set in. It didn't.

Suddenly her happiness knew no bounds. She could hardly contain herself and vowed to make this experience a memorable one, even though she had heard that the first time could be disappointing for a girl.

Nineteen

"Where do you want to start?"

"In here." Catharine took Tyler's hand and drew him through the living room, into the kitchen. Her nerves were atwitter, but not with fear, with anticipation. Still that old enemy, fear, wasn't entirely conquered. What if she failed? Disappointed Tyler?

Love made her desperate. She couldn't wait a day longer. To buy a little time to prepare for the Big Event, she asked, "Would you mind opening a bottle of wine while I... uh... take care of something else?"

He hiked his brows.

Sensing he thought she must be setting him up for another disappointment, she said, "You don't twig it, do you?"

"Twig it? What does that mean?"

"Realize the truth." She smiled, putting all her love into her eyes. "I won't change my mind. I promise."

He nodded, accepting her words at face value. When he reached for the corkscrew and a bottle of red wine, she dashed away, racing through the apartment, unplugging all the phones, gathering a soft velvety throw from her room and blue candles.

"I'll meet you in the living room." She called.

With the open wine in hand, Tyler snagged two new crystal goblets from the cupboard, and followed her.

Standing by the sofa, Catharine drew in a deep breath, and forced herself to shove all her qualms aside. For better or for worse, their vows must be consummated now. The decision was made. Everything else must be set aside. She wanted him and he wanted her. Nothing else mattered.

When he stood before her, she smiled. "You're so handsome, you take my breath away."

Tyler did a double take. Suddenly she realized she'd rarely complimented him.

"You look fantastic." His eyes gleamed with approval, and expectancy. "You always do."

Catharine laughed. She felt wicked, desirable, and a little brazen. "Thank you." She stuck her hands in her skirt pockets, clutched the golden wand and made another silent wish that she wouldn't disappoint him.

To occupy her hands and cover her nervousness, she spread the velvety maroon throw over the sofa, and lit the candles she'd already positioned on the coffee table. Tyler waited for her to finish before he poured the wine.

They sat side by side on the sofa. She leaned forward, picked up both crystal goblets and offered him one. Raising hers to his, she said, "To us."

"To us." He clinked her goblet, his eyes caressing her in a way she'd never seen him do. She almost felt as though he had touched her intimately and her flesh tingled with the thought.

"I love you so much, Tyler."

"I love you too, Catharine."

"I want you to love me all the way, no matter what. Please don't stop, even if you think that maybe you should."

Tyler smiled. "Just remember one thing."

"What?"

"You're not afraid of me. You're afraid of someone else. Don't transfer that fear to me."

"I won't," she promised and she meant to keep that promise, however difficult it might prove.

They sipped their wine, then he leaned close and nibbled on her ear, licked her earlobe, blew gently into her ear. Sensuous tingles shivered through her.

She had only to look into his gray-green eyes to know how badly he wanted her. Her heart started to beat faster, her pulse to drum. She wanted him, too. The realization still startled her. It pleased her, too. "I want you," she said.

"You don't have to look so surprised."

"I'm sorry. I didn't know before."

"I want you, too."

She stared up at him with hope, and without fear. "I'm ready whenever you are."

He made a sound, half groan, half laugh, and caught her close. "You've bewitched me, Cath." He pulled her to him in a crushing embrace. She'd never felt more exhilarated, more desired, more willing to give.

When he released her, she stared at his broad shoulders, his black, naturally wavy hair, and smiled when she thought about the small black curls on his chest she couldn't yet see. This intimacy did have its rewards, she decided, wondering when they would get rid of their clothes.

He didn't rush her. She didn't know whether to be glad or frustrated. He slid his hand beneath her full skirt and touched her legs. Gently. Tenderly. Her breath got trapped in her throat. How could a mere touch make her feel so—so what? Wanton? Aroused? Desired.

With one hand still caressing her thigh, Tyler kissed her cheek, her forehead. He took another sip of wine, and kissed her lips, ever so gently. She tasted wine on his tongue and inhaled his new mint scented cologne.

She was surprised at how he made her body glow with an inner warmth, and wondered if he knew.

He set her goblet on the coffee table, along with his own. "Tell me what you want," he said, watching her.

"I want you as close to me as you can possibly get, because I can't bear the distance any longer."

A flash of pain flickered in his eyes. "I can't bear it either, love."

He tilted his head and gently pressed the tip of his tongue against her slightly parted lips. The gentle intrusion went from teasingly mild to wildly hot in mere seconds. Heat and sweetness spread through Catharine with the swiftness of a volcanic eruption.

Emboldened by their mutual eager caresses, she arched closer, accepting his penetrating tongue, dueling with her own. Tasting the wine he had sipped, she felt faint with wanting, intoxicated by his nearness, his minty scent and humbled by her need.

Tyler made growling noises as he kissed her with the sureness of a man who knew that kisses were not enough, not for him, and not for her. What they were doing, sharing, felt so right that she wanted to cry. But she couldn't concentrate on anything except him and the new sensations he created as he reclined on the sofa and pulled her down with him.

His ragged breathing combined with the ferocity of his kisses made her bolder still. She felt the press of his erection against her and ached for fulfillment. Finally she reached down between them, not sure where she got the nerve, and stroked his arousal through the fabric of his trousers as though she had done it a thousand times. And then suddenly she realized she had—in her dreams—and in another life. Somehow she had blocked those memories until now.

Free to revel in the feel of him, and her power to make him want more, she stroked, beginning to feel like a seductress. Beginning to feel like a bride.

His kisses turned wild, stimulating her beyond reason.

They undressed with hasty gestures as though their clothes couldn't be gotten rid of fast enough. He kissed her flesh as he bared it. She kissed him back, wanting to please him, taking pleasure in each touch, each stroke, each murmur, each caress.

When he stood naked before her, Catharine knew there was no stopping now. "You look magnificent."

"You look beautiful."

It came back in a flash. Every memory they had ever shared, sharp and clear, no longer murky and vague.

His eyes mirrored the agony she felt... for all the opportunities they had missed, for the ecstasy they might have shared.

"I'm sorry," she whispered. "I didn't remember everything before. If I had, I might not have been afraid."

He reached out, touched her cheek, caressing it lightly with her fingers. "I knew you would remember eventually."

His smile stirred her as much as his nakedness. A strange and wonderful heat throbbed through her. Passion soared, shooting her toward the sky when he gathered her close again.

After one lingering kiss, he pressed tiny fiery kisses all over her face, down her throat, over her collarbone, lower, to the sensitive valley between her breasts. Then, when she thought she could bear the wait no longer, he claimed one of her nipples with his seeking mouth. Vaguely she wondered why she hadn't wanted these glorifying sensations before.

The erotic foreplay stole her breath and made her gasp. She loved the way he caressed her, teased her breasts, tormented her nipples. Following his lead, she touched him and kissed him.

When he lowered his fingers and found her secret place, she panted and started to shake. He caressed the crevices. All of a sudden she felt like nothing except nerves. Vibrating. Waiting. Wanting. Needing.

Finally he lowered her onto the smooth velvet coverlet, his weight full upon her. Once again she felt his rigid shaft that had frightened her earlier. Now she welcomed his arousal, welcomed him as she had wanted to eons ago in another life. Why hadn't she remembered how glorious he could make her feel until now?

With her skin burning and his heated caresses tormenting her, she tried to catch her breath and couldn't. She trembled, on the brink of discovery and shook with urgency. In sweet anticipation, she arched her hips.

"It might hurt," he said, his voice thick with need.

"The waiting hurts," she moaned, wondering how she summoned the breath to speak.

Taut expectation rose within her. She waited, felt him probe, but didn't stiffen. Instead she welcomed him, inch by slow inch as he worked his way erotically in and out, keeping her body so tightly wound and excited that she felt her love juices flowing out to him, making the dance more sensual, more erotic.

After the initial pain, the fire he created sent flames spiraling up, spreading out in streams of liquid heat, pulsing through her, satisfying the need that she'd begun to fear could not be quenched. Her urgency peaked, demanded. She moved with him in a frenzy of wild abandon, clutching at his shoulders, his arms. Then she cried out in ecstasy as her world suddenly erupted into a thousand tiny stars.

Fulfillment came in a rush, penetrating her senses, making her feel vibrantly alive. The thrilling sensations tingled through every inch of her body, found their way out to her flesh, ran down her legs, up over her midriff, her breasts, her throat, her cheeks, her forehead.

For a long time she couldn't stop trembling, wondered if she should even try. It felt so delicious, so wonderful, so right. She smiled. At long last she felt like a wife.

Tyler lifted his head and smiled, then leaned closer and kissed her gently.

"Happy wedding night," she said, her voice scarcely more than a whisper.

"Welcome to my lair," he said. "This is where you belong now. Where I'd like you to sleep from now on."

She stifled a happy giggle. "On the sofa?"

"In my arms."

"I want that too, Tyler," she said, her voice serious. "I hated sleeping alone, without you, even for those few nights."

"But it's what we needed to do. It helped make you ready to share this."

She nodded agreement, then decided to confide in him. "I think I overcame my fear because Fey may have made some wishes come true."

"What wishes?"

"Before we wed, I wished that you would always want to kiss me. Please correct me if I'm wrong, but you always seemed to want that."

He nodded.

"A couple of times I wished for other things, and they happened, too. Then today I decided to wish for something big."

"What?"

"This. That I wouldn't be afraid. That I would please you. And that I would enjoy making love to you."

"You still have the fear of other men then?"

"I'm afraid I do."

"I suspect the fear of near rape never really goes away, but if we talk about it, perhaps that will help you deal with it."

She nodded, her heart full to overflowing. "Thank you for being so understanding."

"Thank you for being the love of my life." He smiled, tenderly, adding, "The love of all my lives."

A few minutes later, after her heart had calmed down a bit more, Tyler said, "I'm thirsty."

"Me, too."

They sat up. Each took another sip of wine. And Catharine took her time looking him over from head to toe. She admired his broad shoulders, his long, lean torso, his muscled arms and legs and chest.

"Do you like what you see?" he asked in a husky voice.

Feeling bashful and aroused again, she nodded, staring down at his bare thighs, lightly dusted with fine black hair, and his exquisite male anatomy that now intrigued her so.

Ty tilted her chin until their gazes locked. She wore nothing except jewelry—pearls, the earrings they had bought in Hawaii, the worry bead bracelet, and her wedding rings. He'd never before seen her face ablaze with such happiness. He wanted to see it often. Her wondrous eyes were lit with passion, glowing up at him as they had when he'd entered her. Her mere gaze made him rock hard. She'd trusted him and loved him far better than he had hoped to imagine. "I want you again."

"Right now?"

He nodded.

"I want you, too. If I'd known how good it would be, I wouldn't have been afraid. I'm sorry we wasted so much time."

"The time wasn't wasted, sweetheart. I might have been miserable, but you needed to get used to me. Used to the idea of sharing this." He kissed her then, and she responded as though she, like he, couldn't get enough. As soon as that kiss ended, he planted another hot one on her acquiescing mouth. Then he drew her firmly against his trembling body and caressed her flesh as though she were a finely tuned violin that responded only to her master's touch. With her arms wrapped around his neck, she pulled him closer and took her turn deepening the next kiss.

"I think it's time to try out my bed," he whispered.

"You shan't find me unwilling."

"Is that a promise?"

"Absolutely."

She laughed when he picked her up and headed for his room.

"No more separate beds, I hope," she ventured.

Tyler grinned. "Never again. We'll have a wake for the extra bed and celebrate getting rid of it."

Catharine winked, more laughter bubbling up from inside. "A wake? Sounds fun. But we could keep it for guests."

"I guess we could, but we'll celebrate anyway. And that's a promise I intend to keep."

~ * ~

Much later, Tyler said, "I'm surprised the phone hasn't rung."

Catharine pursed her lips to keep from grinning before she admitted, "I unplugged all of them while you were uncorking the wine. I turned my cell phone off, too."

He grinned. "I left mine in my case in the car. I think we're in for a sexy afternoon."

"I'd like to think you're right, but what about the office? Don't you have to return?"

Tyler moaned. "You're right. I guess I should go back for a few hours."

"I'm sorry I mentioned it. Maybe you could stay here and work twice as fast tomorrow."

"I like the way you think."

She smiled at his wolfish grin. "Maybe we should pretend we have a date tonight, and tomorrow, and stay home so we can do more of this."

"You deserve to go out on a real date." Ty felt guilty for something he hadn't even thought about until she'd mentioned the word date. Except for their dinner in Breckenridge and a few Saturday movies, he had never asked her to go out. He couldn't count the cocktail parties as dates because they had been for political reasons.

"I never courted you. I deprived you of a courtship."

"I don't feel deprived, and I really would prefer to stay right here."

"Here? In bed?"

She nodded. "Is there something wrong with wanting that?"

He chuckled. "No. Not a single thing."

She frowned. "Someone might disturb us."

"We won't answer the door."

"One of the telephones might ring."

"We'll unplug them every night. And turn our cell phones off. Make ourselves unavailable."

And that's exactly what they did. Every night for the rest of that week. And all weekend, too.

~ * ~

On Monday morning, Mack asked, "Did you have a nice weekend, son?"

"One of the best," Tyler said, grinning.

"What did you do?"

Still grinning, Tyler winked at Catharine. "That's a secret, Dad. Why? Did I miss something important?"

"No. But Catharine's grandparents called a couple of times. Once on Saturday, again yesterday. Guess they tried to get ahold of you, but you never answered any of your phones."

Worried about them and trying not to feel guilty for turning all the phones off, Catharine frowned. "I'll call them right now."

A few seconds later, she said, "Hi, Grandmother. How are you?"

"We're fine. How are you?"

"I'm fine. So is Tyler. Mack said you called. Is there anything in particular you wanted to discuss?"

"Yes."

"What?"

"We know you're not our granddaughter. We want to know where Kacy is. If you don't have a good explanation, we're calling the police."

Twenty

Catharine felt as though her heart had jumped up her throat to clog her air passage. "Could—we discuss—this later?"

"How much later?" Porter's gruff voice sounded annoyed.

Startled to hear him on the phone when Eileen had started the conversation, Catharine said, "Perhaps around one. When I get off work. I could come over then."

"We'd appreciate that. Please do. And bring Rachel and Mack with you."

"I'll try."

"What was that all about?" Tyler asked when she'd hung up.

"They—I—" she couldn't decide what to say, and decided on the truth, even if it created problems with his parents. She had intended to tell them and Kacy's grandparents eventually. Might as well be now.

"I'm not Kacy," she blurted. "And her grandparents apparently know I'm not. We switched places... and identities."

"We've suspected that for some time." Rachel crossed her arms, smiling.

Catharine's throat almost clogged again. "You have?"

Mack nodded, smiling as well. "We hoped, of course, that someday you would confide in us. Also that you and Kacy had a good reason for switching identities."

"How? When did you know?"

"Shortly after her trip to England with Jennifer," Mack said. "Kacy came back, then quite suddenly developed a British accent, and a much more shy demeanor. That surprised us, of course. Made us suspicious. But we decided if Jennifer trusted you, we had no reason to interfere."

"Kacy and Tyler were good friends," Rachel added, "but their friendship lacked the magic you two share. Mack and I were both surprised it took so long for you to get around to discovering you're in love."

"She avoided me," Tyler said, "because most men frighten her."

"You're not afraid of me, are you?" Mack asked, his dark brown busy eyebrows hiked in concern.

Stroking the worry beads, Catharine made a quick wish she would never be frightened of him again, and found herself honestly saying, "No. I'm not afraid of you."

"Where is Kacy?" Rachel assumed her attorney expression, and folded her arms again, taking her attorney stance.

Mack, too, seemed to tense while he waited for Catharine to reply.

Discomfited, her mind scrambled for a reply. "That's difficult to explain."

Rachel unfolded her arms, but didn't relax her rigid stance. "Why?"

"Because, look, I only want to explain this once." One of the things Catharine still had trouble with was calling people older than her by their first names, but she forced herself to say, "Porter and Eileen want to talk about this, and they'd like you two to come with me when I leave work."

"We'll be happy to accompany you," Rachel said. "We're interested in hearing about Kacy and where she is now."

Mack nodded agreement, and Tyler reached for Catharine's hand. From the love shining in his eyes, she knew he would support her in every way possible.

The foursome left the office as soon as the afternoon receptionist arrived. "We can all go in my car," Tyler said.

"Good idea," Mack agreed.

A few minutes later when Tyler pulled onto the road, Catharine asked, "Would you mind stopping at home so I can collect Kacy's journal? I think her grandparents might want to see it."

Tyler flashed a reassuring smile. "I'm sure they will."

Catharine grasped the worry beads and wished Rachel and Mack wouldn't make her explanation to Eileen and Porter difficult. That they would remain quiet and not use their legal expertise to drill her.

After they reached the Rose's home, Catharine sat beside Tyler on the sofa in the formal living room, rather than in the family room where they usually congregated. Eileen and Rachel sat across from them on the matching love seat. Porter and Mack remained standing, each behind their wives.

Without wasting time, Catharine looked across at Eileen and asked, "How did you know I'm not Kacy?"

Eileen shot Porter a triumphant look before she spoke. "You talk differently. You don't think like Kacy. You don't act like her either. And you haven't touched the trust fund since the accident."

Catharine resisted the urge to say, *'It isn't mine to touch.'* The elocution lessons Jennifer had urged her to take hadn't worked. Eileen and Tyler had both mentioned her British accent. "Would you mind telling me what made you decide I'm not Kacy?"

"You do look like her," Eileen said, "although you haven't acted like her for some time. We thought the accident was responsible, until a week or so ago when we both started having dreams that you're not Kacy."

Catharine swallowed. At least Mack and Rachel were doing as she'd wished. Not interfering, or bombarding her with their questions.

"What we really want to know," Porter said, "Is did Kacy die as a result of the accident in London two years ago? Is that why you decided you could get away with impersonating her?"

Catharine shook her head, not knowing whether to be relieved yet, or apprehensive. "Kacy and I switched places because she wanted to be where I was and I no longer wanted to be there."

"And where is that?" Rachel's question claimed Catharine's full attention.

"In England."

Her gaze as intent as if she were in court, questioning a witness on the stand, Rachel said, "Then we'll see her again?"

"I sincerely doubt that," Catharine disagreed.

Rachel's smile dissolved in a frown. "Why not?"

"Because Kacy lives in a different century."

"What?" Rachel, Mack, Eileen and Porter all shouted.

"She's living in the mid eighteen fifties," Catharine blurted.

"No way." A disbelieving frown crimped Rachel's face.

Mack looked a bit stunned. "That's too farfetched to believe."

Catharine glanced at Eileen and Porter. They too looked astounded. "While Kacy was in that two-week coma in the London hospital, her spirit traveled back to my time."

Both Eileen's and Porter's silvery brows shot up. "You cannot expect us to believe that poppycock," Eileen said.

"What do you mean, your time?" Porter asked.

"I was born in Kent, England, in eighteen thirty-seven. A little over two years ago I switched places with Kacy so she could return there, to be with the man she loves." Catharine reached inside her backpack and pulled Kacy's journal out. "The details are all in here."

Eileen hiked her brows. "What is that?"

"Kacy's journal. One of the reasons Tyler and I flew to England in February. Kacy left it in a bank vault so I could obtain it. I'm using it to write her story. I intended to tell you eventually so you would understand the story. The journal should help convince you. I apologize for deceiving you, but I promised Kacy I'd treat you as my grandparents, and she promised to treat my mother as her own. However," Catharine's voice shook a little, "when Kacy went to see Mother, she was no longer in Kent. I heard she might be in this time and that I might see her again some day. And then I did."

No one said a word. Eileen, Porter, Rachel and Mack merely stared at Catharine as though she'd lost her mind. The air was so quiet and still, a dropped pin could have been heard.

Tyler draped his arm around Catharine's shoulders. She leaned against him for comfort and support.

"I think we should call the police," Porter said, his tone gruff, his eyes full of distrust.

"That won't bring Kacy back," Tyler said. "And what would you have Catharine charged with?"

Porter frowned as though he expected Tyler to help them, not side against them.

Ty raised a hand to ward off any such suggestion. "Don't expect me to do anything that might hurt my wife. She never said she was Kacy, did she?"

Eileen and Porter both started to nod, then shook their heads. "Don't remember," Porter said.

"Actually she insisted on being called Catharine, even made the legal change," Ty said.

"Guess she did," Eileen conceded, before she pressed her pink lips in a thin, straight line.

"And she worked to support herself and hasn't used a cent of Kacy's trust fund."

"Maybe we can't expose you," Porter conceded, "but even if we were to believe what you have just told us, I don't understand when the switch was made or how. Kacy seemed to be herself when she came out of that coma in London."

"That was Kacy," Catharine said. "We didn't switch places until a couple of months later. It's all in here." She held up the journal. "You will recognize her handwriting, won't you?"

"Yes."

"Of course."

"Then please read this. Afterwards if you have more questions, I'll be happy to try to answer them."

Catharine leaned forward and laid the journal on the square coffee table between them.

Porter glared at Tyler. "How long have you known she isn't Kacy?"

"I knew in February."

"How did you discover the truth?" Mack spoke alone for the first time.

"Catharine told me. At first I didn't believe her, because like all of you, I thought her tale too preposterous to be true."

"What made you change your mind?" his mother asked.

"I saw a video Jennifer made that explained. Then too, the way Catharine responds to me is unique. Kacy never responded favorably. Now I know why."

Porter frowned. "Why?"

"Because Kacy loves another man. And the answers you want are in her journal. I understand you might be concerned about foul play, but please believe me, there was none. Kacy switched places with Catharine of her own volition."

"How? People can't just jump here from the past or travel back there without some sort of miraculous help."

"Kacy's guardian angel facilitated the switch," Catharine said.

Eileen and Porter exchanged disbelieving glances. Rachel and Mack did the same.

"Do you believe any of this?" Porter demanded, frowning at Mack.

He didn't reply, merely held Porter's angry stare.

"We told them this morning," Tyler said. "Like you, I'm sure they'll have a difficult time believing the time travel part, although they already knew Catharine isn't Kacy. We have more to tell you, but perhaps we should wait until you've read Kacy's journal."

Eileen opened the journal to the first page. Tears sparkled in her silvery blue eyes. "This is Kacy's handwriting, Porter."

He turned his frown to Catharine, his posture stiff, his voice gruff. "We appreciate your coming to see us even if we can't believe your trumped up tale."

The tears in Eileen's eyes spilled over onto her wrinkled cheeks. "I miss Kacy."

"I miss her, too," Catharine said.

"How could you?" Eileen cried. "If you came from the past, you didn't know her."

"I dreamed about her long before I met her. Then after we met, I stayed with her for a few days in the past. When we parted I felt as though I'd lost a dear friend. I felt like that when she decided to switch places with me as well. Thankfully, I had Jennifer at the time to help me adjust to this century."

"But now Jennifer's dead," Eileen wailed. "Children and grand-children are not supposed to precede their parents and grandparents in death."

Aching to comfort her, Catharine said, "Jennifer isn't dead. She's in the past. With Kacy. And when I finish writing Kacy's story, I plan to write Jennifer's."

Although Rachel remained seated, shaking her head, Eileen jumped to her feet with a liveliness that belied her advanced age. "What kind of preposterous tale are you spinning now, young lady?"

Before Catharine could comment, Porter cut in. "First you have the audacity to tell us that Kacy asked you to switch places with her so she could leave this century and travel back in time. Now you want us to believe the same is true of Jennifer? That she didn't die in that car crash in January?"

Eileen and Porter's faces were red, their voices strained. Catharine curled her fingers around the worry beads and made a quick wish that they would calm down and believe her. "I didn't mean to upset you more. I wanted to comfort you. And I thought telling you that Kacy and Jennifer are both alive and living in the same time period would make you happy. I'd expected you'd be pleased with the news. Would you rather they be dead?"

"As far as we're concerned, they..." Porter stopped. A smile replaced his frown. "You're absolutely right, Catharine. We should be happy they're alive and together, even if I cannot comprehend how they can be. They should have been dead for years if they've truly gone to live in the past."

"That's something I can't explain," Catharine said. "I haven't a clue what makes it possible."

Rachel stood up and assumed what Catharine considered her attorney stance again. "You're teasing us, aren't you?"

Catharine shook her head.

Rachel began to pace.

"It's true, Mom and Dad," Tyler said.

"How do you know?" Rachel stopped pacing and frowned at him. "Don't try to tell us you traveled to the past and saw Kacy and Jennifer. We aren't buying that cock and bull story."

"I wouldn't tell you anything that isn't true. The girl we buried in January wasn't Jennifer."

"What?" Rachel shrieked, looking astounded.

Mack looked astonished, too. "Who was she then?"

"A girl from the past who knew Catharine. A wizard brought her to this time and he took Jennifer back to the nineteenth century. She's happy there and so is Kacy. They're both married to the men they love."

Rachel latched onto Mack's arm, and sputtered, "Jennifer is with Dirk?"

Tyler nodded. "Only now his name is Drake and he's a duke and Jennifer's a duchess."

Rachel stumbled back to the love seat and sat down. Mack lowered himself onto a chair as though he'd just received a blow to the head and couldn't tolerate moving fast.

"This is all too incredible to believe." Mack looked from Catharine to Tyler. "Did you buy both of these stories about Kacy and Jennifer, hook, line and sinker, Ty?"

Tyler shook his head. "No. I saw Jennifer in England before she went to the nineteenth century for the second time. That's the real reason I flew to England with Catharine in February. Jennifer had Kacy's journal and she gave it to Catharine so she could write Kacy's story. Jennifer also told us all about her five months in the past. As Catharine mentioned, she intends to write Jennifer's story when she finishes Kacy's."

Rachel put her right hand on her throat. Her eyes a bit glazed, she sputtered, "Catharine really intends to write Jennifer's story after she finishes Kacy's?"

Tyler and Catharine nodded.

His frown still in place, Mack asked, "Do you have any physical evidence?"

Tyler shook his head. "Sorry. No material proof. Only our word. And Catharine's memory of what life was like before she came here."

"We still have the VCR tape Jennifer made," Catharine said. "I wish you'd watch it and believe what we've told you."

Rachel and Mack perked up, their eyes as surprised as when they'd had doubts. "I do believe you," Rachel said. "For the life of me I can't figure out why, but I believe everything you've said is true."

Mack nodded. "I'm sure you have nothing to gain by telling such an unbelievable story, yet I find that I believe you as well." He grinned then. "Perhaps some night soon you can tell us about life as you knew it before you came to our time."

"And show us that VCR tape you mentioned," Rachel added.

"We'd like to see the tape as well," Porter said.

"We'd love to show it to all of you." Catharine smiled, grateful that two more wishes had come true. Eileen, Porter, Rachel and Mack believed her. Catharine resisted the urge to look around and see if Fey was there. But in her heart she believed the fairy's help had won all of them over.

"In the meantime, I want to hear all about Jennifer," Eileen said, drawing everyone's attention. "Who was that girl Rachel and Mack buried, if not her? Come, you can tell us while we eat. I made sandwiches and a pasta salad. You must be hungry. It's past lunchtime. You will join us, won't you?"

"We'd be delighted." Tyler winked at Catharine, and as soon as Porter, Eileen, and his parents headed toward the kitchen, he whispered, "Did you make a wish that they would all believe you?"

"Yes."

"Smart girl. Why didn't you do it sooner?"

Catharine shrugged. "Because I didn't think of it. Even when I did, I thought they deserved explanations and answers to their questions."

Tyler squeezed her hand. Catharine smiled as they strolled to the kitchen, delighted she had the nerve and the right to touch him whenever she wished.

Looking around, believing Fey must be nearby and had granted the wishes she had finally thought to make, Catharine reminded herself to thank the fairy the next time she presented herself in the flesh. Every time she thought about Fey, Catharine remembered the wand. She slid her hand inside her pocket and stroked the four golden inches she never let out of her reach. She had passed the hurtle of explaining to Rachel, Mack, Eileen and Porter. She had yet to deal with Dillon McKenzie and Wilbur.

But she would also have the exciting pleasure of introducing her mother to these people who were near and dear to her heart.

<h1 style="text-align:center">*Twenty-one*</h1>

Tyler's life turned hectic. The campaign and election loomed ahead. He stopped being at the office every morning, and wasn't always around to drive Catharine home. Rachel and Mack took turns driving her, but Catharine hated putting them out.

Sloan hadn't been in the office for over a week, not since the day Catharine had wished a pox on her face. The day she and Tyler had finally consummated their wedding vows. Catharine didn't miss Sloan. Apparently no one else did either. Rachel had hired two legal temps and they were doing a credible job of helping to get things caught up.

One day, at home after lunch, Catharine couldn't write because she couldn't concentrate. The walls of the apartment felt as though they were closing in on her. For the first time in her life she felt trapped in a cage, like a bird that had never learned to fly.

I need to do something.

But what?

You could learn how to drive. Then you wouldn't be dependent on Tyler or his parents.

That made sense. She had money. Although most of the lottery check had been invested, she had placed a huge sum in a liquid money market fund so she could buy a house for Eileen and Porter in Arizona. There should be plenty left to buy a new car for herself. But first she needed to learn how to drive.

Hurrying back to her computer, Catharine connected to the Internet, and looked up Denver automobile instructors. She called one named Harry Peabody.

"When do you want to start?" he asked after she explained she needed lessons.

"As soon as possible."

"I had a couple of cancellations this afternoon."

"That's excellent. I'll take both."

"Can you be here by three o'clock?"

"No. I don't drive. Can't you come to my apartment?"

"I could, but it'll cost more."

"How much more?"

"Ten dollars."

"That's within my budget," she said, trying to sound like she lived with one.

"I'll meet you outside, in front of your apartment building."

As good as his word, Harry showed up precisely at three o'clock. "Are you Mrs. Catharine Quinlane?" he asked after he parked by the curb and rolled the window down.

"Yes. You must be Mr. Harry Peabody."

"I am."

"Good." She had made sure the gold wand was in her pocket and she rubbed the worry beads when she wished she wouldn't be afraid of him. Notebook and pen in hand, Catharine climbed in the passenger seat.

Harry grinned. "You should be behind the steering wheel, Mrs. Quinlane."

"I'm not ready for that yet. You see I'm from England, and I've never driven. I need to learn everything from the very beginning. I'm afraid I'm not even familiar with the parts of an automobile."

"All right." He grinned again. "We'll start with basics. This is the steering wheel, and this is the ignition."

She felt a flush run up her cheeks. "Thank you."

"And this is how you turn the engine on."

A couple of hours later, after she'd driven all the way around one block, and felt very proud of her accomplishment, she said, "When can I have my next lesson?"

"Tomorrow, if you'd like."

"I would. Same time?"

He nodded. "You want to meet here again?"

"Yes, please."

"It'll cost an extra ten dollars and I'll only have time for one lesson."

"That will be fine." Catharine opened her backpack and paid him for her first two sessions.

She was so excited, she wanted to tell Tyler. But she decided to keep it a secret and surprise him instead. Her wish, that she wouldn't fear Harry, had worked and with the wand in her pocket she felt safe from Wilbur and Dillon.

~ * ~

After her second lesson Harry extended a driver's handbook. "Read and study this. I'll be asking questions to see if you do your homework."

"I will," she promised, smiling.

For the next fortnight Harry gave her lessons every weekday. He drilled her verbally. Taught her how to maneuver the car and tutored her when she couldn't remember something she'd read in the handbook.

Delighted with her progress and her secret, Catharine decided she must tell Tyler... soon. But not until she had a little more confidence.

~ * ~

Ty knew something was going on with Catharine. Something she was trying to hide. He started to call her every afternoon. She never answered the apartment phone or her cell phone.

On Friday, he left work early and saw her getting out of a strange car as he drove by the apartment complex. He felt a little betrayed. She'd promised not to go anywhere without first telling him. He also felt disgusted. The guy dropping her off didn't even have the decency to get out and open the car door for her.

Instead of proceeding to the underground parking garage, Ty parked in an empty visitor's space, and raced into the high rise lobby. He confronted Catharine as she walked through the front door.

"Tyler." She smiled. "You're home early. How wonderful."

"Who the hell is that guy?"

"His name is Harry Peabody. Good old English name, isn't it?"

Frowning at her smile and the glow twinkling in her eyes, Ty demanded, "What were you doing with him?"

"I can't tell you." She winked impishly. "It's a secret."

He clasped her arm and marched her to the elevator. "The hell you can't," he growled as soon as they stepped inside, out of earshot of the people mulling in the lobby.

Catharine looked startled. "You're not jealous, are you?"

"No," he lied.

"Good. You have no reason to be. Harry's happy."

"What about?"

"I mean delighted."

"Is that so?"

"Sorry." She scratched her forehead. "I mean gay. He has no interest in me. He's only interested in men."

"Then I'll repeat my question," Tyler said, confused. "What the hell were you doing with him?"

The twinkle in her eyes faded. "Must I tell you?"

"Yes!"

"I'm taking driving lessons."

Ty could hardly believe his ears. "What?" His loud question reverberated like thunder in the hollow metal elevator.

"I said I'm taking driving lessons."

"Why?"

"So I needn't be so dependent on you, or your parents. It must be terribly annoying for you to have to drive me everywhere I go, and I really don't want to use taxicabs." She smiled again, her expression hopeful. "But now that you know my secret, will you help me buy a car?"

Ty didn't know whether to be pleased or stay furious. On one hand he was proud she'd taken the initiative to learn how to drive. On the other, he felt less needed, and very concerned about her safety. "You promised you wouldn't go out without telling me."

She had the grace to blush. "I know, but Fey gave me a magic wand to protect me from Wilbur and Dillon. And meeting Harry Peabody, and taking lessons, has proven that I've grown beyond my fear of strange men."

Almost at a loss for words, Ty grumbled, "What kind of car do you want?"

"I haven't a clue. I was counting on you to help me make that decision."

"We'll go look at cars tomorrow, if you'd like."

She threw her arms around him and hugged him fiercely. "Oh, Tyler, thank you, thank you." She planted kisses all over his face, and he was too stunned to do anything except enjoy all the attention.

When the elevator stopped, she stopped too, but she didn't look as though she wanted to do so. Ty grinned. "Feel free to touch and kiss me any time you please."

Not long ago each touch had been torture. Each pulling away sheer hell. Now it was only a prelude to what would follow.

Inside their apartment a few minutes later, Ty shut the door and gathered her close. No matter how often they made love, each time still felt new and exciting. He kissed her deeply, passionately. And she responded as she always did, with eager enthusiasm.

~ * ~

By Saturday night they had visited more than a dozen car lots and Catharine felt more confused than ever. Back home in their living room, too keyed up to sit still, she paced in front of the dark TV. "How can I make a choice from all those cars? There are too many to choose from."

"Don't think about them for a while," Ty suggested, tossing his keys onto the coffee table. "We'll go look again next weekend, or maybe one night this week."

"Okay. Thanks for taking me browsing today. It was fun, if confusing."

Ty grinned wickedly. "You know how you can really thank me, Cath?"

"Yes, I know." She smiled, striding close, wrapping her arms around his neck and urging his willing mouth down to hers.

Clearly he enjoyed kissing. So did she. His mouth was firm. Demanding. Possessive. Perfect.

She opened to his questing tongue as a flower would to the warm, welcome sun. The kisses made her knees feel weak. Had Tyler not held her close, she might have fallen to the floor.

Her breath came out in a quiet sigh. She loved what he did with his lips, his tongue and hands. How feminine he made her feel. She moaned, low and deeply. What erotic sensations he evoked. She longed for satisfaction, but he seemed to be in no hurry.

He caressed her back, her shoulders, her arms. A tremor of need made her throat and breasts quiver, and he hadn't even touched them.

Tyler tugged her red blouse loose from the waistband of her black skirt. Sweet anticipation made her shiver. She ran her hands down his back, up over his powerful shoulders, across his arms, up to his cheeks, hoping he enjoyed her caresses as much as she enjoyed his.

He forged a trail of kisses down her throat, his hands busy with the red buttons on her silk blouse. Seconds later, he teased her nipples through her lacy black bra. They turned to rigid nubs, aching to be released from their confinement, yearning for more attention.

Tyler didn't disappoint her. He unfastened her bra, cupped her breasts, lowered his mouth to suckle first one, then the other.

Trembling with need, Catharine fumbled with the buttons on his shirt, impatient for him to remove his clothes. Still he took his time, drawing out their pleasure, giving her breasts all the attention they craved.

Breathing raggedly, she tugged his long-sleeved shirt off, kissing his shoulders, his chest, giving his nipples the same treatment he had given hers.

His breath sounded labored. Delighted that she could make him pant, she whispered, "Let's get rid of our clothes."

"In due time," he murmured, claiming her lips in another soul stirring kiss.

Finally, after what seemed a lifetime, they were both naked. Tyler's gaze flicked over her like a molten flame. "Have you any idea how lovely you are?"

His voice, low, masculine, deep and husky, sent shimmers of pleasure cascading across her flesh. With a gentle shake of her head, she asked, "Have you any idea how magnificent you are?"

He smiled, a slow, sexy smile, and nodded. "I feel magnificent with you, Cath. Only with you." He claimed her lips again, lowering her to the sofa, positioning himself close beside her.

His love play drew moans of pleasure from her. Adrift on a sea of sensuality, she marveled at the glorious things he did to her. Wanting to give him as much pleasure as he gave her, she followed instinct, fondled him, caressing his flesh, stroking his erection.

With a groan, he finally positioned her atop him. "Tonight you ride me." He slipped inside her. And thrust.

Catharine followed his lead, meeting each trust with one of her own. And then she went wild, thrashing and thrashing, unable to stop. The pressure built until she thought she might explode.

And then she did, in a thousand tiny flashes of light.

Tyler held her tight, while their bodies convulsed. And then he loosened his hold, slightly. "I love you, Cath."

"I love you too, Ty."

Sheer bliss transformed her from a mere mortal who had known and lost her love in many lives, to a reincarnated being who knew she now dwelt with her immortal soul mate. Nothing equaled what she felt. Nothing could be more splendid.

Reaching for something to cover them, Tyler found her full skirt. He lifted it off the floor. The small wand fell out of the pocket.

He picked it up, staring at the slim golden stick. "What's this?"

"The magic wand Fey gave me to protect me from Dillon and Wilbur. I take it everywhere I go."

Tyler hiked his brows, his grey-green eyes glinting as he teased. "Everywhere?"

Catharine blushed. "Well, everywhere except to bed."

"We don't need any magic there." He smiled, wickedly. "We make magic of our own."

"Yes, we do."

~ * ~

Sloan still hadn't been in the office. No one knew why. Only that she called in sick every morning. On Monday she showed up an hour late.

"Look at me," she spat the instant she strode through the front door. Catharine couldn't help but look. Sloan's face was covered with ugly red marks that were scabbing. She looked truly awful.

"Did you put a hex on me? Are you some kind of freaking witch?"

"That's enough," Mack said, coming to Catharine's rescue as he walked out of the photocopy room, a mug of coffee in hand.

"I've been to doctors, skin specialists, even to the hospital and no one can get rid of this."

"You can't blame Catharine for your malady," Mack reasoned.

Catharine inhaled, quietly. She liked having her father-in-law stick up for her.

Sloan flicked a glance at her, then turned her attention back on Mack. "She said she wished a pox on my face and the minute she said that my cheek started to itch."

"Catharine isn't a witch. It's probably your meanness coming out to spite you," Ty said, joining them to see what the ruckus was all about.

His mother had come to the lobby, too. "I think it's time for you to clean your desk out, Sloan. We agreed that if you didn't work out here, you would leave quietly."

"If I leave, I'll sue you."

"I wouldn't advise that," Mack said. "I have a number of the snide comments you've made to Catharine on tape."

The red scabs on Sloan's face turned purple. Ty hadn't thought that possible.

"And I have your signed agreement that you would leave without recompense if your trial employment didn't work out," Rachel added.

Sloan shot Catharine a venomous glare. "You'll regret taking Tyler away from me."

"I was never yours to lose." Ty wrapped his arm protectively around Catharine's shoulders.

She smiled up at him. Now she felt as though she truly belonged in the Quinlane family.

"Thank you," she said after Sloan marched to her office with Rachel following.

Tyler squeezed Catharine's shoulder, smiling down at her. "I'm sure we'll all be happier without her."

Catharine did something that surprised even her. She arched up on her toes and kissed his cheek while his father watched. "I love you."

Tyler smiled as well. "I know you do. I love you, too."

Her heart threatened to turn over. As far as she was concerned, her life was perfect. More perfect than she could ever have imagined or dared to wish. If not for the fear of Wilbur showing up without warning, and the fear that Dillon McKenzie's trial might go awry, she would have no worries at all.

When those problems were taken care of, they would be happy beyond her wildest dreams. She finally felt that in her bones as well as in her heart and soul.

Guilt descended after Mack and Tyler returned to their respective offices. Catharine felt sure her pox wish had created Sloan's rash. If so, she wished it would clear up. She fingered the worry beads, and stroked the wand, while she made that silent wish. Although she disliked Sloan, she had no wish to ruin her complexion. At least as long as she stayed out of their lives. And left Tyler alone.

About ten minutes later, after she'd apparently cleaned her desk out, Sloan stormed through the reception area. Rachel was still with her.

Sloan opened the front door, then turned and spat at Catharine, "You're the one who's going to regret meeting me."

"Don't let the door hit you on your way out," Rachel said in a mild tone.

Sloan glared at Catharine, but didn't speak again. The door slammed behind her. A shudder bolted through Catharine. Had that glare been a threat? Did she now have more than Wilbur and Dillon to worry about?

Twenty-two

"Pull over to the curb." Without his usual smile, which Catharine thought odd, Harry Peabody pointed to a spot in front of a strange house on Kearney.

"Why?" she asked, concerned. Today he hadn't smiled once. He'd been somber throughout the entire driving session. Did I do something wrong?"

"No. You've come a long way, Mrs. Quinlane. You're now an excellent driver."

"Is there something wrong with the car?"

"No. The car's fine and I'm confident you'll pass your driving test with no problem."

Catharine's mood soared as she signaled, braked to a stop near the rounded curb that had no sidewalk, and shifted into park. This was her last driving lesson. She had her learning permit, and Tyler made sure she got lots of driving practice. Now she felt confident enough to drive almost anywhere by herself. If not for the threat of seeing Dillon or Wilbur, she would feel as free as a bird. The ability to drive was a liberating experience.

She smiled at Harry. "Thanks for your patience and all you've taught me."

"You're welcome," he said, "and good luck."

"Thanks." Thinking he seemed nervous, she set the brake, and collected her backpack to pay him.

To her utter surprise, someone yanked the door open from outside. A frisson of fear whipped up her back. She looked up. Dillon McKenzie towered above her.

"Get out," he ordered.

She didn't because she couldn't move. Except to turn her head to stare at Harry. Her nerves atwitter, her heart sank. She recognized the look in his eyes. Betrayal.

"I said get out," Dillon growled again.

The only thing to fear is fear itself, she reminded herself as she slid her hand into her pocket, planning to use the wand as protection. But before she could clasp the wand, Dillon latched onto her arm and jerked her from the car.

Catharine stumbled, righted herself, closed her fingers around the four-inch wand. To her horror, Dillon slid his hand inside her pocket too, wrapped his fat fingers over hers and squeezed until the small wand snapped in two.

Shock jolted through her.

"Did you really expect that useless stick to help you?" He wrestled the broken wand from her pocket, and flung the two pieces over the top of Harry's car.

Scared out of her wits without the wand to protect her, Catharine glanced frantically at the houses lining both sides of Kearney. Not a soul in sight. The only car was parked on the street across from them. Was that Dillon's?

Holding both her arms with one hand, he jabbed something sharp against her rib cage. A knife!

Terror exploded inside her. Did he intend to rape her? Or did he mean to kill her?

She shot her gaze back to Harry, still seated on the passenger side of his car. His tortured eyes held regret. She wanted to shout at him to help her. But Harry had set her up. He wouldn't help.

"I have your mother," Dillon growled. "If you don't come with me, she's dead."

Mother? Dead? The words echoed through Catharine's fevered brain. Part of her knew Dillon could be lying.

But she'd expected something like this to happen. Had felt it in her bones. If only his trial date hadn't taken so long to get on the court calendar. He should already be behind bars. But he was here and he intended to make her suffer.

She would have screamed but her throat felt too dry, too paralyzed. She shuddered and tried to speak. Her voice sounded like a frog's croak. "Where is Mother?"

"I'll tell you later."

"If I don't go home, Tyler will know something's happened. He'll call the police."

"No he won't. He'll try to rescue you on his own. But he won't succeed." Dillon's ugly sneer sent a blast of his bad breath straight to her nose. Her stomach recoiled.

Dillon shoved the knife closer, deeper into her flesh. Catharine felt warm blood trickling down her cold, sweaty side.

"Let's go," Dillon snorted.

Alarm scooted up Catharine's spine and froze her heart, but not her thoughts. *How could she escape?*

"And don't try to get away." Dillon snarled his threat.

His snarl reminded Catharine of Wilbur. The thought came so suddenly, it chilled her to the bone. "You're Wilbur, aren't you?"

He laughed, an ugly sound. "So you finally made the connection. I was beginning to think you never would."

Dillon, the pompous, troublesome ex co-worker is also Wilbur, my step-papa from the past! Panic set her skin on fire.

Fear and fury blasted her mind. Tyler wouldn't know she was in trouble until he got home from work. Would she ever see him again in this life? She couldn't bear to believe they had shared all they were meant to share. She wanted more. A whole lifetime more.

"Come on." Wilbur tightened his hold and dragged her toward the car parked across from them. Catharine's fear turned to stark terror. She fought him. The worry bead bracelet got hooked on something and came loose, clattering softly on the ground. A hundred wishes flashed through her mind, but before she could form a single coherent one, Wilbur shoved a handkerchief in front of her nose. To her horror she inhaled something sickeningly sweet and noxious.

He swept her up off her feet. Then her world went blank.

~ * ~

Seated behind his desk at work, reading a contract for a new real estate client, Tyler's whole body jerked when he heard a voice say, *::Catharine's in trouble.::*

Not a voice, a telepathic message from Jennifer in the past; his cousin, who possessed the gift of sight. *::Catharine's been abducted. She's unconscious, and being lifted out of the back of a black, sporty car. It looks like she's being carried inside a motel room.::*

Tyler jumped to his feet, grabbed his cell phone and dialed Catharine's number. The phone rang and rang but no one answered.

He sucked in a ragged breath, and forced his mind to clear, concentrating on telecommunicating with Jennifer. *::Do you know where Catharine is? The name of the street? Or the name of the motel? Anything at all?::*

::No. Nothing yet. But I'll stay tuned in. If I see anything else, I'll let you know.

Thanks. I'll tune back in after I call the police.::

Ty turned his cell phone back on. Before he could dial 911, his office phone rang. He snatched the receiver. "Hello."

"Tyler Quinlane?" a deep, male voice asked.

The kidnapper? Ty thrust his panic aside. Forced himself to answer calmly. "Yes."

"This is Sergeant Mason with the Denver Police. We have a man in custody who says your wife has been abducted."

"What's his name?"

"Harry Peabody."

"That's my wife's driving instructor. She had a driving lesson set up with him today."

"Harry said he didn't know the other man's name, but he'd threatened him and his family if he didn't cooperate and help him get your wife. Do you know anyone who might want to abduct her?"

"Yes. Dillon McKenzie." Tyler explained the break-in, Dillon's subsequent arrest, and posting bail. Then he asked, "Did Harry Peabody tell you what happened?"

"Yes," the sergeant said. "In addition, two different parties from the same Kearney neighborhood called. Each one reported seeing a man force a woman out of a car, and drag her to another car at knife-point. Fortunately the witnesses wrote down the license plates of both vehicles. That's how we found Harry Peabody."

"Have you found the other car? The one my wife might be in?"

"Not yet, but we're looking. Sometimes abductors head out of town as fast as possible. More often than not, though, they hide out nearby and send a ransom note."

"Dillon isn't after money."

"What is he after?"

"I told you. He tried to rape my wife. I think he must be crazy. He can't be dumb enough not to know that kidnapping her will land him in prison."

"If he's caught," Sergeant Mason said in a grim tone. "Can you give us a description?"

"Yes."

Twenty-three

Catharine awakened in a room that was pitch black except for a small sliver of light between what she assumed must be drapes covering a window. Lying on a mattress with her hands and ankles tied to what appeared to be bedposts, she decided she must be in a motel.

She'd been gagged. The cloth tasted awful, smelled terrible, too. She forced the bile that climbed up her throat back down. A blanket covered her, but she was still fully dressed, even had her shoes on. Thank goodness.

Clenching her fists, she wished Wilbur, alias Dillon McKenzie, would disappear off the face of the earth. Then she wished she was back home with Tyler, safe and sound.

Nothing happened.

She wished she knew where she was.

That wish didn't come true either. She hadn't really expected it to without the worry beads or the wand.

Still, she wished she knew where her mother was.

She wished she could get free, away from Dillon.

Again, nothing changed.

Without the beads and the wand, every wish seemed to be countered by a higher power. Recalling the wizard who had made Jennifer's life miserable, Catharine wondered if an otherworldly being was playing havoc with hers.

How could the wand have broken? It was magic and supposed to protect her. And where was Fey?

Determined not to give up hope, Catharine wished she could communicate with Tyler through mental telepathy. She knew he'd been telecommunicating with Jennifer since February. *Am I capable of mental telepathy?* After several attempts, it appeared she wasn't.

In the solitary dark, she felt so alone. Her throat clogged, tears streaming down her cheeks. Everything seemed utterly futile. Her whole world had gone haywire.

Full of doubts, she turned her head to stare at the slender sliver of light across the room. Tears slid off her face, down onto the bed. An ocean of regret pulsed through her. Would she ever see Tyler again? Was their love as hopeless as it was timeless?

After a while, Catharine swallowed and summoned hope again. Surely her fairy godmother would know she was in danger and come to her aid. "I wish I could see or talk to you, Fey," she mumbled around the awful gag.

Above the bed a tiny light blinked on and off, then stabilized. In the inky dark, Catharine saw the two inch fairy flapping her tiny wings in slow motion, while holding onto a lighted match stick as though it were a life-saving torch.

"Fey," Catharine breathed through the gag, hardly daring to believe her eyes.

"You summoned me." The fairy sounded breathless.

Catharine nodded vigorously. The spirited movement dislodged the gag. It wasn't tied, just stuffed in her mouth. She forced it further away with her teeth and tongue, then had to force bile back down. "Oh Fey, I desperately need your help."

"Why?"

"I've been abducted by Dillon McKenzie, who is also Wilbur. I don't know where I am. Tyler expected me to be home. He's probably frantic with worry."

The fairy blinked several times. Finally she said, "I cannot decipher what Tyler thinks. I only know that Wilbur also abducted your mother."

Catharine didn't know whether to be relieved or more upset. "Is she—Mother here?"

The fairy shook her blonde-haired head. "No. She's locked in a motel room on the other side of town."

"Do you know where this room is located?"

Fey nodded. "On Colorado Boulevard."

Catharine's heartbeat sped up. The smelly gag, although no longer in her mouth, was still so close, she feared she might retch. The taste in her mouth was vile. "May I see Mother? Can you take me there, wherever she is?"

"At the moment, no."

"Why?"

"I've been in the past. It takes time for me to recover from time traveling. Also, something bad happened. For several hours in time there was no magic anywhere on earth, nowhere in the world. During that fiasco, I was injured by another worldly creature. One who doesn't like fairies. I must recover. Restore my strength before I use more magic."

"Oh, Fey, I'm sorry," Catharine sympathized, disgusted with herself for being so self-centered and not thinking about the fairy's welfare. "Will you be all right?"

"Eventually, yes. In the meantime your mother is resting for the first time since Wilbur abducted her. You should sleep while it's dark. And I must rest as well."

The fairy waved the match out. Plunged back in total darkness, Catharine fought her fear. Was she alone again?

"Where is the wand I gave you?"

Catharine nearly cried in relief. Fey was still with her. "Dillon—

Wilbur found it, snapped it in two and tossed it away when he first abducted me."

"That must have happened while magic was dead."

Catharine swallowed, convulsively. "Do you know where Wilbur is?"

"Yes." The fairy sighed. "He's playing poker with a bunch of cronies in the room next door. Don't worry, he won't bother you for a while. He expects you to sleep through the night."

In the meager light slanting through the slit drapes, Catharine saw the fairy close her eyes wearily. "I must rest now, or I'll be no good to myself, or anyone else come morning. Try to rest. Tomorrow may bring more chaos than you've ever faced before."

"Do you think you could untie my hands?"

"Not yet. I haven't the strength."

Appalled by her selfish thoughts, Catharine said. "I'll be quiet now so you can rest." Still tied to the bed spread-eagled, she lay in the dark, her thoughts on Tyler. Somehow she had to communicate with him. Staring up at the black ceiling, she twisted her body, trying to get more comfortable.

"You should rest," Fey admonished, even though Catharine could barely see her.

Too upset to try, Catharine asked, "Fey, will you stay with me?"

"Of course, sweetling. At least until the miscreant meets his future."

"What does that mean?"

Fey coughed, quietly. "For all the good and wonderful things in the universe, there will always be opposing forces. Bad and evil." She sounded as though she had to force the words out. "Do you understand what I'm trying to convey?"

Catharine nodded in the dark, sensing Fey saw her. "Mankind and all who dwell on earth will always have choices. Whether to be good and kind, or corrupt and evil."

"Precisely. Now, let me rest. I shall not desert you. By morning my magic may be restored. If not, we could be in a heap of trouble."

With all her heart and soul, Catharine hoped Fey's magic would return. Too keyed up to sleep, she lay in the dark wondering what the dawn would bring.

Throughout the long hours left of the night, she focused on trying to communicate telepathically with Tyler.

::Tyler, please hear me,:: she pleaded. *::Please tune in. I'm in trouble. I need you. Dillon abducted me. He abducted Mother too, but I'm not with her. Fey's here, but she's been injured so her magic won't work yet. She says Mother's in a different motel across town. Please help me, Tyler. Tell me what to do. My wishes aren't working. I need you.::*

Over and over again, Catharine repeated her thoughts, praying Tyler heard them.

Near dawn, she thought she might have succeeded when she heard Tyler's voice in her head. *::Don't panic, Cath. Try to concentrate on where you are so I can find you. Concentrate hard and remember this, I'm on my way and I will find you. Keep your mind open so we can communicate.::*

Catharine heaved a huge sigh of relief. Tyler knew she was in trouble. And he would come. Not for a minute did she doubt that. She only hoped he arrived before it was too late.

::I love you, Cath. Remember that. Now concentrate on your surroundings. I'm on my way. I have a feeling you're east of our apartment. Give me some clues so I can locate you.::

Buoyed up by that telepathic message, Catharine sent one back. *::Fey said I'm on Colorado Boulevard.::*

::I heard you. Colorado Boulevard. Do you know where?::

::Not yet.::

Catharine tried to relax and concentrate on her exact location. Knowing big clues often hinged on much smaller ones, she focused on her surroundings. The smoky-smelling room. The uncomfortable, lumpy mattress. The dirty sleazy feeling of everything that surrounded her.

"I wish I knew my exact location," she mumbled. And then, as though a neon light blinked on inside her head, she knew. She sent the message to Tyler. *::I'm south of Target, on the west side of Colorado Boulevard.::*

The door opened while Catharine was waiting for a reply from Tyler. Dillon—Wilbur flipped one lamp on, then another. Used to the dark, it took a few seconds for Catharine's eyes to adjust. When they finally did, she could almost see the mental cogs ticking in his brain. He looked astounded that she was no longer gagged.

And then she saw someone behind him. Sloan. Her face was still pockmarked with red welts and ugly unsightly scabs. Catharine decided her wish for them to go away probably hadn't worked because she'd added the caveat that Sloan leave her and Tyler alone.

"How long have you been awake?" Wilbur demanded.

Catharine drew in a long slow breath. "I don't know. I don't remember," she fibbed.

"She's a witch," Sloan screeched, shooting Catharine a poisonous glare. "I told you she's a freaking witch."

Ignoring her, Wilbur said to Catharine, "How do you feel?"

She didn't answer. This wasn't a social visit. When he moved closer, terror held her in its grip, and her heart threatened to stop. Revolted by the smell of his unwashed body, his oily scalp, and the alcohol on his breath, she tried not to wince.

Wilbur turned his gaze to Sloan. "You've seen her, now get out."

"Get out?" Sloan shrieked. "I thought you were going to let me get even with her."

"I'm not. She's mine. Go now or I'll throw you out."

"It was my idea to threaten the driving instructor and bring her here," Sloan blabbered. "You owe me. We had a bargain."

"You'll get what you wanted. I'll have her and you'll have her husband."

Sloan's glare, full of hatred and impotent fury turned to one of gloating. "Yes, I'll have Tyler. He'll have my shoulder to lean on once she's gone. But if something goes wrong and you don't hold up your end of our bargain, you'd better make sure you're not around to feel my displeasure."

Wilbur raised his hand, waving a deadly looking knife. "Are you trying to tempt me to use this on you?"

Sloan cowered back, then turned and stomped out.

Wilbur turned to Catharine after he slammed the door behind Sloan. "Are you going to cooperate?"

Fear almost choked her, threatened to close off her air passage, stop her breathing. Too scared to speak, she strained against the ropes that bound her to the bed. The snug ropes burned her wrists and her ankles. She hated being Wilbur's prisoner, but she wouldn't give him the satisfaction of seeing how frightened she was.

"Or will you fight me?"

She forced her expression not to change, although it took considerable effort. If he wanted sex, he'd have to exert force, and she'd make sure he had a rough time. She might not have the wand, but she wasn't helpless. If necessary, she'd fight him to the death.

He leaned closer and sat down on the creaky chair beside the old bed.

He smelled awful. Like he always had in the past after he'd drunk too much. Had he been drinking all night? Would that make him do something rash?

She watched him like a hawk.

Wilbur grinned. "I was lucky at the poker table. Won enough to keep me happy for a while. Then we'll have your fortune to live on. I'm never gonna work again. And I'm gonna screw you senseless. But not yet. I'm gonna give you time to think about it, anticipate it, worry about pleasing me so I don't have to use this." He sliced the knife through the air in front of him, an evil gleam in his bulgy bloodshot eyes.

To her horror, he turned the knife toward her, aimed it at her chest, and moved closer, slowly. She swallowed a convulsive sob, tears gathering in her eyes.

His grin turned evil. Moving closer, he used the tip of the knife to flip the blanket off her.

She closed her eyes, bit her lips, and waited. *For what?* For him to plunge the knife into her? Or use it to cut her clothes off? Both fears revolted her. She strained against the ropes again, her wrists and ankles stinging.

Wilbur laughed evilly and touched the knife to her shoulder. She cringed.

And then, to her utter surprise, he raised the knife above her head, and cut the ropes that bound her wrists to the bed.

Too astonished to speak, Catharine rubbed her chafed wrists while he cut the ropes binding her ankles to the foot of the bed.

In an abrupt mood swing, Wilbur announced, "We're leaving. Get up."

Still rubbing her wrists, Catharine asked, "Where are we going?"

His villainous grin made her skin crawl. "To Mexico."

She had to keep him talking, stall him until Tyler found her. "You'll need to sleep first, won't you?"

Wilbur bent over and touched her cheek with a clammy cold hand. She forced herself not to cringe, flinch, or bite his fingers, which she yearned to do.

"I appreciate your concern, sweetie, but I can sleep on the plane."

Her breath got trapped in the back of her throat. "Plane? she gasped.

He nodded. "You're gonna be with me for a long time, Miss High and Mighty. You might as well get used to it." He leaned down, closer. His foul breath nearly made her retch.

She grimaced.

He pulled back, the sound of his ugly laughter a crippling blow to her heart.

"Do I frighten you?"

She shook her head. "You disgust me."

"Now, why doesn't that surprise me?" He laughed again, an ugly, cruel sound. "You can come with me peacefully, or I can drug you again. Which is it going to be?"

"I'll come peacefully," she lied.

Wilbur frowned, his eyes narrowed in disbelief. "Promise?"

She nodded.

"If you're lying, you'll wind up sorry."

Afraid he might read her intention to try to escape, she turned her head. "When can I see Mother?"

"Did I say you could?" he sneered, running his fingers along the edge of the shiny sharp knife still in his hand.

"You indicated as much."

He shook his oily-haired head. She wondered how long it had been since he'd washed his hair, or showered. His awful smell filled the air inside her nostrils and she gagged. If she didn't go peacefully, would he drug her again? Could they fly on a plane if he had to carry her on?

She fell back on the bed. Hoping to buy time, she curled up in a ball, pretending to be ill. Where was Fey? Would she help her? Could she? Had her magical powers returned or was she still incapable of subduing Wilbur?

"That's it," Wilbur growled, startling her. "Your mother's a dead woman."

His words struck like a lethal blow. Catharine's fear exploded. She forgot everything except her need to conquer him. She uncoiled and looked up, ready to fight, in spite of the knife.

Twenty-four

Full of determination, Catharine slid her legs over the edge of the bed. Her full denim skirt slid up above her knees. Wilbur's mouth fell open, his eyes filled with lust. Fearing he might bend down and paw her, she shoved her skirt back over her legs.

Wilbur dropped to his knees. To her sickening horror, he rammed his hand under her skirt, roughly along her thighs, toward the juncture of her legs.

Her stomach turned and she nearly retched. Fighting the bile in her throat she jerked away, and gasped, "You said you intended to wait."

Wilbur blinked before he stood back up. Waving the knife threateningly, he bellowed, "Get up."

She jumped up so fast, she stunned him. Before he recovered, she kicked him in the groin. Hard. Harder than she knew she could.

He reeled backwards, dropped the knife, and bent over, holding himself as he had when she had kneed him the night she returned from England.

Terrified of his retaliation, she wished she could be invisible.

"I'm gonna get you for that, bitch." He glanced up. His pain-filled face turned white. "What the hell? Where are you?"

Catharine looked down. Her silent wish had come true... she'd turned invisible. She didn't take time to relish it though. Instead, she kicked him again, wishing she could render him incapable of forcing himself on any woman ever again.

An electric current steamed up from her invisible foot. Like jagged lightning it slashed the lower half of Wilbur's body. He jerked as if shocked or burned.

Yelping in pain, he fell on the dirty carpet, thrashing around as though wrestling with an invisible demon.

Catharine could only stare. Finally the brilliant electrical spiral disappeared. But Wilbur stayed on the floor, curled in a fetal position. Had her wish rendered him incapable of forcing himself on any woman ever again? With all her heart, she wished that could be true.

"You have succeeded," she heard Fey say. Then, as though a radio were playing inside her head, she heard Fey talking to Tyler.

"You've found the right motel. We're in room one-ten on the ground floor. Catharine's invisible and Dillon, or rather Wilbur, is doubled over in pain. I'm pleased to say, he will be that way for some time."

Still white-faced, Wilbur uncoiled part way and bawled, "What the hell's going on? Who's talking?"

Perversely satisfied that he couldn't see her or Fey, Catharine said, "Your sex organs have been rendered useless. You'll never force yourself on another woman. Actually, you may wish you were dead before my fairy godmother and I finish with you."

"If you expect..."

The sound of running feet pounding outside halted his tirade. Catharine vaulted around him. Hoping Tyler had arrived, she yanked the door open. Her mother, more disheveled than Catharine had ever seen her, dashed inside. Without uttering a word, she pointed her four-inch gold inch wand at Wilbur. "Tell me where my daughter is or suffer the consequences."

"How the hell do I know where she is? She was here a minute ago. I took my eyes off her and she disappeared."

"Liar." Eliza waved her wand in small circles in a continuous motion, and chanted, "Suffer now and for the rest of your days. Live out your years in a sharp, painful haze."

Still holding himself, Dillon curled up in a tight ball. His body thrashed in spasmodic jerks.

"Mother," Catharine said. "I'm here."

Eliza looked all around her. "Where?"

"Right here. Beside you. I'm invisible."

Before Eliza could comment, Tyler burst into the room. He glanced from Eliza to Wilbur, still lashing about on the dirty carpet. "Where's Catharine? Is she all right?"

"I'm fine." Catharine launched herself at Tyler. His arms came around her just as she wished she were no longer invisible.

The fury in his eyes faded, turning to a look of wonder and awe. "You—are you all right?"

She nodded. "I am... now that you're here." She hugged him fiercely.

He kissed her, on the mouth, the cheek, the forehead.

"Oh, Tyler, we communicated using mental telepathy. Isn't that great?"

"Sure is." He hugged her tighter, as though if he loosened his hold he might lose her.

"Well," Fey said, waving herself visible, "I must say you didn't much need me, sweetling. You subdued the miserable miscreant all on your own."

Blood rushed to Catharine's head, making her feel faint. "I did?"

"Of course, dear one. You control more magic than you've ever given yourself credit for. You didn't need the wand or the worry beads for all those wishes you made."

Fey turned her grin to Tyler. "If I were in your shoes, I'd take advantage of her power to keep your political opponents in their proper place."

Then Fey waved her silver wand at Wilbur. He stopped jerking and lay very still. "That'll give you some peace and quiet until the police arrive."

"Is he still alive?" Catharine asked.

Fey nodded. "Only out cold. But when he wakes up, he might wish he were dead." Then she smiled and explained, "Kacy has the Gift of Healing. Jennifer possesses the Gift of Sight. You, sweetling, have the Gift of Magic. Use it well, with discernment and care, lest it backfire and cause great harm."

Catharine swallowed. Awed by the power she possessed and had discovered in slow degrees, she vowed to heed Fey's wise counsel.

The fairy winked, her eyes twinkling. "I shall go now. I'm no longer needed here." She waved her wand again and vanished.

"I think it's time for me to go as well," Eliza said, heading for the door.

"Where are you going?" Catharine asked.

"Home. To Boulder. I have clients to see to."

"We'll see you soon," Tyler promised.

Catharine blew her mother a kiss, too happy to be in Tyler's arms to move from them.

"I should probably call Mom and Dad," Tyler said. "They're worried sick about you."

"Let's do it outside," Catharine suggested. "I don't want to look at Wilbur any more than necessary."

Tyler opened the door. They stepped out into the cool, morning fresh air. Catharine kept her arms wrapped around his neck. She couldn't bear not to be touching him.

He kissed her, then pulled his cell phone out. One arm held her close while he called Rachel and Mack. As soon as he ended the call, he kissed Catharine again.

Casting a quick glance at the closed door, she asked, "Do we have to stay here until the police arrive?"

Tyler nodded. "I'm afraid we do." Then he smiled. "I hear a siren. That must be them."

Fortunately it was.

~ * ~

After Catharine explained what had happened, the police carried a handcuffed, unconscious Wilbur out of the motel room.

"Let's get out of here," Catharine said.

Tyler nodded. "My car's right there."

She grinned, impishly. "I wish we were already home."

And then they were. In their bedroom.

Tyler smiled. "How'll we get my car home?"

"I'll wish it home." She did, then grinned. "It's in the parking garage.

"I think I could get used to your wishes coming true. Your magic is something else."

Catharine followed his gaze to the mirror above the dresser. He tightened his hold as they stared at each other in the mirror. She smiled, too. "In the future I'll try to be careful what I wish for."

"Good idea. What do you wish for right now?"

"That you would make love to me."

Hunger filled his eyes. "Far be it for me to think otherwise."

Catharine felt the craving build inside her, warming her from the top of her head to the tips of her toes. "But first I want to do something."

"What?"

She laughed. "You'll see." She dashed to the bureau, pulled the bottom drawer open and found the white shorts Tyler had bought on their honeymoon that she'd never worn.

He whistled.

She turned around, met his gaze and smiled when she saw the hungry sexy glint in his eyes.

She unhooked her skirt, let it slide down over her hips. When she heard Tyler's in-drawn breath, she pulled the shorts on, then got rid of her petticoat and looked up.

Tyler's fierce gaze was all consuming. Catharine's craving transformed into a blaze of white-hot hunger, so fierce it threatened to melt her brain.

"Tyler?"

"Yes, love?"

"Love me. Please. Love me again and again."

"With pleasure," he murmured.

She ran back across the room and launched herself into his arms.

He kissed her hard. "Damn, you're sexy in those shorts," he murmured, kissing her again. "Wear them when I have more patience to appreciate your bare legs."

He kissed her once more, his hands cupping her full breasts, turning her insides to mush.

"I will," she promised between kisses, while he caressed her bare legs, toyed with the waist band of her shorts, and teased her senses until she felt like she was nothing more than nerves with tingling aroused sensations.

When she thought she couldn't wait another second, he peeled her shorts off. Impatient, she tugged at his trousers until they were in a heap at his feet. He stepped out of them and flung her shorts aside. Then he worked her blouse loose, off her shoulders, down her arms.

Her heart clanking, Catharine responded as a woman deeply in love. With warmth and eagerness, excitement and passion.

They made it to the bed, and fell onto it wrapped in each other's arms.

"Sometimes I can't believe how much I love you," she murmured.

"You can't possibly love me more than I love you."

~ * ~

Much later, after they'd sated their hunger for each other, Catharine smiled. She still lay in Tyler's arms, and she didn't want to budge from them. "I don't deserve you."

"Yes, you do. And after all we've shared, you can't possibly doubt that we were meant to be together, can you?"

She smiled at the wonderful memories they'd made. "No. I always wanted to share your life. I just never had the courage in past lives to admit how I felt."

"You didn't want to hurt other people in those lives," Tyler said. "You're too kind hearted, Catharine. That's only one of the things I love about you."

Basking under his praise, she smiled, delighted when he added, "I also love your eyes and your smiles, and the way you respond to me. The way you responded even when you were afraid."

"Anything else?" she prompted, loving the things he said and the blissful way they made her insides tingle.

"Yes. There is something else."

"What?"

"You need me. I love being needed by you. I think you needed me in past lives, too. But I was too encumbered with other responsibilities to realize that, and you were too shy in all those other lives to admit your own needs and desires."

He raised her hand to his lips and kissed it. Then he cupped her cheek. "And there's something else I love about you."

"What? she asked, staring at his tender, serious expression. "I love knowing you'll never betray me or be unfaithful."

She smiled back. "How do you know I won't?"

"I just do."

Catharine saw love shining in his greenish gray eyes. She made a wish that she would never hurt him, that she could always live up to his expectations. And she sealed the wish with a silent prayer for the very same thing.

He leaned forward and claimed her mouth in a soul-stirring kiss.

"Ah," she sighed when their hands were as involved as their mouths.

Tyler raised his head to gaze down at her. "What is it? Is something wrong?"

"No." She shook her head, smiling. "I was just marveling at the things women learn when they become wives."

Epilogue

Thirty Years later

Seated beside Catharine in their luxurious home in Sun City West, Arizona, Ty smiled. He had retired early, two years ago. Turned the law practice over to his two sons and only daughter. Five years ago he'd resigned from the State Legislature after serving in it for twenty-five years. Catharine had published a score of books. Romances, women's fiction and children's stories. They'd had a good life, and were looking forward to more of the same, but with more time spent together.

He smiled as he glanced at Catharine. She grew more lovely with each passing year.

Soft music played in the background. Delighted to be alone with her after the frenetic pace of the holidays, he slipped his arm around her shoulders.

After thirty years, he knew Catharine still loved quiet nights at home, alone with him. Beside them, by the big family room bay window, lights twinkled on the tall Christmas tree they had decorated a month ago.

"The holidays are over," she said.

Ty groaned. "Time to take the tree down. Should we get off our duffs and get busy?"

Catharine shook her head. "I'd rather wish it down this year, if you don't mind."

He grinned. "You won't get any resistance from me. Decorating's fun, but un-decorating's work."

She grinned, too. "I wish the tree and all the Christmas decorations were down, packed and stored in the attic above the garage."

Magically the tree, along with all the other Christmas decorations, vanished.

"Good work."

She leaned back, rested her head on his shoulder. "There's usually a let down after Christmas and New Year's Day. The children and grandchildren all go home and get caught up in their own lives and we won't see them again until summer."

"Frankly, I think that's great," Ty said. "Makes them appreciate us more now that they don't see us as often as they used to."

"I guess you're right."

"And we are taking that extended vacation you've talked about for years," Ty reminded. "Three months. Do you really want to travel that long?"

"Yes. Don't you?"

"If you do. I know you want our destination to be a surprise, but if you don't tell me where we're going, I won't know what to pack."

"You don't need to pack anything."

"Guess that means you intend to pack for me."

"Actually, no, it doesn't."

"What does it mean?"

When she didn't reply, his grin grew. Sometimes she surprised the dickens out of him. He had racked his brain, trying to figure out where she wanted to go for three months, and finally had given up. Wherever it was, he felt certain they would enjoy themselves.

She stood, turned the CD player off, then extended her hand. "Come, take my hand."

He looked puzzled. "Why?"

"So we can begin our journey."

He hiked his brow. "We're leaving now? Tonight?"

"Yes."

"Are you sure you don't want to tell me where we're going?"

"I'll be happy to tell you now. Once, years ago, you asked if I could wish Jennifer and Drake to this time for another visit. Do you remember?"

He nodded. "Yes, and you said that would be a misuse of your wishing power."

Catharine nodded. "But now I have permission to make the wish in reverse."

Ty scratched his forehead. "I'm not sure I follow that logic."

Catharine beamed a happy smile up at him. "It means, we're going to the past. To visit Jennifer and Drake. And Kacy and Claythorne."

Ty's heart began to thump almost beyond recognition. What a blast it would be to go back in time. They'd travel light. Use Catharine's magic to conjure clothes and whatever else they needed. He grinned at all the possibilities. "How will we get there?"

"Take my hand and I'll show you."

He did.

Meet Evanell

Born in Utah, Evanell graduated from Orem High School, and attended both Brigham Young University and the University of Utah. After working as a secretary in Salt Lake City, and putting her husband through college, she moved to Denver, and worked in the oil and gas industry, operating her own consulting firm.

From Colorado she and her husband moved to England, where she joined the American Women's Club of London. In addition to serving as both Treasurer and President of the AWCL, she wrote articles for and worked on the staff of the London Bridge, a magazine for women living in the U.K.

Upon their return to the U.S., they bought a home in Boulder City, Nevada. Four years later they relocated to Arizona where Peggy joined RWA as well as two local chapters, Desert Rose and Valley of the Sun. She is also a member of the West Valley Authors Association (WVAA), plus a weekly critique group, and she mentors other writers.

Peggy has three sons and nine grandchildren. Married to her current husband for twenty-six years, she also has four step children and three step grandchildren.

Peggy has always loved to read and vowed to give the characters in her head their own written stories someday. Her hobbies include golf, Mah Jong and being a Queen Mum for the Red Hat Ya Ya's.

Works From The Pen Of Peggy P. Parsons & Evanell

Written as Evanell

<u>Glimpse of Eternity</u>

Startled, and still on the bed, his gaze level with hers, he said, "If you like my kisses, why did you stop me?"

"Because that's not why I'm here. And I'm sure my guardian angel wouldn't approve if we did anything more."

Clay breathed in and out, slowly. "Why then, did you thank me?"

"For the reunion."

Puzzled, he frowned. "The reunion?"

She nodded. "I think we've known each other before. In prior lives. But I don't expect to stay in this century. So I don't think we should kiss again. I He wanted to kiss her again. Giving in to the impulse, he lowered his head.

She thwarted him by scooting off his lap, jumping to her feet. Instead of dashing away, she stood before him, her mouth swollen from his prolonged kiss, her eyes blazing with unfulfilled passion. And then to his utter amazement, she said, "Thank you."

need to try to help solve your problems, not complicate them, so I can go home."

<u>Glimpse of Forever</u>

Having loved and lost Drake in other lives, including her current life in the twenty-first century, Jennifer is delighted when she finds herself catapulted into his life in the middle of the nineteenth century. Mistaking Jennifer for his intended, Drake finds her much easier to deal with after she falls from a tree in his woods. Although he thinks she tricked him into agreeing to wed her, he plans to have *a marriage in name only. Now he discovers he wants her to be his wife in every way.*

With her gift of sight, Jennifer knows Drake's charge is impersonating her in the future. When she convinces Drake she isn't his intended, he promises they will fight the evil wizard who wants her soul together. Then he is thrown from his horse and wounded. Fearing the wizard will never let them live in peace, Jennifer returns to the future only to discover the girl impersonating her is dead and she has no life to reclaim.

Glimpse of Never Ending Love

Still standing close but no longer touching, Catharine said, "Tyler?"

"Yes?"

"Will being together be this exciting if we are married?"

"Yes," he promised. "We'll make it this exciting or more."

Neither said another word, but both knew a commitment of sorts had been made.

He reached inside his breast suit coat pocket and removed the betrothal ring. "You'll let me know when you're ready to wear this, won't you?"

She nodded, staring at the huge diamond solitaire sparkling up at her.

Written as Peggy P. Parsons

One Stolen Night

Having broken up with her high school sweetheart after graduation, Pamela Tate follows her dream of attending the University of Hawaii where she meets the legendary Robin, who steals more than her bruised heart.

Yours Till Niagra Falls

Embarrassed by her attempt to warn Jade about a conniving college classmate, Kia flees to her beloved Camp in the Adirondack's to mourn the loss of her family. When Jade shows up uninvited and unexpected, she agrees to let him stay in one of her log cabins. Although she isn't ready for love, she wants to trust Jade, but his association with her unscrupulous ex-boyfriend, makes it difficult to believe he isn't there for a sinister reason.

Paper Marriage
Chandler's eagle gaze checked Analyn's compact living room. "Is your whole apartment decorated in red, white and blue?"
"What if it is?" He'd broken her heart. Would he insult her taste, too?

Yesterday's Secrets
Story begins with Janalou boarding a bus in Spartanburg, SC. She meets seven people and they form a friendship and stay together after they transfer to a different bus. That evening Janalou has an attack of appendicitis and is rushed to the hospital, then ends up traveling by car across the country with Kree to give her body and her facial bruises time to heal before she meets his family and starts to work with them.
When Janalou discovers her father/papa and stepmother have been arrested for her murder (even though no body was found--there was blood in the house), she feels compelled to return to Spartanburg. The next day at the court house she meets her real family, including her identical twin, and discovers she was kidnapped when she was four. Her twin tells/reminds her that for their last Christmas together they were given twin dolls, and dresses in their own size to match the dolls.

Letter to Our Readers

Enjoy this book?

You can make a difference

As an independent publisher, Wings ePress, Inc. does not have the financial clout of the large New York Publishers. We can't afford large magazine spreads or subway posters to tell people about our quality books.

But, we do have something much more effective and powerful than ads. We have a large base of loyal readers.

Honest Reviews help bring the attention of new readers to our books.

If you enjoyed this book, we would appreciate it if you would spend a few minutes posting a review on the book's **_Amazon page_** or on its Wings ePress, Inc. webpage **_at www.wingsepress.com_**

Thank You very much.